how to
save
a life

"Zarr delivers a moving, funny, and
emotionally honest story about three women
whose understanding of family, and of themselves,
shifts in profound ways."
Publishers Weekly, A Best Book of 2011

"I could probably write a review for this that just says,
'You guys, you have to read this. Please please read this'.
And you would, and would agree with me that this
book is amazing, and that Sara Zarr should be crowned
Queen of All of the Things."
Swoontini

"Woven together from two simple threads, the resulting
tapestry is as beautiful as it is real. A story that will
resonate beyond its final page."
Kirkus

how to save a life

Sara Zarr

USBORNE

Jen, this one is for you, with love.

First published in the UK in 2012 by Usborne Publishing Ltd., Usborne House,
83-85 Saffron Hill, London EC1N 8RT, England. www.usborne.com

Published by arrangement with Little, Brown and Company Books for Young Readers,
Hachette Book Group, New York, New York, USA. All rights reserved.

Text copyright © Sara Zarr, 2011.

Jacket Design by Alison Impey. Jacket © 2011 by Hachette Book Goup

A CIP catalogue record for this book is available from the British Library.

ISBN 9781409546757 JFMAMJJ SOND/12 00751/03

Printed in Reading, Berkshire, UK.

"The life you save may be your own."

Flannery O'Connor

From: MMK333

To: heart_homeDen

Subject: Re: [lovegrows] Christmas wish

Date: Jan 1 03:09:47 AM UTC-6

I am writing in response to your Love Grows post from Christmas Day.

I think I might have what you're looking for.

It should be available on March 1. Or around March 1.

Right now I am living in Omaha, but this is not where I want to be. So if you pay my way, I will bring it to you in Denver. If that is where you really live. No offence but a lot of people on this site lie. I know they all say don't send money and don't send tickets and don't do this and don't do that. Rules don't always apply, though, and you never know what another person has gone through to end up here. After reading your post, I knew you would understand this.

No lawyers. No agencies. That's why I am on this site. If either gets involved, I will disappear with the item in question. I don't mean to sound threatening. That's just the situation.

I would like to come a little bit early and have the

matter taken care of there. This way we can get to know each other. I'm not asking for money. Just expenses. It's getting hard for me to stay here much longer.

This offer is good until one week from today. After that I will seek other solutions. I'm sorry if I'm rushing you, but you have to understand – I'm trying to do what's best. I have attached a picture of myself and as you can see I am white and in good health and not bad-looking.

A lot of people in my situation might have a problem with some of the facts you mentioned in your post about you. Not me, because I think I understand.

If you accept me, I accept you.

Please write soon.

Mandy

Jill

Dad would want me to be here.

There's no other explanation for my presence. Sometimes it's like I exist – keep going to school, keep coming home, keep showing up in my life – only to prove that his confidence in me, his affection for me, weren't mistakes. That I'm the person he always said I was. Am. That I know the right things to do and will always do them in the end, even if it takes me a while to get there and even if I fight the whole way.

We were the same that way. Are. Were. He was, I am. When he was here, I knew who I was. If I forgot, he'd remind me. In theory, I should be the same person now I was then. He died, not me. So I'm trying to be that person, still, even though he hasn't been here for ten months now.

But let me tell you: it's epically, stupidly, monumentally *hard*.

Hard to deal with people who are only trying to be nice, comforting. Hard to not hate all my friends who still have their dads. Hard to smile and say "thank you" to all the random strangers I deal with in a day who don't know any better than to act as if the world is a good place.

The hardest thing of all is loving my mom without him to show me how. Loving, maybe, isn't the best way to put it. Obviously, I love my mom. Understanding, appreciating, showing kindness and compassion and basic friendliness towards – which, you know, are the things that express love, because otherwise it's just a word, right? – those are the challenges.

Especially understanding. Especially when she's making lunatic decisions, like the one that's led us here to the train station at seven o'clock on a Monday morning. Instead of celebrating Presidents' Day the way it's meant to be celebrated – with sleep – we're waiting for the human time bomb that's about to wreck our lives. Wreck it more, I mean. That's my opinion, and it's no big secret. Mom knows how I feel about this; she just doesn't seem to care.

It's a grief thing. Anyone from the outside looking in can analyse what's going on and see it, except she claims this isn't about that, not directly. Eventually I had to stop arguing with her; my rants only make her more stubborn about seeing this through. Not that I'm unfamiliar with stubbornness, and not that I've done such a fantastic job handling my own grief. But at least I've tried to limit the stupid shit I've done so that I'm the only one who gets hurt.

This? This affects three lives. Soon to be four.

"Sun," Mom says now, stretching to see out the high, narrow panes of the station windows. There's a glimpse of winter sky growing blue. When we got here, we found out that because of security rules, we couldn't actually wait out on the platform, which somewhat shattered Mom's romantic vision of how this whole thing would go down. Threat level Orange tends to do that.

I know I shouldn't say this – I know it as surely as I know the earth is round and beets are evil – and yet here it comes: "It's not too late to change your mind."

Mom, still staring up at the windows, lets her bag slide off her shoulder and dangle from her elbow. "Thanks, Jill. That's tremendously helpful."

If I had any sense, the edge in her voice would shut me up. Alas. "You're not obligated, like, legally. You didn't sign any papers."

"I'm aware."

"You could put her up for a night in a hotel, then pay her way back home tomorrow. You could say, sorry, you made a mistake and didn't realize it until you actually saw her and it hit you."

Mom hoists her bag back up and walks closer to the doors under the TO TRAINS sign. Once there, she strokes her left jawline, where I know there's a small mole, almost the same colour as the rest of her skin, so you don't really notice it, but it's raised enough to feel. When she's nervous, agitated, pissed off, or deep in thought, she runs her fingers over it non-stop.

I sink my hands into the pockets of my pea coat, trying to warm them up and also feeling for my phone. *Don't check it*, I think. *Don't check for a message from Dylan because there won't be one.*

Mom looks so lonely over there. No Dad beside her to rest his hand on her shoulder, the way he would. I could do that. How hard can it be? I move closer. Tentatively lift my arm. She turns to me and says, "You're the sister, Jill."

My arm drops.

The sister. It's so hard to get there mentally. Yes, when I was a kid, I desperately wanted a baby brother or sister, but at seventeen it's a different scenario.

Mom looks at her cell phone and fluffs her cropped hair. It's a new look for her, one I'm not used to yet. "Why don't you go ask if there's a delay."

I leave her there to her mole and her thoughts.

The station, with its soaring ceilings and old marble floor, is echoey with pieces of conversations and suitcases being rolled and the *thwonk*ing of a child's feet running up and down the seat of one of the high-backed wooden benches. "No, no, Jaden, we don't run indoors," the mother says. *Thwonk thwonk thwonk.* "What did I just say, Jaden? Do you want to have a time-out?" Pause. *Thwonk thwonk thwonk thwonk.* I can see the top of Jaden's head bobbing along as his mother counts down to time-out. "One...two..." *Thwonk.* "Three." *Thwonk thwonk.* "Okay, but remember you made the choice."

Jaden screams.

This is what we have to look forward to.

Why my mother would want to put herself through all this again is a mystery to me, no matter how she's tried to explain it. When she announced over tuna casserole six weeks ago that she was going to participate in an open adoption, I laughed.

She frowned, fiddled with her napkin. "It's not funny, Jill."

"This is just an idea, right? Something I could potentially talk you out of?"

"No." Her hand went to her left jaw.

If I didn't know my mom so well, I wouldn't have believed her. But this was completely consistent, *so* something she would do. She's never been one to solicit opinions before making major decisions. It drove Dad crazy. She'd go trade in her perfectly fine car for a brand-new one, or book a non-refundable vacation on a total whim. Then there was the time she decided she wanted to paint every room in the house a different colour and started one Saturday while Dad and I were at the self-defence class he made me take. We came home and the living room had gone from white to Alpine Lake Azure. Surprise! I didn't really care, but Dad was so aggravated.

This, though, I cared about, and when I realized she was serious, I said, "It's insane."

"War is insane. The fact that there's still no cure for AIDS is insane. This is not insane."

"You're old, Mom!"

"Thanks, honey. Early fifties is *not* old."

"When the kid is my age, you'll be—"

"Seventy. I can do the math, Jill."

"Seventy is *old*."

Everything was in its normal place: the old wooden farm table in front of me, the iron pot rack over the stove, the cigar box full of stamps at the end of the counter near the phone. Our quiet street outside. Yet this conversation? Not normal. She remained so perfectly calm through it all that I had to say several times, "You do realize you're talking about *adopting a baby*?" to make sure we were living in the same reality.

"Yes."

"A *baby* baby."

"Jill. Yes."

We went on like that for a while, and I got angrier and angrier, though I couldn't say exactly why.

"I'm not asking you to do anything, Jill," she said. "You're leaving after graduation. You know Dad and I talked about doing something like this for years."

Yes. And they really got into their volunteer work with foster kids a few years ago. "That's different." What I wanted to say was that with Dad gone, it didn't seem so much that she was carrying out their plans as trying to replace him. With a baby. Which just seemed like a really, really bad idea, for so many reasons. But I couldn't say that. Sometimes even I know when to shut up.

As I got up from the table and took our bowls to the sink, something I didn't want to feel pushed up from underneath the anger. Anger I can deal with. Anger is easy for me. It can actually be kind of energizing to fume and feel superior and think about all the ways you're right and other people are wrong. But the truth is I felt like I was going to cry. The feeling pushing up, the one I avoid at all costs because I don't know what to do with it, was hurt. That she'd decided this huge, life-changing thing without consulting me.

My mom is not a stupid person and not a selfish person. Things she does that might seem that way on the surface come from a really good place in her heart. One year she boycotted Christmas because she was fed up with consumerism. A cool idea from a good place, yet it also kind of sucked because, you know, no tree, no presents, not even a stocking. And one time she decided we'd eat only one meal a day for a month and send our grocery money to Sudan, where a lot of people eat only one meal a day all the time. Again, chronic hunger wasn't so terrific for helping me get homework done, and I'm pretty sure my dad was sneaking lunch on the job, but you have to love that heart.

And I know that's the heart that led her to make this decision. Adding someone to a family, though? Is major. Life-changing. Permanent. When someone's been subtracted from a family, you can't just balance it out with a new acquisition. In the months after Dad died, a couple of people told us we should get a dog. A dog!

How is this all that different?

I rinsed the dishes and beat down the hurt with more anger. "I can't believe you're doing this, Mom. It's just so impossible."

Grim, resigned, she got up and headed to me with the casserole dish. She spooned leftovers into a plastic container. Snapped on the lid. Put it in the fridge. Handed me the casserole dish to rinse. "I want to give a good home to someone who might not otherwise have one," she finally said. "Why see that as impossible? Seeing good things as impossible is exactly what's wrong with our world."

What could I say to that?

She put on the kettle. I watched her middle-aged body move, her back half-covered by silvery hair Dad would never let her colour, and I could almost see his hand smoothing it down as he bent to give her an after-dinner kiss before taking down the cups and saucers – pottery from their tenth anniversary trip to Brazil.

"Mom..." I stopped short, not sure what to say. I knew how much she missed Dad. I missed him, too. And I knew how different our missing him was, and that made it even harder. Couldn't it be just us for a while, missing him together, in our separate ways? Couldn't she at least wait until after graduation? Let us get used to each other, the people we are without Dad. "Mom," I tried again, but she probably thought I was going to keep berating her and said, "No, Jill, I've made up my mind. It feels right. A death, and now a life."

The next day, she chopped off her beautiful hair.

Mandy

The train's horn is always two long, one short, and one long. A lonely sound.

It fits, because almost everyone is asleep but me, and it's lonely to be the one who's awake.

The man next to me has been sleeping for the last few hours, and I've passed a lot of that time watching him in the near dark. He's nice-looking, with black-grey hair and short sideburns. Skin like he might be Hispanic, or Indian like Christopher, or even the other kind of Indian. He could be in his thirties or forties, and two times his leg has brushed against mine without his knowing it. When I got on in Omaha, he was already sitting there, and as I walked the aisle, he looked up and smiled. So I stopped, and he let me sit by the window.

There's no wedding ring on his left hand.

Someone else is awake – the woman in a seat across and

in front of us has been crying off and on. It started with sniffles, and the sniffles got more frequent, and then she put her face down into her scarf and pressed it against her eyes. I wonder what kind of crying it is. Anger or hurt or betrayal or feeling lost. Those are things that might make me cry, but not in public. My mother says a little bit of sadness is okay, and sometimes it can help men notice you. But crying is too much, she says. Crying makes them scared. They feel helpless, and you never want to make a man feel helpless.

She didn't have to warn me about public crying. I haven't done that since I was little. I barely even do it in private.

At the train station in Omaha, I came close. The cab picked me up in the afternoon, the way I'd arranged it, so that I left before my mother or Kent got home from work. In my mind I said goodbye and searched inside myself for pieces of me that would miss it, miss them, and didn't find any. That's not what made me want to cry.

The drive across the river from Council Bluffs and into downtown Omaha is short; the cab got to the station, and we unloaded my bags and I paid, tipping the driver two dollars, and he said nothing, and it wasn't until he pulled away and I walked to the door of the station that I saw it was closed. It didn't open until nine thirty at night. I'd planned to stay there, waiting for the ten-thirty train, and it was only just after four. I should have shouted and waved my hands in case the driver looked back, but mostly in life I don't protest things. I go along, or at least I make people believe I'm going along. Sometimes it's better if people think you're dumb or don't care.

A light snow had started to fall on top of the snow already on the ground. My bags were big. I didn't have a cell phone to call another cab. Why couldn't the driver have waited to make sure I got into the station? Did he notice it was closed? I would have noticed if I were him, driving a pregnant girl from Council Bluffs to the train station. I would make sure she was okay. This is what I'm saying. This is what made me want to cry. It felt bigger than only a cab driver, a stranger, leaving me in the snow. It felt personal. Abandonment. Knowing no one really cares if you stay or if you go or if you freeze to death in a train station parking lot or if you simply disappear. I've been knowing that a long time. Mostly it doesn't bother me, and my mother says don't be the squeaky wheel because you might get the grease but you'll also get the grief.

At the train station, though, seeing the cab drive away, that hurt me where I already hurt.

Still, I didn't cry. Instead, I dragged my big bag behind me in the snow and put the smaller one over my shoulder and walked uphill to the corner and went into a place called Joe Banana's, where I ate a pizza as slowly as possible so I could stay. Some people stared. I stood out. At nine fifteen, I dragged my bag back down the hill in the dark and waited for the station to open.

I'm not sure what I expected from a train station. Something different from what it was: small, cold, and ugly like a hospital waiting room, like a classroom. After a while more people started to come in: a few old people, and a group of boys my age who had matching jackets, like they were on some kind of sports team. One of them, a tall one with a wide face like Kent's, stared at me too long and then started typing on his phone. Another boy near him began to type on his. I knew they were sending each other text messages about me. I'd been walking around school for months looking like this, so I was used to it. Still.

I closed my eyes so I couldn't see them seeing me.

I thought I'd sleep on the train. But now, even after hours on board, I can't and I don't want to. It's my first time riding a train and my first time more than a hundred miles from Council Bluffs, and I don't want to miss anything. The snow-covered plains light up the night, and the carriage is dim, so I have a good view of spiny trees and run-down farmhouses and empty fields. I try to imagine Denver. It has mountains, and a big football stadium, and a river running through parts of it, just like in Omaha. That's all I know. Though I'm not a nervous kind of a person, when I think about getting to Denver, I feel sick. Because what if it's all the same? My mother says you can lead a horse to water... and I forget how that saying ends, because she hardly ever finishes it.

I have to remember what I've told Robin, so that I don't get tense and mess it up when we meet. For example, that I'm thirty-seven weeks pregnant, when the facts are different. Not that different. Close enough, I think. There are a few other pieces of information that are more wishes than facts, plus one I don't know myself.

The man next to me stirs. "Did you say something?" he murmurs.

"No." At least I probably didn't. Sometimes things come out and I don't notice.

"Oh. Dreaming, I guess." He sits up straight; I smile and rub my belly, which is something I've learned calms people. They like to see a healthy pregnant young woman, and it doesn't hurt if she's pretty.

Glad to have someone to talk to and glad it's him, I ask where he's going. This train started in Chicago and goes all the way to the California coast.

"Salt Lake." He pats at his hair, smoothing out the sleep ruffles. "My sister's getting married. I don't fly."

"Me neither." And I only mean I've never been on a plane. "I'm getting off in Denver. Two more stops."

We talk softly so we don't bother sleeping passengers.

He should ask, "Business or pleasure?" and I would say, "Neither," and I'd run my hand over my belly again, once, and then maybe with a look of concern he'd ask, "Where's the father?" I'd glance away. Then I'd reply, "Afghanistan. He's a soldier." Because another thing I've learned is that's one of the best answers you can give. People look at you like you're a hero yourself.

He doesn't ask, though. Only shifts in his seat and opens up a magazine.

So I ask him, "Are you married?"

It's a question to make conversation is all, but after I ask it, I know I should have thought of another type of a question. My mother says I have no social sense. She says I make people uncomfortable. And I want to say, *Well, you make me uncomfortable when you tell me things like that, so maybe I got it from you.* Actually, I never think of what to say to her until a few days later; by then it's better to not bring it up.

The man pauses the uncomfortable pause I'm used to before he says, "Yes."

"You're not wearing a ring."

He holds out his hand, looks at it. "No. I never have. My wife doesn't, either."

"Why not?" If I were married to someone like him, I would wear the ring.

"We just don't." He shrugs and goes back to his magazine. When he flips the page, a sharp, spicy smell comes up from a cologne sample. "Whoa. Maybe I should rub some of this stuff on. Another eighteen hours to my next shower."

"I like the way men smell just naturally." When he pretends not to hear, I realize that's another thing that should stay in my head and not come out of my mouth. "What's your name?" I ask. "I'm Mandy Madison." Madison is actually my middle name, but I like the way the two names sound together without *Kalinowski* on the end.

"Oh. Alex."

"Alex what?"

He lifts his magazine. "I'm sorry, I really need to—"

"You don't have to tell me. I was only wondering if you were Indian. Like in Nebraska, we have Comanche, Arapaho, Pawnee..."

"No. I'm a plain old Mexican American. Third generation."

I don't know why he won't just say his last name. "Really my last name is Kalinowski," I offer. "It's Polish. I don't know what generation."

When he doesn't reply, I tell him, "I'm going to try to sleep now. Enjoy your article."

I close my eyes and imagine him watching me, wondering about me, thinking how pretty I am while I sleep. My mother says men like to see you like that. In sleep you look vulnerable, and it makes them want to take care of you.

When I wake up, Alex has his tray down, and there are two styrofoam cups on it. Above them, steam is making curls in the air. "I got you some tea. Herbal."

No one's ever brought me anything before without my even asking. I take the cup. "Thank you."

"I don't know if you heard the announcement – we're running behind schedule. We might be an hour late getting in to Denver." He's put away his magazine, and other passengers are up and stretching and getting coffee and tea. The train seems to be barely moving. "I have a phone if you need to make any calls or anything."

"Friends are meeting me."

"Um, hey." He shifts his body so that he's sitting on his side, facing me and leaning close. "It's Peña, by the way. My last name. And I'm..." He laughs. Lines appear around the corners of his eyes, and there's tea on his breath and stubble on his chin. "This is stupid. I'm not really married. I just said that because I thought you were trying to hit on me or something, and it seemed kind of weird because...

well, then I thought obviously picking up some stranger is the last thing on your mind right now. And you're probably half my age, and most likely you have someone, anyway, given..." He gestures to my belly. "That."

This. *This* rolls inside me, stretches a limb. I touch where it moved and wonder if it can feel my hand there.

"I'm nineteen." Almost.

"There you go. That's exactly half. I'm thirty-eight." He sips from his cup. "So, how long before you're a mother?"

I smile. I'll never be a mother. "About a month, I think."

Alex scratches at his stubble. "Most women I know can tell you to the minute."

"I'm different." Being so specific with dates is silly. No one measures a life in weeks and days. You measure it in years and by the things that happen to you, and when this life is a whole year, I won't be in it.

"Well, good luck with everything. There's something about being a young parent that's so great. Too late for me, but my brother had all his kids in his twenties, and now they're like pals, you know, listening to a lot of the same music and stuff like that."

I like his voice. It's energetic. "It's not too late for you."

"Maybe not. Just gotta find the right girl."

"I don't think nineteen and thirty-eight are so far apart. My grandpa was twenty-eight years older than my grandma."

I picture us at Alex's sister's wedding in Salt Lake, everyone I'm his date and how we met on the train. It's disloyal to Christopher to think this, because Christopher is like a dream, and I need to think about my real and actual future. Alex's sister's wedding would be colourful and festive with dancing, a perfect place for romance. "Are there going to be Mexican wedding cookies?"

"What?"

"Those cookies rolled in powdered sugar? One of my mother's boyfriends made those once. They're good." His face is blank. "At your sister's wedding?"

"Oh. I don't know." He pulls out his magazine again, turns away.

"I thought since they were called that, they'd be served at a Mexican wedding."

"It's more like a Mormon wedding."

"I see." I look out the window. The winter sun has come up, flat, grey dawn creeping over the landscape. When we pass dark clumps of trees, so slowly, I can see my reflection. I'm still pretty, even after being on a train all night. Alex's reflection is behind mine. I imagine our reflections bending towards each other, his smiling at mine so I can see those lines around his eyes again. To the window, I say, "I just don't think nineteen years is that big of a gap."

He quietly flips his pages.

Jill

The train is a little behind schedule. "A little" is the way the station agent describes it at first, but when I press for details, he admits there's trouble at one of the switches and it could be another hour. We sit on a bench while we wait; Mom pulls her bag into her lap and digs through it until she's recovered a well-worn envelope – pictures of Mandy that she stares at every day. "Look at her, Jill," she says, holding the snapshots out to me.

"I've *looked* at her, Mom."

Giving the photos an insistent little shake, she says, "Why are you here today if you aren't going to participate? I'd rather do this alone than have you here being so...I don't know, Jill. So sulky, so hard."

"So *me*, you mean?"

"This is not you, Jill." She retracts the pictures, but I

lean over and grab them from her hand before she can put them away.

They're the same pictures I've seen a couple of times – snapshots Mom printed from e-mails. Mandy and her big belly at the park. Mandy and her big belly on some bridge. On a couch. Standing in a bare hallway. In all of the pictures, she's wearing the same outfit, and her big belly is the exact same bigness, as though they all were taken on the same day. And in all of the pictures, Mandy and her big belly are alone. I don't know what I'm supposed to make of this girl, what I'm supposed to feel.

"She has good hair," I say, an offering, the best I can do. Her hair is palest blonde, thick and glossy and halfway to her waist.

"Prenatal vitamins will do that."

When I hand the pictures back to Mom, she shuffles through them yet again, staring hard, as if she's seeing the face of a long-lost relative or searching for the answer to some private, momentous question that, for whatever reason, can't be answered by me.

She looks at her watch. "Let's walk over to Common Grounds for some blueberry coffee cake. It might be my last for a while," she says, standing. "I don't want the baby to develop a sugar habit so early, the way you did."

"I turned out okay."

"Mmm." It's a non-committal sound, like maybe I did and maybe I didn't.

When we get back to the station, Mom convinces the security guy to let us wait on the platform. Maybe she told him our whole sob story; maybe she dropped her buddy the mayor's name – I don't know. But when I come out of the bathroom, she hustles me through the waiting area and towards the TO TRAINS sign. Security Guy searches Mom's bag and pats down my pockets before we can climb the ramp. We emerge outside to see the train crawling towards the station at what seems like two miles an hour.

We wait forever for it to go a hundred metres, Mom perched at the very edge of the yellow strip you're not supposed to cross if you don't want to fall onto the tracks and wind up with a severed limb. She's maximally nervous. I know this because she hasn't said one word in the last fifteen minutes, since we walked back from the coffee shop. The sun is fully out now, sky blue, Lower Downtown – LoDo – looking its best and ready to make a good impression on Mandy.

I will try to do the same.

I move a little closer to Mom and hope she knows I wouldn't be here if I didn't care.

Finally the train rolls to a stop; within moments people emerge from the silver carriages. A lot of them light up cigarettes immediately and cluster in groups without their luggage – you can tell these are the ones who have the good fortune to not have Denver as their final destination. Not that I don't like it here. It's a good city. But when I'm free to leave, I'm going to.

The passengers with luggage are slower to come out.

Mom glances back at me. "Be nice to her, Jill. Welcoming. Put yourself in her shoes. Imagine what she's going through. Set aside your opinions about this and try to think—"

"Mom. Calm down. I'm not a monster."

Of course you're not, Jill, she could say. *I don't think that.*

"I'm going to check the front carriages." She walks purposefully towards one end of the platform, her low boots *clop-clop-clop*ping away, and I go to the other, pulling my hood up to keep my ears warm, and there she is. Mandy. I recognize the hair.

She's standing on the platform not looking around the way you'd expect someone in her situation would. Instead, she's staring into the train carriage, until a man comes out with a big duffel bag in one hand and a smaller shoulder bag in the other. I walk towards them, slowly, watching. Now that she's around other people, I can see how petite she is; shorter than me – and I'm no giant – and all-round tiny. *Elfin* would be the word, except for her disproportionately voluminous hair and, of course, her belly, and even the belly doesn't seem that big for someone due in three weeks. Maybe it's the dress – a pastel flowered thing the likes of which I've neither worn nor seen since fourth grade. Totally wrong for winter. No decent coat, either, just a light jacket.

The man with the bags says something to her. She touches his arm and finally takes a gander at who else might be on the platform – the people there to meet her, house her, and raise her child, for instance.

I wave.

When I check over my shoulder for Mom, I see she's still at the other end of the platform, talking to one of the stewards, showing him a picture. Of Mandy, I presume. I don't call out to her. I want to get an up-close view myself, first. "Mandy?" I walk the three or so metres between us, narrowly escaping being rammed by a stroller.

I have got to get out of this town before the strollering of Mandy's baby happens. Attempting to be supportive of Mom, yes. Pushing a stroller? No.

Mandy nods, smiling. Before I can introduce myself and make her feel welcome and put myself in her shoes, she touches the guy's arm again and says, "This is my friend, Alex Peña." Her voice, like her body, is small.

"Hi. I'm Jill." Does Mom know Mandy brought a friend? Is this the baby's father, or what?

Alex appears no less confused than I feel. He sets the bags down. "Take care, then."

He starts to turn away; Mandy stops him. "Maybe you can take the bags to their car?"

"I have to get back on the train."

Alex clearly wants to get away, and I'm highly doubting he's the father, seeing as he's got some grey hair and a few wrinkles. He catches my eye with a pleading look.

"I got it," I say, and turn to look down the platform. Mom has spotted us and is hurrying over.

Mandy smiles at me and touches her belly. "Thanks." Her eyes are ice blue, light and clear, the kind of eyes you see on certain sheepdogs. Her smile makes me uncomfortable. Then there's this fully awkward moment in which Alex puts down the bags and Mandy hugs him. Or tries to, up on her toes, though everything in his body language says *Get away*.

"Good luck," he says, more to me than to her.

Exit Alex. Enter Mom. Who starts crying.

They hug. Mom continues to cry. Mandy smiles and remains dry-eyed while even I tear up. As I said, I am not a monster, and it moves me to see my mom happy after a long, dry spell of sorrow.

"You're so small," Mom finally says, getting her tears under control.

"I don't feel small."

"You're so beautiful."

"Thank you."

"Your hair..."

"Thank you." Mandy puts her hand to her stomach and says, "He's kicking. He's excited to meet you."

"Really? Can I feel?" She palms the sides of Mandy's belly while people mill around us. This look crosses Mom's face, this look that is simultaneously ecstatic and petrified. I brush my one tear away while they're not looking.

Mandy says to me, "Do you want to feel?"

"I'm good."

"Jill." Mom drops her hands.

"It's okay," Mandy says. "I think he stopped, anyway."

Mom puts her arm around Mandy's shoulders. "Let's get out of here. You must be starving. We have lots of options at home and can be there in fifteen minutes. Or would you like to go out?"

I'm full of coffee cake and more than ready to get back into bed, but of course Mandy wants to go out, and today is all about Mandy – as are the next three weeks, and who knows how long after that? Every time I ask Mom for specifics about the after-plan, she tells me not to worry and changes the subject.

They start down the ramp and, after several steps, remember my existence. Mom turns back and says, "Jill? Grab Mandy's bags, will you?"

Sure.

We wind up at Pancake Universe because that's where Mandy wanted to go – never mind that we have a dozen great diners that serve killer huevos and kick-ass pancakes. "It's just that I've seen the commercials my whole life," Mandy said, "but I've never been there and I thought—"

"You're not missing anything," I said, but Mom caught my eye in the rear-view and said if that's where Mandy wanted to go, that's where we'd go, and got me to use the GPS to find the closest one.

For someone who's never been to Pancake Universe, Mandy makes her decision pretty fast, barely looking at the menu before closing it and setting it down. Everything sounds gross to me, and the table is sticky. PU doesn't have the kind of hash browns I like. I like chunks of real potatoes, and these are the shredded crap that comes out of the freezer. "They look and taste like shoelaces, but at least shoelaces have a purpose," Dad says. Said. We were on the exact same page when it came to hash browns, among other things.

I order a side of sausage and a tomato juice. Mom orders a two-egg breakfast. Then comes Mandy:

"Double strawberry pancakes with extra whipped cream, and can I get that butterscotch sauce on the side?" She glances at me. "I saw it on the commercial."

So much for Mom's sugar-free baby.

"Don't you want some protein, honey?" Mom asks. Already Mandy is "honey"? Traditionally, *I* am "honey". "Some eggs? Or ham?"

"No."

Mom lets it go and smiles hopefully. "How have you been feeling?"

"Good."

She waits for more details, but Mandy isn't giving up anything other than that unsettling smile.

"So," Mom says, "we want to welcome you." I catch a tremble in her voice, very slight. Only I would notice, given that I've been hearing her talk for seventeen years. She's still as nervous as she was at the station, maybe more. I could reach my hand right over to her leg and give it a squeeze under the booth to let her know that it's going to be okay. Dad would do that. Except I'm not Dad, and I don't know if it's going to be okay, so I leave my hand where it is.

"We have a little more setting up to do at the house," she continues, "but if you're tired, you can lay down in my room while Jill and I take care of that. And if there's anything you need, you let one of us know. We want you to feel at home." She slides out of the booth. "Be right back."

"Thank you, Robin," Mandy says as Mom heads off to the bathroom, where I'm pretty sure she's going to cry some more.

The waitress comes back, setting tomato juice down in front of Mandy and orange juice in front of me. After switching the glasses, I shake hot sauce into my juice, and Mandy sips hers.

"That's not good for your heart," she says.

"What?" I stop mid-shake.

"Hot sauce."

I laugh. "Where'd you hear that? It's fine for my heart." She watches as I stir in the hot sauce, squeeze my lemon wedge into the juice, and then drop the whole thing into the glass, stirring again.

"Are you hung-over?" Mandy asks.

"No. I just like my tomato juice this way."

What a weirdo. I wish Dylan could see this. Right now she's fixed her stare on my eyebrow ring. To get her to stop gaping, I raise the eyebrow in question and think I might say, "Does it offend you or something?" Then I hear my dad's voice in my head, the way I have for the last ten months. "Try a little tenderness, Jilly." So saith Otis Redding, Dad's favourite. Dad understood my natural inclination away from tenderness because it's just like his was. Neither of us will go down in history as "nice", even though he had the best heart, absolutely. "Try a little tenderness" was our polite way of saying to each other, "You're being an asshole."

So I try. Maybe girls from Nebraska or Iowa or wherever she's from are more sheltered. Maybe she never learned how babies are made. Or what birth control is. Maybe none of this is her fault. Suddenly I'm dying to ask her all these questions: *How did it happen? Who's the father? Why did you decide to have it?* But Mom comes back, looking a little splotchy, and I don't think she'd view my curiosity as welcoming.

Mandy, however, has no such worries about inappropriate curiosity. As soon as Mom gets her napkin back in her lap, Mandy asks, "Is Jill adopted, too? She looks nothing like you."

Before we can react, the waitress appears with our food, setting my sausage in front of Mom and Mom's eggs in front of me. She gets Mandy's order right. "Anything else?" I switch the plates. "Oh," she says. "Oops."

"Just keep the coffee coming," Mom says.

When the waitress is gone, I tell Mandy, "I look like my dad."

His dark eyes. His shorter, thicker build. Mom is willowy. Me and Dad: more oaklike.

"You've got my nose, though," Mom says, "and it looks better on you." She's been saying that as long as I can remember. Her nose is fine on her. A little wider than she'd like is all.

Mandy isn't even paying attention. She's drowning her pancakes in butterscotch sauce, enough to cover the plate. I steal a look at Mom, expecting to see it killing her not to say anything while Mandy ingests so much sugar, but all that's on her face is that same shy rapture I saw at the station. The nerves are gone and it's lighting her up, I can see it, thawing out the places in her heart that Dad's death left numb, warming her in a way I haven't been able to.

Because although I have Dad's build and hair and eyes, his bluntness and his impatience, his good common sense, I don't have the piece that matters: his heart.

Mandy

Robin's house is like a house you see on a TV show. Like a mansion. In her e-mails she called it an old Victorian that she and her husband had "fixed up a little". It's nicer than any house I've been in, with two fireplaces and a formal dining room and a polished wooden staircase and darker wood floors. And I haven't even seen the upstairs yet.

"We'll set you up right here for now so you can rest a bit," Robin says, patting the couch. "Jill and I will finish getting your room ready. If you decide going up and down the stairs is too much, we'll figure out something else. At the moment there are no real beds down here..." She stops and stares, and starts rubbing a spot on her face. I stare back. I'm really here, is what we're thinking. "I hope this is all okay, Mandy. You'll tell me if it's not?"

"It's fine. Thank you."

I'm still getting used to her voice and also her hair.

During this whole thing, we never talked on the phone. I told her I couldn't because of reasons beyond my control. Everything was through e-mail, and that was hard enough because I only did it from the library, even though we had a computer at home. Kent could be very nosy, especially when it came to me.

In the pictures Robin sent, her hair was long, and I imagined her voice softer and higher than it is. There's nothing wrong with it. It's just not how I imagined, and I spent a lot of time imagining everything about her. Maybe she spent a lot of time imagining me, too. I wonder if I'm like she hoped.

"Put your feet up," she tells me. "I'll get you a glass of water."

The couch is leather, with a matching chair and the thing you put your feet on – I forget what it's called. Real leather. My mother showed me in the furniture store one time the difference between real and fake. Once you touch and smell and even hear them both, you never forget, and afterwards what's fake stands out, even if you never noticed it before. The living-room furniture in Kent's apartment was vinyl. If you sat on it very long, especially in warm weather, your rear would be damp when you got up. A lot of things about Kent were fake.

In front of the couch here at Robin's is a low coffee table

with a vase of real flowers and some magazines I've never heard of, with names that all start with *the*, like *The Economist* and *The New Yorker* and *The Atlantic*. There's no TV.

When Robin comes back with my water and finds me holding *The Economist*, she says, "I know you told me you're not much of a reader, but we've got lots of books all over the house if you change your mind. Jill's dad had a little bit of an addiction."

Then I notice the built-in shelves on both sides of the fireplace, the books behind glass doors. I set the magazine down. "Is there a TV upstairs?"

"No, this is it."

I look around the room again, nervous.

"Oh!" She laughs and goes over – quick steps, everything she does is quick – to a dark red wooden cabinet against the wall and opens its doors. "Here you go. We hide it when we're not watching."

At Kent's apartment we were never not watching it. If the TV is off and there's no radio, the silence is so heavy. It makes you scared.

Robin hands me the remote and looks ready to cry again. I don't know what to say. Whatever I would think of is the wrong thing, probably, the way I kept saying the wrong thing to Jill at breakfast and it was just like my mother told me: I make people uncomfortable. Actually what she said was: "You give them the creeps. Just act right."

I close my eyes to think.

"I'm sorry," she says, and I open my eyes. She's pressing her hands to her cheeks. Every move she makes is part of the puzzle I'm putting together: her voice, her hair, her quick steps, the way her hands move, plus all of our e-mails and the way she started writing "Mandy, Dear" instead of "Dear Mandy" in the last few weeks. It's adding up to something, finally. "You're exhausted. I'll try to contain my excitement and leave you alone for a while. I'll run up and get the sheets on the bed. I should have had it all done, but I decided at the last minute to get you new bedding, and I wanted to wash everything first... Okay. You rest." She's lowered her voice to a whisper. "I can't get over how tiny you are."

She goes upstairs. It's the first time I've been alone since the cab dropped me off at the train station in Omaha.

I'm here. I did this. When I sent my first e-mail to Robin, I only had a small hope she would reply; and after she replied, I had only a small hope she would agree to everything the way I wanted it; and when she agreed, I only had a small hope she wouldn't change her mind. And here I am, all of those small hopes getting me from one day to the next, the way they have my whole life.

In the pocket of my dress is another small hope – the white sticker from Alex's magazine that has his address on it. I peeled it off while he was in the bathroom.

When will you be coming through Denver again? I'll write. *We can meet for coffee.*

I have to keep thinking of my future.

The only little worry mixed in with my hopes is Jill. Robin never said very much about her in the e-mails. At breakfast, after Jill said she looked like her father, I asked her about him, and she wouldn't say anything. Robin had already told me some and in a way I felt like I knew him, but I wanted to make conversation with Jill. She changed the subject. Then I offered her some of my pancakes. She made a face and said she didn't like pancakes. What kind of a person doesn't like pancakes? Not a good kind.

It could be that she's jealous. The way she stared at Alex when he got back on the train made me think of what my mother says: When it comes to men, never trust another woman. "Especially if you're pretty," she told me, jealousy will always get in the way. "And you are a woman, Mandy," she said when I got my period. "You stopped being a girl today and that's something, but don't expect the world to throw you a parade." I didn't. Friendships were the first thing to change, she said. When I got to school, I told my best friend, Suzette, I'd started, and she said, "Gross," and told everyone. My mother turned out to be right that time.

Anyway, Jill is not Alex's type, with an electric-blue streak in her brown-black hair, and that eyebrow ring, and dark, chipped nail polish. She's doesn't take care of herself or understand the importance of first impressions. My mother says you should always take a moment to look in the mirror before you leave the house and try to see yourself through the eyes of strangers.

The baby moves and I touch it back. When I first started to feel it, it was sometimes like a heartbeat and sometimes like tiny waves from a miniature ocean, as if the baby was swimming inside me, already graceful. Now it's a kick. Every time it moves, I imagine how it will look. How I hope it will look. Just because I'm giving my baby to Robin doesn't mean I don't think about it the way anyone in my state would, imagine holding it or the way it might look at me. It's been a part of me since July. Now it's February. That's a long time to think about someone every day.

Robin made a doctor's appointment for me, and it's tomorrow, and we'll find out the sex. I told Robin I already knew. In our e-mails, I told her I've been going to all my prenatal appointments. I told her I'm due in three weeks. I told her it's a boy. She already has a girl, and I thought that she would want one of each and that if I told her it was a boy, the chances of her saying yes would be better.

Heavy footsteps clomp down the stairs, and Jill says from behind me, "How many pillows do you want?"

"What?" I ask, turning to her. She's got her hands in the pockets of her sweatshirt. Slouching and frowning.

"On your bed. How many? Mom says some pregnant people like to sleep with one between their knees."

"Okay."

"Okay what? One for your knees and one for your head? Or more?"

How many pillows do they have? "Either way."

She sighs. "Can you just give me a number?"

"Three."

"Great."

Jill clomps back up. I lean into the soft, real leather of the sofa and close my eyes, wondering what my mother would say if she could see me now.

Jill

The excitement of watching Mandy take over our lives has to be temporarily abandoned so that I can come to work. Work is good. I urgently need distraction from the situation, which until this morning was all dread and imagination. Like the SAT or a dentist's appointment. For weeks and weeks you imagine how horrible and impossible it's going to be, and then you're doing it and it's hard to tell in the moment: Is this as horrible and impossible as I thought it would be? Worse? Not so bad? I don't know.

I've tried convincing myself it has nothing to do with me. It's Mom's right to do this. Yet I can't help thinking, *Am I not enough?* Mom and I have had our issues. I know she didn't want me having a serious boyfriend in high school. I know she would have preferred me to have friends with better grades. I know she wants me to go to college, and I'm not, at least not right away. She knows I know all these things, though we never talk about them. You're familiar with the elephant in the living room? We've got a whole herd. The biggest one is this: Dad was the parent I was closer to.

And I think, for my sake, Mom feels guilty about being the one who lived.

It has occurred to me that she sees the baby as a second chance; an opportunity to correct my failings and to finally have a child that's all hers.

These are not pleasant thoughts. Work gives me a little bit of a break from it all.

Margins is a bookstore – part of a big national chain, which Mom isn't super thrilled about, given that she's on the Buy Local board and had me marching around Washington Park with a sign reading SAVE MOM 'N' POP! when I was eight. But my parents wanted me to have a job, and Margins was hiring. At least it's books, Mom said, something we can believe in and not deep-fried sandwiches or mortgage banking. Plus, Dad quickly realized I could put the employee discount to good use keeping him up to his neck in World War II memoirs and quantum physics theory and crime novels. And, to our collective surprise, it turned out that for a person who doesn't like people, I'm pretty good at this customer service stuff.

It's a slow night. We've got a Presidents' Day special

going on – twenty-five per cent off any title at all related to a president. The problem is, Corporate didn't define "at all related" or "president", and right now there's an old guy trying to get a discount on *Happy Birthday, Ms. President*. The cover photo is of a hot woman in skimpy lingerie holding a briefcase. I look at the back for a description while the customer rests his knobbly hands on the counter.

"So, this is actually about the president of a company," I say.

"Still a president."

"Yeah, but. Of an underwear company."

He corrects me. "Fine lingerie."

My manager, Annalee, is on her break, meaning this case is mine to judge. The guy looks like someone's nice grandpa. Maybe this book is his only hope for some jollies. In the end I give him the discount; Margins isn't going to miss its $1.99 that much. Normally I'm tough about these situations – questionable returns, expired coupons, complicated lies about lost receipts. But it will make me feel good to help this man get the most out of his allotment of happiness – which I've learned over the past year is limited for all of us – and I want to feel good.

"Happy Presidents' Day." I slip his receipt into the bag.

"You, too, sweetie."

Aw.

What I need is to talk to Dylan about Mandy. About how it felt to take her stuff up to the guest room. About her flowered dress and eerie eyes. About how I'm torn between wanting to keep an eagle eye on her to protect Mom and wanting to say, *Fine, you didn't ask my opinion, and now it's your problem.* About how I've felt for months now that some universal force has been slowly inflating a balloon inside me to see just how much I can take before I pop.

Not much more.

After making sure there are no approaching customers, I pull my phone out of my apron and start a text to Dylan.

Store basically empty if you want to come hang out. I'll buy you a sugar cookie.

By the time I thumb type *sugar cookie*, Annalee is walking in, and I shove the phone back into my apron pocket without hitting Send.

"It's getting cold out there. Still dead?" She looks around the store while unwinding her striped scarf.

"One customer since you left."

She pulls her brunette braid over her shoulder and fingers the end. Annalee, who I think is like twenty-seven or something, probably won't ever be a legend in the bookselling business, as she doesn't know that much about actual books, but she's a great manager: completely reliable, never gets sick, is never short at the end of the day, never messes up the schedule, never loses her cool with employees or customers, and rarely takes a day off. So it surprises me when she says, "I'm thinking of leaving early. I can count out register two and have Ron close up the coffee counter. Can you handle the rest?"

"Of course." I've been working here nearly two years. I could run the place if I had to. That's another thing that makes Annalee a good manager, if not an expert on literature – she's taught me how to do everything she does. "In case something happens to me," she said once, matter-of-factly. "Like we're robbed and I get shot." The only thing I don't know is how to get into the safe; I'll just throw all the cash and paperwork into the drop for her to deal with in the morning.

"Doing anything fun?" I ask. "Or not feeling well?"

One corner of her mouth turns upwards. "Don't laugh."

"I won't." Though, it must be said that I would love to laugh. I would love to hear something funny right now – truly funny so I can laugh something other than the bitter "Life Is Unbelievably Shitty" laugh that's become my standard.

"There's a *Doctor Who* marathon on tonight, and I forgot to set my DVR. I don't want to miss it."

Now that's funny. I laugh.

"Jill!"

"Sorry. I shouldn't have promised."

"It's the *original*," she says, defensive.

"Enjoy." Later, when she's gone, I straighten up the display tables, turn out the lights in the back way earlier than usual, and stay at the counter chatting with Ron, keeping my eyes on the doors in the hope Dylan will walk through. Then I remember I never sent the text.

Two older ladies come in together and buy the latest City Read and a fifty-per-cent-off cat calendar.

One of them points to the white fluff ball on the cover. "This one looks exactly like our Edgar."

"You should hang it where Edgar can see," I say.

"Oh, he passed." She looks down as I slide the calendar into a bag.

"Christmas Eve," the other lady says, touching the first lady's shoulder.

Maybe they're sisters. Maybe they're friends. Maybe they're life partners. Whichever, there is such real affection there, real tenderness, that the sight of them inflates that balloon a little bit more and presses against my heart so intensely that I put my hand to my chest in an attempt to mash it back down.

"I'm so sorry." *Don't let my scary-teenager hair and piercings fool you*, I think. *I know loss.* "Have a nice night."

I lock the door behind them and tell Ron, who has to get home to his kid, to take off, I'm closing up.

"Twenty-five minutes early?" he asks.

"I won't tell if you won't."

Poor Ron. He's in his thirties and started here about four months ago; it was the only job he could get after losing his actual career in the recession and winding up the oldest employee here, yet lowest on the totem pole. It's grown on him, though, and it turns out he's this incredible visionary when it comes to store displays. Last week he combined our bestselling sci-fi, fantasy, and graphic novels into one beautiful geek heaven.

He leaves, and as I crank out the closing paperwork at lightning speed, the situation with Mandy re-emerges to obsessive consciousness. Did I do enough to try to talk Mom out of it? I think I did. Yet the more I pointed out what a colossal disaster this could become, the more she turned into a brick wall. There was no one but me to attempt to break through. All my grandparents are dead, and so is my dad's brother, and my mom is an only child. She has friends, but she sort of shut them out when Dad died. Like I did with my friends. Only with her, it was about suddenly being "busy with work", whereas I directly told my friends to leave me alone. My exact words might have been "Leave me the hell alone".

Mom and I, different as we are, are twin planets orbiting the same universe of grief but never quite making contact. Maybe this baby is a good thing and I'm just not seeing it. Maybe it'll be a new little sun for us, or at least for Mom. Or maybe it will be a black hole that will suck us in and tear us to bits. Either way, we're at the point of no return. Hello, event horizon.

At home earlier, I caught Mandy sniffing the couch. When she realized I was watching her, she said, "Real leather."

"Yeah."

I mean, it's nothing sinister, but it's weird, right?

And before I left for work, she hinted that since I work at a bookstore, maybe I could borrow some magazines for her to read, the celebrity gossip kind, then I could return them tomorrow.

"It's not a library." I sat on the bottom stair, lacing my boots.

"I wouldn't wrinkle the pages."

"We do have a library about a mile away," Mom said. "It's closed for the holiday, but we can go tomorrow, on our way back from the doctor."

Mandy shut up about the magazines after that and started in on Mom with special grocery requests. All stuff we never eat, like kids' cereal and frozen lasagne and snack mix. I watched Mom's face as Mandy rattled off her list. Mom just kept smiling. I'm dying to see, when I get home, if Mom is so eager to please Mandy that she violated her deeply held wholefood principles.

Now I put on my coat and remind myself to stop fixating on Mandy. Ultimately it's not about her but the baby. The baby and Mom. And I guess I fit somewhere in that scenario, too.

Outside, in the retail development where Margins is one of the main stores, the chill is startling. It's at least twenty degrees colder than it was at the train station this morning. I lock the doors behind me quickly, wishing I'd brought gloves. There might be a pair in my messenger bag, but it's too dark and deserted to be standing around digging in my bag like a perfect target, asking to be bludgeoned. Dad signed me up for self-defence when a serial rapist was on the loose in downtown Denver, and not only did he go with me every Saturday for six weeks, he *participated* in the class by volunteering to be repeatedly kneed in the nuts by a bunch of outraged women. He wore padding, of course, but still.

The instructor never failed to remind us to be aware of our surroundings. So when a guy approaches from what seems like out of nowhere, my muscles are already tensing.

"Aren't you open ten more minutes?"

I relax a little. It figures that the one night I close early, we have a late customer. His face is in shadow, but he seems young, and he's tall, dressed in a suit that I can't imagine is keeping him warm without an overcoat.

"Usually, yes." I apologize and suggest he come back tomorrow, hoping he's in a good mood, because closing early is definitely a serious offence.

When I start moving away from the door, he stays close. I unrelax. One thing we learned in the self-defence class is to trust your instincts, and my instincts tell me this is creepy. There's no one else around. I think about my keys in my hand and how I can use the big store key to gouge out an eye if I have to. As cold as it is, sweat prickles under my arms.

I start walking towards my car, which is also towards him. If he follows, I'll know something is up. With my keys in hand, I take a few purposeful steps his way.

He puts out his arm to stop me. "Oh, um, I need to search your bag? I'm R. J. Desai? From Corp—"

But the second his hand touches my shoulder, my reflexes kick in and I throw an elbow strike to his face, the forces of fear and adrenalin behind it. He drops without a word, stunned.

Wow. That completely worked. A hundred elbow strikes to a punching bag, my dad standing behind it to hold it still, are apparently engraved in my muscle memory even after a year. The next thing you're supposed to do is either (A) run like hell or (B) try to do a little more damage while he's still vulnerable. Since I'm a slow runner and he's already getting to his feet, I mentally prepare to go for the groin and the eyes.

But when he's up, he backs away, holding his face. "Why'd you *do* that?"

It could be a diversionary tactic. I stay in my defence position, feet apart and knees slightly bent. We're both breathing hard. I stare him in the eyes and don't see a trace of a threat, only pain and bewilderment. Also? He looks a tiny bit familiar. What was he saying before I decked him? "Because you're stalking me in a dark mall in the middle of the night," I say.

"Are you Jill MacSweeney?"

"Maybe."

"R. J. Desai." He reaches under his suit jacket and pulls a card from the chest pocket of his shirt. "Margins Loss Prevention."

I step up and whip the card from his hand.

R. J. DESAI
LOSS PREVENTION ASSOCIATE
MARGINS, INC.

"How do I know this is you?"

From his back pocket he pulls out a wallet and produces a driver's licence. I take it and hold it next to the card. It's him. Ravi Jagadish Desai, nineteen, with a Washington Park address.

"You could have had this card made at any copy shop. A real Margins employee would not do a dumb-ass thing like show up with no warning and start grabbing at a girl in the middle of the night."

"I wasn't grabbing at you."

"Yes, you were."

"I didn't mean to."

"Well, you did. With no warning," I repeat.

"If we gave a warning, we'd never stop employee theft." His voice is unsteady. I think I really scared him.

"Now you're accusing me of stealing?" I look at the licence again. "Wait, do I know you?"

He takes his driver's licence out of my hand; I hold on to the card. "At least half our property losses last quarter were from employee theft and carelessness." He takes a deep breath and expels it in a puff of white into the cold air. "We went to the same high school."

"We did?"

"We were in computer science together." He touches his jaw cautiously.

I study him, trying to conjure up the computer lab and the people in it, including myself – the self I was. "With that student teacher? Ms. Schiff?" I begin to shiver in the cold even as a trickle of perspiration makes its way past my ear.

"Yeah. My senior year. I think you were a sophomore." He waits while I keep staring.

Sophomore year. Eons and eons ago. "If you say so." I turn to head to my car; he follows.

"Jill, I think I still need to search your bag."

I laugh. The bitter one. "I don't think you do." I keep walking. My hands are shaking. Even though I know the moment of crisis is over, my body doesn't – adrenalin pumping, knees weak, and even tears working up. A purely physical reaction to being scared and mad. Not only at him. Maybe I didn't do the right thing. I never know any more what the right thing is, let alone if I'm doing it.

R. J. jogs a little to catch up with me. "I – hang on. I was just trying to do my job..."

"Fail," I say over my shoulder. Because it's a lot easier to be mad at him than at me. "Is that really what they train you to do? Stalk people? Jump out at them in the dark?"

"No," he says, next to me now, indignant. "Procedure is to come into the store. You closed early. You—"

"Don't try to blame this on me." I get to my car and fumble with the keys for way longer than I want, thinking that I wish I hadn't closed early and I could really get into trouble. When I finally get the door open, I throw my messenger bag onto the passenger seat before getting in.

"Wait." R. J. holds the corner of my door, keeping me from closing it. With my adrenalin-fuelled super powers and all the other emotions roaring, I yank it shut and start the engine. I hear his muffled pleas. "Wait! I'm sorry. You're right." That gets me to look at him. He's grimacing, holding one hand with the other and now tapping them both against the window as I back up. "Are you going to report this? I can't lose my job right now, Jill."

He says my name as if he really knows me. Ms. Schiff's, sophomore year. The year I got together with Dylan after we took driver's ed together. The year I got my piercing without Mom's or Dad's permission and suffered through a two-week grounding thinking it was the worst thing in the world that could happen to me. The year Laurel and I sneaked into an eighteen-and-over club on Colfax and had the best night ever and totally got away with it. The year I had no idea how much of my lucky life I'd lose.

"Jill?" R. J. asks again. "Seriously, it's my first week. Please."

Realizing I have the power in this situation, I roll down

the window just enough so he can hear me clearly. "Tough shit."

He stands there, holding his hand and watching me take a speed bump too fast. Then I turn towards the exit and he's gone.

Halfway home I pull over on a residential street, too amped to drive. My elbow hurts where it connected with R. J.'s face. *Idiot.*

I start crying.

Not because of fear or anger any more. Because: when I get home, my dad won't be there to get outraged on my behalf, to be impressed when I re-enact my elbow strike, to say I told you so about making me take that class, to tell me I did the right thing and the store stays open too late, anyway, for school nights. I won't get to see him turn red. I won't get to talk him out of calling the police or Margins headquarters. I won't get to say, *Dad, calm down. I lived. It's fine.*

I'll walk in the door and his chair will be empty.

I beat on the steering wheel a few times, blow my nose on a napkin I find in the glovebox, and head home. On the way I stop at a mini-mart and buy Mandy three magazines and a package of cupcakes.

Why I do this, it's hard to say, except I know that it's exactly the kind of thing my dad would have done.

* * *

Later, when I can't sleep and I've tried all the usual tricks – listening to talk radio, counting backwards, drinking warm tea – I pull out my sophomore yearbook so that I don't wind up lying awake thinking about my dad all night.

I find my class picture and stare and stare and stare, like Jill MacSweeney is someone from my long-ago past. A forgotten pen pal. An old summer-camp friend.

Here's something I remember: Laurel and I swapped shirts the morning of picture day. For no reason other than to make fun of the whole idea of school pictures and how everyone at school was trying so hard to look good. I can see us in the girls' room, laughing and standing in our bras. In my picture I've got on her favourite retro Specials T-shirt. In her picture, she's wearing my signature green hoodie. It hurts to look at that too long. All I can remember is what I lost, not who I was.

Desai, Desai. I flip pages until I find him. Ravi – not R. J. – Desai.

His senior quote is beneath his picture:

> *As we journey into the future,*
> *may we all encounter new adventures,*
> *and our true selves.*
> *Thanks Ma and Baba, Miti, Neil, Anand.*

He had glasses back then, big, bushy hair, a round face; he signed his picture. I feel kind of bad not remembering him. He was obviously a different person back then, though. And so was I. The pre-dead-father Jill. Who is as much a stranger to me now as Ravi is.

Mandy

Today we have a doctor's appointment, and it's the one last thing I have to get through before I can unpack. Robin offered to help me last night. "Don't you want to have everything in order before you go to bed?" she asked. "You'll sleep better." We were in the guest room, my room. Jill had gone to work. Robin made us turkey sandwiches and fruit salad for dinner. I've never had a fruit salad like that; it was just cut-up fruit, no Cool Whip or marshmallows or anything.

I told her no, I'd wait and do it today, after I'd had a chance to think about where to put things. Robin left me alone after that, and I lay awake for hours listening to cars go by. Not that that's what kept me up; I like that sound, and knowing there are people out there coming and going. Kent's apartment was on the third floor of a building off I-29. He liked to be close to the casinos. "An apartment community", my mother called it, reading from the website before we moved in with him. "It has a broad range of amenities." It was quieter than you'd think, with carpets everywhere and neighbours not really talking to each other. Sometimes I got the feeling that even if I screamed and screamed no one would hear me.

What kept me up last night was worrying about this appointment and whether afterwards Robin is going to let me stay. I have to get it right. The appointment is a reminder of why I'm really here. I'm not here for me. Robin's not here for me. The guest room isn't here for *me*, and it doesn't matter if Jill likes *me*, and all this is leading up to a moment when I'm gone. That's the point. Me being gone. The baby staying here. That's the part I don't want to mess up.

The doctor turns out to be a woman. Her name is Megan Yee, with an office in a hospital, and we're all sitting at a small, round table in the exam room. She's young and too pretty to be a doctor, with sleek hair in a ponytail and natural lipgloss on. I thought the doctor would be a man. I hoped. Men like me better than women do, all around. I answer Dr. Yee's questions the same way I've been answering Robin's all along.

Amanda Madison Kalinowski.

Eighteen.

Thirty-seven weeks.

A boy.

The father can't be located but, as far as I know, is in good, normal health.

Yes, I've been taking my vitamins, going to appointments, and not drinking or smoking.

Only a percentage of those things are true, but I try to say them all exactly the same way. Making eye contact but not too much eye contact. Breathing normally. Resting my hand on the baby and sometimes looking at the painting of lilies hanging on the wall behind Dr. Yee's head. When I say "thirty-seven weeks", she glances up from the laptop where she's entering information, and her eyes flick to my belly, to my face, and to my belly again. Then back to the computer.

"Have you had a glucose tolerance test?" she asks, typing.

"Probably."

"You'd remember. They give you a drink? Tastes like flavoured sugar water?"

She could smile and be friendlier if she wanted her patients to relax. Every time I answer a question, I feel like it's the wrong answer. "Maybe not."

Robin's been sitting quietly in the chair next to mine. I've avoided looking at her, even though I would like to stare and stare, keep seeing the pieces of her add up. I want to add up for her, too, and don't want to let her down, even though it's bound to happen eventually. In all our e-mails since January, I've tried to be what she wanted me to be, because all that mattered was getting her to take the baby and getting away. Except she asked me so many questions, more questions about me than I've ever been asked by anyone in my whole entire life put together. Little things, like what kind of music do I like, and my favourite subjects at school; and bigger ones, like what is my idea of God and who are my heroes in history and if I could be anything I wanted, what would I be? One time she sent a short e-mail that said only *There were magpies out in the snow when I was on a walk this morning. Have you ever seen Monet's painting* The Magpie? *It's one of my favourites.*

I didn't know how to tell her that I've never even been to a museum. Maybe on a field trip once a long time ago, but I didn't know if that counted.

Questions like that, and like who my heroes in history are or what I want to be, I didn't answer, because I don't have an answer. I didn't want her to think I'm dumb. I didn't want to say the wrong thing. Her e-mails made me nervous sometimes, even though they were also exciting to get and to read. And even though none of this is supposed to be about me, it was hard not to let it be a little bit about me. I never talked to anyone who had so many thoughts about so many different things before. Everything felt like a test, and I must have kept passing because I'm here.

Now this appointment feels like a test, too, and I'm sure I'm going to fail.

"Stand up, please." Dr. Yee takes a tape measure from around her neck and measures my belly. "Thirty-seven weeks?"

"Yes."

"If you're sure about the approximate date of conception, I'm concerned about IUGR." The last part she says to Robin.

"Oh." Robin sounds worried. "It means the baby isn't growing at the rate he should," she says to me. "Are you absolutely sure about the timing?"

"I could be off a little." I picture my room at Robin's house. Taking my unpacked bags downstairs. Getting on a train to go back. Never getting a "Mandy, Dear" e-mail from Robin again.

Dr. Yee puts the tape measure around her neck again. "Since Mandy doesn't have any records, I'd like us to start with a clean, or at least informed, slate and run all tests. Including an ultrasound. Okay?"

Robin nods, her lips mashed together. Not angry. Scared. I didn't mean for her to be worried. "I probably figured wrong," I say. "I'm never good at math." She tries to smile, but still I can see there are thoughts running through her head like maybe I lied on purpose and the baby isn't healthy like I said it was, or I slept with more possible fathers than I said I did. Or that I lied about all my doctor's appointments. Which I did.

"Cola, orange, or lime?" Dr. Yee asks. "You get your pick for the glucose tolerance test."

"Orange."

She goes out and a nurse comes back, and over the next ten minutes I pee in a cup, have my blood pressure taken, and drink the sweet drink, and then the nurse takes Robin and me down the hall to the ultrasound room, where I get undressed enough to give them access to my belly. Robin gets up to leave with the nurse. "No," I say. "You can stay." She looks at a chart on the wall while I strip off my dress, leaving on my underwear but taking off the long camisole I've been wearing because my bras are too small now. I stand in front of her and hug myself. "It's cold."

She stares at me, not moving. "Your body is so..." She laughs, embarrassed. "Your skin. You don't even have any stretch marks. It makes me feel old." She gets up and takes a folded-up sheet off the table, and drapes it around my shoulders.

She *is* old. A little bit old. Older than I pictured, even though she told me her age and I don't mind it. Standing as close to her as I am now, I can see every line on her face. "I have good genes is all. So will the baby."

There are three short knocks on the door, and then Dr. Yee comes in with a man following behind. "This is Nils. Our ultrasound pro."

Nils, short and blond and wearing a pink top and bottom, winks at me. "I'm sure you're a pro by now, too, Mandy. Presuming you've done this at least once?"

I don't say anything, letting them think that's a yes. I get on the table and Nils arranges the sheet so I'm mostly covered except for my belly. He slathers it with cold goo. To stay relaxed, I think about train rides and the Missouri River and fields of corn, turning myself into a person who knows nothing other than what she's been told, not a liar. The sensor glides over my belly while I stare at the speckled ceiling tiles until Robin sucks in a breath and says, "There he is." She holds my hand.

On the monitor, a form in black and white and grey undulates and throbs.

I think of summer. The warm night, the stars.

"He?" Nils asks. "Are we sure about that?" He moves the sensor around.

Dr. Yee studies the monitor. "Nope." She turns to me. "When did they tell you it was a boy?"

"I don't remember. Last time."

"Well, they got it wrong. It happens."

"It's a girl?" Robin asks quietly. I can't tell from her voice if she's happy or disappointed. When I look, there are tears in her eyes, and I think, I hope, they're the happy kind of tears. The shape on the screen – the baby – makes something in my heart move, too. The truth is that it's the first time I've seen it. Her. A part of me but not. Connected but also an alien. Alive. Real. Evidence of something...of one thing or of another.

"A girl," Robin says.

"There's her face," Dr. Yee says, pointing. "See the nose?"

We all watch quietly for a few seconds, maybe longer. I try to see who she looks like.

Then Nils says, "Was the person who told you it was a boy the same one who said you'd be thirty-seven weeks now?" A look passes between him and Dr. Yee.

"It might have been the beginning of July," I say. "The conception. Now that I think of it."

Dr. Yee nods. "That would make more sense. You're measuring at around thirty-three."

I keep my eyes on the monitor to avoid Robin's. Nils presses some buttons to print off pictures. Then he takes the sensor away and the baby disappears.

* * *

We have to wait awhile longer so that a full hour has passed between when I had the orange drink and when they draw blood. Robin types on her phone, papers spread out on the chair beside her. "Sorry," she says. "I've got a lot of client messages to deal with. There's always a backlog after a holiday."

"It's okay." I like seeing her work. Mostly what I've seen of my mother's work, at least since she got the casino job, is her coming home in her smoky uniform and taking off her make-up with cold cream, the same kind my grandma used. Then she'd take a bath and refix her hair and put on fresh make-up so that when Kent got home he didn't have to think about the fact that she'd been walking the floor all day serving drinks to other men.

"But that's how he met you," I said. "He knows."

"I know he *knows*, Mandy, but I don't have to throw it in his face."

Robin's job is a whole different kind of a thing, even though it seems a little bit right now like she's doing it to avoid talking to me. I wish I could think what to say that would make her know she's right to trust me, even if I might have been wrong about a few details. She's not making a mistake, I want to tell her. This baby, boy or girl, belongs with her and will make her happy, and just because the dates are a little bit off and the sex is different doesn't mean there's anything to worry about. Maybe I should tell her that I have doubts, too, that there are small moments when I remember July and feel sure what this baby is evidence of and want to keep it. That it's the only evidence I have. And that's why, in the end, even though there are those small moments, I want to protect it by keeping it far from me and where I've come from.

We're in the same boat, Robin and me, with fears and doubts, even if they're different for each of us. We're both going into an unknown future. But I know if I try to say all that, I'll mess up the words somehow and only worry her more. Lots of times in life, the best thing to do is stay silent. "Don't open your mouth if only nonsense is going to come out, Amanda," my mother says.

When time's up, the nurse takes my blood. Dr. Yee talks to Robin about me. "She can keep, or start, exercising moderately. Watch her nutrition. Jenny will have some pamphlets for you at the front desk and will call you with the results of the blood draw in a couple of days. On your way out, make an appointment for two weeks from now." Dr. Yee pats me on the shoulder. "Okay, Mandy. Take care of yourself and that baby."

"I will."

*　*　*

In the car Robin reminds me to buckle up. "We'll get you home and fix you something to eat, then I've got to run out to a meeting."

"Okay."

There's a lot of traffic coming out of the hospital, which is in Aurora, about a twenty-minute drive from the house. Robin told me about it on the way there – how it's the best, how it's a straight shot on Colfax and easy to get to, how the birth centre there has the newest of everything and big tubs in every delivery room, if you want to do it that way. On the way home, she's quiet. It isn't until we pull into her driveway and she turns off the car that she asks me, "Did you really not know your real due date?"

Honesty doesn't always work. Times I tried to be honest with my mother about important things, she didn't believe me, and it only made situations worse. I think Robin is different. I know she is. That's why I'm here. Still, I'm too scared to say anything but yes. I'd rather she think I'm stupid than that I lied. She'd see it as taking advantage, but that's not it. It was survival, that's all. I couldn't wait any more.

She nods. "I'll have to rearrange my schedule."

"I'm sorry." I run my hand along the shoulder strap of the seat belt. "Do you want me to move somewhere else until the date is closer?" Not that I could. Unless I sold Kent's watch, which I'm not ready to do, not yet.

Robin looks at me, surprise on her face. "No. No no. You'll stay right here. It's fine." Her phone chimes from somewhere in her bag; she ignores it. "But, Mandy, you've got to understand how much trust this takes for me, doing this the way that you want to do it. What I'm risking."

"I know."

"I can't lose someone else." Her voice is steady.

"I know."

She takes off her seat belt and gathers up her bag, her coat, her sunglasses, and looks at me and I can see she's still happy, she doesn't hate me. "So," she says, "I guess we'd better start thinking about some girl names."

Jill

It's fairly easy to stalk someone when you've dated him for almost two years. And Dylan, being a creature of rigorous habit, makes it child's play. Tuesdays in cold weather are pho days, and as I am the only one of his friends who shares his great passion for pho, he'll be going alone. Alone is a recurring theme for me, too, when it comes to lunchtime. On Friday, I made an attempt at offering myself up as available to eat with Laurel and Cinders, but they didn't take the bait. Namely, me standing in our old meeting place near the girls' room by Laurel's locker, trying to look bait-y and available. They saw me. Oh, they saw me. *Upon* seeing me, they exchanged a glance and kept walking.

I guess I could have come right out and said, "Hey, I miss you guys. I'm sorry. Totally, totally sorry. I was wrong. Being left alone was a bad idea. Can I eat with you? Or near you? Pretty, pretty, pretty please?"

However, that's not so much the kind of thing I'm good at saying.

Hoping to do better with Dylan, I wait by his car in the student lot, freezing my ass off and betting on his addiction to Vietnamese soup. Enough time passes that doubt sets in, as does the cold. I break into his car – a simple task, owing to a back-door lock that's never worked right – and grab his UC-Boulder fleece blanket from the back dash, pulling it over my head and curling up on the back seat.

I've told myself all morning that I only need his friendship right now, his advice about Mandy, his insight. That I'm not here to try to get back together. That even if he wanted to, I wouldn't, because too much has happened now and sometimes things come to a natural end and that's how it is.

But as soon as I smell the blanket...

Okay, the blanket itself is a little musty, but beneath that there he is.

Ohhhhhhhhgod.

The moulding paste he uses on his hair. The environmentally correct eucalyptus dryer sheets his mom likes. Coffee. Cinnamon gum.

We've broken up and gotten back together twice since... Dad. You could say we're on our third break-up now, though technically I think this is more like an "I can't take you right now" break than a break-*up*. All I know is that whatever I said before, and whatever may happen in the future, I need him today.

Just as I'm working myself up to a purifying, private cry, I hear the driver's door open, and sense someone drop into the seat. I knew it. Rigorous habit. He starts the car and turns on the heat and pulls forwards while I consider making my presence known, and then it's kind of too late. Though I am tempted to bitch at him for pulling forwards out of the parking space, which drives me crazy because it drove my dad crazy. "You're supposed to back out," Dad would say. "That's what the rules are, and that's what all the cars around you expect, and you should always try to behave predictably when driving." He was a great driver. Mr. Highway Safety. And it's not fair that he died in a car accident. I wonder if he's out there and knows how it happened. Maybe he's lecturing the old lady – also dead – who got disoriented by a bright beam of morning sun, crossed the central reservation, and hit him at freeway speed.

Don't think about that, Jill. Think about:

How out of it Dylan is. If he weren't, he'd check the back seat to see what's up with the oddly shaped blanket hump. Can't he, like, *sense* that he's not alone? Now I'm afraid if I say something, he'll be startled and veer into oncoming traffic. I mentally follow the stops and turns – yes, definitely pho. It's almost funny how oblivious he is. I imagine all the ways I could reveal myself, from throwing back the blanket and yelling "Surprise!" to snaking out a hand to rest on his neck. It strikes me as hilarious. Or awful. I'm on the edge, teetering between laughing like a maniac and bursting into scary, heaving sobs. A laugh or a sob rises in my throat when I imagine Dylan's reaction to finding me; I clamp my lips shut, hard, trying not to shake. Tears squeeze out of my eyes. I think I'm crying. I don't know.

The car comes to a stop. Dylan jerks the parking brake up, and the door opens and closes. I feel the blast of cold air. Finally, I let out a sob-laugh and sit up, relieved to be breathing without the filter of the blanket. Two more sobs. Definitely sobs. *Shake it off, Jill.* I don't need to be acting a fool in front of Dylan right now. I need to show him I'm sane and stable and ready to be human.

After a few minutes of deep inhaling, exhaling, I get out of the car and walk to one end of the street and then back, oh so casually entering the restaurant. Dylan is in a small booth, already sipping hot tea while he looks at his phone.

"Oh, hey," I say, acting surprised. Badly.

It's been a couple of weeks since I've seen him straight on like this, outside of the classrooms and hallways of school. He's so beautiful. He's got on a smudge of black eyeliner and has a new bleached streak in his dark hair, but he's not wearing his lip ring, the one I like to tug lightly with my teeth when we kiss.

"What are you doing here, Jill?"

It's not quite the hello I'd hoped for.

"Just one?" the waiter asks, handing me a menu.

"Um..." Dylan is going to make me ask what I couldn't ask Cinders and Laurel. "Can I sit with you?"

"If you want." He puts away his phone. A good sign, like he's willing to pay attention to me.

I sit, order a bowl of my favourite pho and a hot tea.

"Did you follow me here?" he asks, staring at me over his teacup.

"*No.*" As if. "I really wanted some soup. You think you're the only one that can come here? You own this place now?"

He laughs. It's a beautiful sound. "Jill, you are so full of shit. You think I didn't see you sitting in my back seat before I even got into the car?"

I smile. "I wondered what the hell was wrong with you that you didn't notice."

"It's a little creepy."

"I almost thought you weren't going to come. But I know you and winter and Tuesdays and pho."

He shrugs. "What can I say? Pho is rock."

Dylan has this whole rating system for everything –

food, bands, clothes, teachers, movies, cars, songs, life events – based on the game rock-paper-scissors. Whatever is the utmost in awesomeness, whatever is profoundly good, whatever is right and true, is rock. Because rock, though it can be beaten (or "hidden", as Dylan prefers to say) by paper, can never be destroyed.

I wonder what would happen if I bumped my knee against his under the table, or touched his arm. I wonder whose job it is to make the first move. I wonder if I even want that.

"I didn't mean to be creepy," I say, keeping my limbs to myself. "I was waiting for you and it was freezing and I knew the blanket was in there. Then I was going to say something but didn't think it was safe to scare you while you were driving." Remembering something Dylan once said about how I never say I'm sorry, that I make excuses instead – true – I add, "Sorry."

The waiter sets two steaming bowls of beef broth on the table, along with plates of noodles and limes and bean sprouts and thinly sliced meat. We quietly go through the ritual of unwrapping and breaking apart our wooden chopsticks, rubbing them together to smooth out any splinters. We move items from the plates into our bowls. I lean my head over mine, inhaling the fragrant steam and closing my eyes for a second. I make a wish. A pho wish.

I wish for Dylan to speak to me as if I'm a person he might still like a little bit. I don't need for him to love and adore me. Only to tolerate, be my friend.

Maybe the best way to encourage that to happen is to talk about something somewhat neutral, at least as it pertains to our relationship.

"Remember how my mom is adopting that baby?"

"Pretty sure I'm not going to forget that."

"The mother, the pregnant girl, got here yesterday."

That gets his attention. He sets his chopsticks down. "Oh, man. I didn't realize that was happening *now*. Wasn't it only, like, six weeks ago or something your mom told you?"

"Yeah. It's happening."

"It must be crazy. To realize it's for real and everything."

"Totally crazy."

"I want to meet her."

"You do?"

He picks up his chopsticks, slurps noodles. "Yeah, I mean, it's a big deal. And even with, you know, the way everything is, I still kind of feel like part of the family? If that's okay."

Yes, I know the way everything is. "It's okay. It's good."

This is going so well. So unbelievably perfect. I barrel ahead. "My mom took her to the doctor this morning. To check everything out. This girl, she's from another planet, I'm telling you."

"Yeah?" He takes a bite of bean sprouts.

"Sniffer of leather. Eater of the worst kind of junk food. Lover of tabloid magazines."

"She's our age, right? And she's only staying there a little while. You can handle it."

"Seriously, Dylan, she's *weird*." I drop a slice of beef into my broth; now I'm on a roll. "Not much going on upstairs. Her big ambition was to go to Pancake Universe."

Dylan pushes his lower lip out and nods. "Uh-huh. And how long have you known her? Like, a total of five waking hours or something?"

His tone has totally changed. So I change mine, too. "Are you saying I don't have the right to judge?"

"No. And even if I were saying that, I know it wouldn't stop you. I'm just saying maybe you should think about how she feels. She's probably scared as hell. She probably needs a friend. Not everyone was born independent like you."

Well. What am I supposed to say to that?

He picks up his bowl and drinks, then sets it down. "Wow. Have I rendered you speechless?"

"Ha," I say weakly, and it's all I've got. So I'm independent. The way my dad raised me to be. No daughter of his would ever be stuck on the side of the road in the dark flagging down potential rapists to help with a flat. He opened my first current account with me when I was twelve and taught me how to make a budget and balance my account using a spreadsheet. He taught me not only how to drive but how to drive in snow, on ice, off road, in a flood. I know how to change my oil and brake pads; I understand the wonders of compounding interest; I'm in charge of keeping the smoke alarms and heating filters fresh in our house; I can load and clean guns and shoot them if I have to; and I know how to drop a man with an elbow strike to the face.

Okay, I also know that's not what Dylan means. He's talking about emotional independence. It's not like I chose it. I want to say, *When someone you love and depend on emotionally dies, get back to me.*

New subject needed. Maybe telling him about my encounter with Ravi, aka R. J. Desai, loss control associate, will get him interested in my life again.

"Do you remember a guy from—"

"Jill, I gotta get back to school." He puts money on the table and stands. Just enough to pay for his lunch and tip. I get up, too, and immediately realize I've left my messenger bag in my locker. Fantastic.

"Can I borrow, like…seven dollars?" Miss Independent, that's me.

Dylan is fixing his jeans so that they rest exactly right on his hips. "What if I don't have it? What are you going to do?"

"Do you have it?"

"What if I don't?"

"*Do you?*"

He takes his money from the table and goes up to the register to pay both our bills with his debit card. Five minutes ago, he was one of the family. Now we're...the way we are. I stand by the door trying to look as if it doesn't bother me. When he comes back, he says, "You need a ride back to school, too."

"No I don't," I say instantly, and just as instantly regret it. Why can't I simply say yes to him? What am I proving, except that I still don't know how to concede that, like anyone else, I don't want to be spinning off into the universe all alone? That sometimes I'm wrong, that sometimes I screw up, that sometimes I require mercy. From friends. From my mom, my dad. That right now I want Dylan's most of all. Even with all of these brilliant, self-aware insights, I push open the door of the restaurant and say, "I don't need anything."

Mandy

It's not my fault about the peanut butter. Robin *wants* me to eat things like peanut butter on apple slices for a snack, instead of cupcakes or hot chocolate. Their peanut butter isn't even that good; they get it from the health food store, and if you leave it out too long, it gets oily.

Jill's standing between me and the TV. "Why'd you stick the empty jar back in the fridge? Put it on the counter so we know we're out. Or write it on the list by the phone."

I've been here only two days. I'm not sure how I'm supposed to know where they keep the grocery list. At Kent's we didn't even have a list. If there wasn't food, he yelled about it and my mother went to the store.

"I think there's enough, if you scrape the sides, to put on a cracker?" I try to see in the space between her arm and body what's happening on the talk show that just started.

"No, there isn't." She walks over to the couch where I'm

stretched out with my feet up, and holds the jar in front of my face with the lid off to show me. The smell makes me hungry again. "Where's my mom?"

"She had a meeting. She said to tell you she left a note in your room."

Still holding the peanut butter jar, Jill stomps upstairs. This morning after Jill left for school, Robin sat by me on the couch and said, "About Jill..."

I propped myself up and paid attention.

"You have to understand," Robin said, "that I sort of dropped this on her out of the blue. So I can't totally blame her for not knowing how to handle it. I'd hoped she'd come around by now." She said to give her time, that Jill's actually a nice, caring person who hides it well. I said, "How much time?"

Robin smiled and then stopped smiling and said that she wished she knew, that she'd been waiting a long time herself for Jill to come back.

On Monday night, I was up in my room and in bed before Jill got home from work, and I didn't wake up until after she was gone in the morning, but there were magazines for me on the kitchen table. From her. So I had something to read at breakfast while Robin read her paper. That was nice. Then yesterday was the doctor, and when Jill got home from school and found out everything about the baby really being a girl and not being due for seven more weeks, she didn't hide that she was mad about that, and hasn't said very much to me since.

It doesn't look like that's going to change today.

The guest on the talk show is a bra expert, and women from the audience come down and get measured and everyone needs a bigger cup size than they thought and I don't know why, but they don't seem happy about it. I've always had the right size. In fifth grade, I got home from school one afternoon and I'd taken off my sweater because it was late spring and I wanted to feel the air on my arms. My mother saw me in my T-shirt and pulled me into my room – actually it was half my room and half Gary's office – and lifted my shirt. We went straight out to get me fitted. "Why didn't you say something, Amanda?" she asked me on the way to the store. "I hope you haven't been running around like that in front of Gary." Gary was her boyfriend that year. What I remember about him is a necklace with a real gold nugget on the chain, and the smell of Chinese tea. He drank it all the time because the antioxidants balanced out his smoking, he said.

After we got the bra, my mother took me out for ice cream. She made me order a triple-scoop sundae with everything on it, even though I wasn't hungry, and she got a diet pop for herself. "Eat up, Mandy, while you can," she said, her eyes fixed on my ice cream, looking lonely for it. I slid it across to her and offered my spoon. She pulled back, like it was poison, and shook her head. "You know what that will do to my hips. And to yours, pretty soon. You'll see." She said from then on I had to watch my weight. And I couldn't be friends with boys. And I should never come out of my room less than fully dressed. And I had to use deodorant and wash my hair every day and not sit cross-legged or run around the schoolyard. After that she did take my spoon and a big bite of ice cream, hot fudge, chopped nuts. "I'm going to tell you what my mother told me," she said, gripping the spoon like she wasn't going to give it back. "Your childhood is over."

I was only just eleven.

When a commercial comes on, I get off the couch and stretch my back. "Jill?" I call towards the stairs. There's no answer. At the bottom of the stairs I try again. "Jill?" She's ignoring me. Getting up the stairs isn't so hard, but by the time I get to the closed door of her room, I have to catch my breath for a few seconds.

There's music playing and, underneath the music, something else.

"Are you crying?" I ask through the door.

She doesn't answer, so I turn the knob and push the door open. Jill is sitting on the floor, in the corner between the bed and the closet, her back to the wall and her head down on her knees. Fingers in her hair. Every couple of seconds, she clenches them.

It's sad, how alone she looks.

She lifts her head, and there's mascara on her cheeks. "Get out."

"Are you okay?"

"I said get out."

It's the first time I've been all the way in her room. Her desk is a mess of homework and food plates and her laptop computer. The empty jar of peanut butter sits next to it.

"Is there a reason you're not getting out?" she asks.

"I was wondering if you had some paper to write on."

She stares at me a second, hard, then points to a desk drawer. I take out three sheets of beige stationery.

"And an envelope?"

"Same. Underneath."

I dig through a little more and find a matching envelope.

"And a stamp?"

"Seriously?" Jill sniffs and wipes her nose on one of the balled-up tissues next to her. "Try the kitchen. Cigar box by the phone. Near the grocery list. And put peanut butter on it." She licks her fingers and runs them under her eyes to clean off the mascara, but there are a few black streaks left.

In the back of the drawer is the edge of a cardboard

picture frame. Opening the drawer a little more, I see it's a close-up picture of Robin and a man with a grey beard and big stomach. A middle-aged Santa of a man. There's a girl in the picture, too, maybe twelve years old with dark blonde hair and braces. It's Jill; I recognize her greenish-brown eyes. "Is this your dad?" I ask, holding the picture up.

She nods.

"Why do you keep it in the drawer?"

"Because it's *private*." She stands and takes the picture out of my hand, pressing it to her chest. "Do you need anything else? A fountain pen? A thesaurus? A map to the mailbox? If not, can you please leave me alone?"

"Sure." I force myself to smile, trying to make friends, trying to give her time. "I like your hair colour in that picture. Maybe you should go back to it."

She holds the picture out to look at it. "Thanks for the tip, Mandy."

"Sure."

Dear Alex,

It was so nice to meet you on the train. How was your sister's wedding? I'm sure it was beautiful. I love weddings. There's nothing more special than seeing two people pledge their love to each other for life. I know you said you're not married yet because you have to meet the right girl. Give it time and be open to the unexpected.

I didn't tell you this before because it's hard for me to talk about, but I'm not keeping this baby. The truth of the matter is that the baby's father was killed in the line of duty. I can't face raising a baby without him and the only fair thing is to give us both a fresh start. So in a couple of months I won't be pregnant any more, and I won't be a mother, and I'll be looking for a new beginning. My life is an empty horizon.

I just wanted to tell you.

You can write to me at this address for now.

Sincerely,
Mandy Madison (from the train)

It takes all three sheets of stationery to get the letter right, with perfect handwriting. Before Robin, I never knew how to write a good letter. I wanted her to think I was smart, or at least not stupid, so I asked at the library for a book to help me, and the lady found me more than one. The books were old and mostly about business letters, but every time

I did an e-mail to Robin, I had the books open, and the dictionary, and I would copy phrases and words from the sample letters in the books. There were different categories, like "letter of thanks" and "friendly letter" and "letter of apology". One thing I learned was that in a friendly letter you should refer to something that was mentioned last time you wrote or talked. That's why I said the thing about weddings, even though I've never been to one. But I've seen them on TV and I do love them.

I bet Alex hasn't gotten a handwritten letter in a long time. Me either. I used to get them from my grandmother a few times a year before she died, but that's it. The kind of life I want is to be a person who would get a personal letter every day. Even an e-mail. I never thought about that until I was getting them almost every day from Robin. I never had a connection like that to anyone, where every day you think about what you'll tell them and you wonder what they're doing, and you know they're wondering what you're doing. I think that's how it's supposed to be between people. That's what I want for my baby. That's what I want for me.

Jill

It's crazy busy at Margins; there's a line at the cafe and tills all night. I like it this way. Annalee has us tuned like a well-oiled machine: attentive but efficient, throwing in a book recommendation here and there when there aren't too many people waiting, and offering but not pushing the frequent-buyers club. It's one of those nights when every customer goes away happy with blue plastic bags full of books and CDs and random crap from the impulse-buy section – overpriced chocolate, fancy bookmarks, mugs, journals.

For nearly three entire hours, I don't think about Mandy. When things finally slow down a bit and I do remember her, the word that won't leave me is *sister*. Mandy's baby will be my sister. The discovery that the baby is a she and not a he has softened me up a tiny bit. I know that logically this shouldn't change anything in terms of how I feel about the situation, and I definitely think Mandy's full of shit about not knowing her real due date, but what girl doesn't want a little sister? It's a chance to be worshipped and adored, to buy miniature pink hoodies and spiffy toddler tights, to instruct a clean-slate brain on How to Be Awesome and Not Lame. By the time I'm my mom's age, a seventeen-year gap won't be a big deal, and it could be, I don't know, *good*. To have someone built into your life like that, permanently, even if you didn't always get along. Family.

And if something happens to my mom, the way it did to my dad, I won't be all alone.

I pull myself back from this thought and work on rekindling my annoyance at Mandy, which is a much easier and more pleasant mental space to dwell in. If my sister turns out to be exactly like Mandy, forget it. Based on what I learned in psychology class, it could go either way. Nature, nurture, a mash-up of both...it's all a mystery no one truly understands.

First we have to get through the next seven weeks.

Half an hour before closing, the lines finally dwindle, and Annalee sends everyone but the closers home. That leaves her and me and Ron. I'm straightening up my register area and restocking bags when I feel eyes on me. Annalee asks, "Can I help you?" in a super-friendly, flirty way, and I know it's Dylan. I just know. There's no one else whose presence I can feel that way, down into my bones. I purposely keep my head down a few extra seconds so that he can soak up this view of me in my element and have time to forgive me for being a bitch yesterday.

"Um. I'm here to see Jill?"

My head jerks up. It's not Dylan. It's R. J. Or Ravi. With a yellowish bruise on his jaw.

"Why were you staring at me like that?" I blurt.

"Like what?"

Now that we're in normal light, I can see the resemblance between the current R. J. and Ravi circa my sophomore year. His face has thinned out, the glasses are gone, and the hair is under control. But it's him.

"Never mind. This is R. J. Desai," I say to Annalee. "Loss prevention associate." To him, "This is my manager, Annalee Calonita. But you probably know that, since you've been spying on the store."

They shake hands. "Are you new?" Annalee asks. "What happened to that Doug Richards guy?"

"Doug Richmond. He's...no longer with us."

"He *died*?"

"No no no. He's pursuing other opportunities."

She laughs. "You don't have to use corporate-speak here. He was canned, I get it. So what's up?"

While testing the pens in my pen cup and tossing the duds, I build my defence in case he's here in a pre-emptive strike to get *me* into trouble for closing early.

"I need to speak with Jill if you can spare her for about five minutes."

He's pulling down on his suit jacket with his fingertips. That's when I realize he's nervous – not here to get me in trouble but to beg me, the way he did when he was chasing down my car, not to get *him* in trouble.

"Go ahead." Even though Annalee sounds cheery, I can tell she's wondering why someone from Corporate would want to talk to me and not her.

R. J. and I wend our way through the store towards Philosophy and Religion. It's in a quiet corner, a good place to talk. Normally I'd deeply savour such a moment as this: me, upper hand all the way, with something another person wants that I can choose to bestow or withhold. Except I'm not feeling the power. What I'm feeling is flustered that I could have been certain those were Dylan's eyes on me. It's so unnerving that I actually stumble on a carpet seam and have to right myself in a graceless move that involves clutching at a shelf and knocking over a paper coffee cup someone has left behind. It's half full of cold coffee, which splashes onto my hand. I curse.

R. J. whips a handkerchief from his chest pocket and

starts dabbing at my hand. "Here."

"Can you just...not." I grab the hankie from him and use it to mop up the coffee before it can ruin half a shelf of books. "Help me with these."

He picks up five books with one hand and rescues two with the other. I finish cleaning the shelf and myself, rearrange the books, and give the now brown and wet hankie back to R. J., asking, "Why'd you change your name?"

"So you do remember."

"Not really." I crumple the empty coffee cup in my hand. "I had to look in my yearbook. How's your 'journey into the future' going?"

"What?"

"Nothing." Ron comes down our aisle with some books for shelving. "Anyway, you look pretty different. So you can see how I wouldn't have recognized you, right?"

He nods and presses his lips together.

"I like Ravi better," I say. "'R. J.' sounds like a Texas oil baron."

"Okay, call me Ravi. Most people do." He's still fiddling with his suit jacket, with his tie, with his sad-looking hankie. "About the other night..."

"Excuse me," Ron says, brushing by and disappearing around the corner.

Ravi clams up again, staring at me like he wants something, expects something.

"What?" I ask. When he remains silent, I give him the impatient swirling hands of *Go on.*

"It was a poor –" he glances towards the ceiling, blows out a breath, then continues – "execution of my duties. I should have thought before startling you like that."

I point to his bruise. "Does it still hurt?"

"Oh yeah." He says that with a charming little half smile, and a tone of awe, like he's impressed. Whatever is left of my indignation deflates.

"Let's forget it. Only because I don't want to deal with the whole nightmare of making a report for HR. And I know closing early was dumb."

His body relaxes and he loosens up in his suit, looking slightly less like a person living out some kind of pathetic CIA make-believe game, his black hair cut high and tight and a cell phone clipped to his belt. "Noted."

We stare at each other. He's got that same expectant look. I can't comprehend him as someone who occupied the life I lived before – before I was all Dylan's, before my dad's accident, before I changed. Before I leaped over that jagged place between then and now and didn't look back. I want to tell Ravi not to take my failure to remember him personally; I don't remember me, either.

The lights in the back of the store blink off, the subtle signal to customers to get the hell out and go home. I put my hands in my apron pockets. There's no reason for our conversation to continue. *Thank you and good night.* Yet my lips keep moving, and my feet stay put. Like, if I talk to Ravi long enough, maybe I'll catch some glimpse of myself from back then. "So do you go to UC or DU or what?"

I watch his face, listen to his voice. Strain to see or hear a memory of Schiff's computer lab, the view from my keyboard, the sound of whirring CPUs, maybe. Anything.

"Neither," Ravi answers. "None. Just working right now. Finally. It took for ever to find this job. That's why I'm a little intense about it, I guess."

"A little."

"That's also why I changed my name. After about twenty applications and no interviews, I thought I'd mix things up a little. See if someone named R. J. could get more play than someone named Ravi." He pulls another business card out of his jacket pocket. "Here. If you need anything at the store or see any suspicious activity or something. There's been a lot of merchandise disappearing in our region, so I'll be around a few times a week, at least." Very professional, very thorough. Like someone twice his age.

"Okay." I put the card in my apron pocket just as Annalee comes towards us, smiling.

"Sorry to kick you out, but we need to get closing under way."

"Right." He gives her a card, too, and repeats what he told me.

I follow him to the door to let him out and to lock up. Before he leaves, he turns and, sounding nineteen again, says softly, "Look at the tennis team page. In the yearbook."

"Tennis team. Okay."

After he's gone, Annalee says, "What was that all about? Are you trying to get my job?"

"Ha. No, thank you."

"Well, whatever. That is one tall, steamy, delicious chai latte."

"Really?" I look at the door Ravi's just walked through. I guess he looks good. Better than he did two years ago, anyway. "I don't think you can say that without violating some company policy."

"All I mean is he's my type."

"He's a little young for you," I say. "But go ahead."

I count out my register, mopey and disturbed that I still can't remember Ravi and what that means about what I remember about me, that I closed early Monday, that Dylan and I can't figure out what to do about us, that I wasn't nicer to Mandy after school today, that I can't seem to talk to my mom any more.

Or, for that matter, talk to anyone, be nice to anyone except here at work.

The sad fact about me and work is that I'm my best self when I'm here.

I can be human to strangers and co-workers, just not to the people who actually care about me.

Mandy

There's a daydream I've had ever since I was little. I don't know where it comes from – maybe I saw something like it in a movie or on TV, or maybe I read it in a book. Except I haven't read very many books so that's probably not it. Maybe I thought it up all on my own. In it I live in a log cabin by a small lake, and on the other side of the lake is another log cabin, exactly like mine. A perfect square. A man lives in it, and he carves tiny animals out of wood. For me. A bear, a deer, a raccoon. And puts them in a boat to float them to my side of the lake. I can never think what to send back, because I don't have anything, but I'm never lonely. Every time I walk out of the cabin door and look across my lake, he's there on his porch, carving. Water and wild flowers between us, but we're still together.

The baby will always have Robin. Jill, too, even though now she acts like she doesn't care. She will. In a way the baby will have me, also. I'll be like the man in the cabin across the lake, and for once I can be the one sending things across – letters, money, presents – and the baby won't have to send anything back. I can give and give and give and never have to take, because I won't really be the mother. We won't fight like mothers and daughters do. I won't be able to hurt her or mess up her life with my bad decisions. For instance, if I pick the wrong boyfriend, it won't affect her, and I won't be able to make her feel bad about herself; she'll always be protected by the space between us.

I'll only send good things across. Starting with Robin and this house.

This is Thursday. I got here Monday. I'm already feeling at home. I've got my favourite end of the couch, and I have the cable set up to record my shows. More and more I think of my room as my room and not as the guest room. Which I think will be the nursery. There's a routine: Robin gets up early and works in her downstairs office while Jill gets ready for school. Jill leaves, and I get up and shower and set my hair. Jill and Robin don't have rollers or even a curling iron, and Jill looked at me funny when I asked. "Curlers?" she said. "What is this, 1988?" All I know is how my mother taught me to do my hair. So I've been saving toilet paper rolls and in the meantime using hair grips.

After my shower, Robin and I have breakfast together

and she tells me her schedule for the day. I'm not sure exactly what she does for a living. She's told me more than once, only somehow it doesn't stick. It's something important, I know that, and she has a lot of meetings with neighbourhood boards and city officials and things like that. If she's not home around lunchtime, she calls me and we chat for a minute and she makes suggestions about what I could eat, and reminds me to take a walk and a nap.

This morning, while she put our breakfast dishes into the dishwasher, she asked me if I'd thought more about my plans for after. "You don't think you'll go back to Omaha?"

"No." I can't do that. Can't and don't want to.

"How about what we talked about in terms of college?"

"Maybe." I can't do that, either, though. At least not until I finish high school, but Robin thinks I have, and I want her to keep thinking that.

There was a silence then, and I knew exactly what Robin wasn't saying. She wasn't saying, *You could stay right here in Denver. Be a part of the baby's life.*

We already talked about that in our e-mails before I got here. With open adoption, one of the points is that you could do that. You *could* be somewhere on the fringes, in the corners, lurking there and being called an aunt or a friend, or sometimes the baby even knows the truth. I told Robin I don't want that. I don't think.

"I just want you to know, Mandy," Robin said, closing the dishwasher, "that I'll do whatever I can to help you get settled somewhere. When you decide what you want to do. I don't want to pressure you, but it would be smart to have a plan worked out fairly soon."

"Okay."

It's not that I don't have a plan. I have Kent's watch. I guess that's a safety net more than a plan – one that I think is best to keep to myself.

I like watching Robin around the house, doing things like making breakfast or sitting at her desk downstairs and looking at her computer. Everything she does, she does with confidence. Like she's sure of who she is and not waiting for someone else to tell her.

During my afternoon talk shows, the doorbell rings. It's an old-fashioned *ding-dong*. Not like the buzzer at Kent's apartment, which was so loud it made you jump.

It takes time to get from the couch to the door, and when I open it, there's a boy walking away. "Wait."

He turns, surprised. "Oh. Hey. You must be...okay, I don't remember your name, but you're the one who...with the baby. And everything."

"Mandy."

"Right. I'm Dylan." He takes a few steps towards the door. "Is Jill home?"

"Not yet. Do you want to come in and wait?"

"Um..." He looks over his shoulder at the street. "She's not expecting me or anything. I could call and stop by later."

"Come in. I don't mind." Honestly, I would like the company; waiting for the baby is a little bit boring.

Dylan is Jill's boyfriend. I recognize him from the pictures hanging on the door of Jill's closet. There are some on the inside door, too, which I saw when I looked around in her room yesterday. Like I said, this can be boring, especially between *The Young and the Restless* and lunch, and Jill's room gave me something to do. Originally I only wanted more stationery, but I found some other stuff. The pictures of Dylan and some letters from him, too, inside Jill's desk drawer. Also there was a school yearbook on Jill's bed. I found her picture, and in it she's got lighter hair, but what really makes her look different is her big smile. I spent an hour looking at the yearbook. Her school is just like mine; there are cheerleaders and sports teams and a drama club and academic clubs and homecoming. I never had a yearbook, though, because it was eighty dollars.

A lot of people wrote in Jill's. Stuff like *Stay great* and *I'm glad I sat by you in fifth* and *Wasabi Funyuns R.I.P.* She has a lot of friends. If I'd had a yearbook, I wonder if anyone would have written in it and what they would have said about me.

Dylan comes up the path and inside. He looks like a male Jill. They dress the same – skinny jeans and sneakers and hooded tops, both with dyed dark hair sweeping across their faces, both with eyeliner. Dylan has a ring in his lip to match the one in Jill's eyebrow. I don't know why anyone would pierce their face; I don't even want to do my ears.

He sits in the leather armchair in the corner.

"They never sit there," I say.

"What?"

"Jill or Robin. I've only been here a few days, but I can tell it's the most comfortable chair in the room and they never sit in it."

"It was Mac's. Jill's dad's." He runs his hand over the arm. "Don't worry, I was always allowed. It's a guy thing."

I lower myself onto the couch as gracefully as I can and smooth out my skirt. "What was he like?"

They never talk about him, just like they never sit in his chair. You can feel him here, though, when they're home. In the late afternoons, after Robin has come back from wherever she is and before Jill goes to work, it feels like they're waiting for someone, like a person is about to walk into the room but never does.

Dylan shrugs. "He was kind of awesomely grumpy. Rough on the outside but a total teddy bear once you got to know him. Smart as hell but didn't have to show it off. Really great person. Really great."

"Did he smoke? I found ashtrays on the bookshelves."

"Cigars. Only on the weekends."

Dylan is nice-looking, with mostly clear skin and sincere eyes. I try to imagine him with normal hair colour and no make-up. When I was in school, I didn't spend very much time talking to boys, or to anyone, and I'm not sure what to say to Dylan now. I smile. He smiles and slowly nods, drumming his fingers on the arms of the chair.

"Why don't you call Jill and find out when she's coming home?"

"We're kind of...we're in a complicated place right now. With our relationship. I was passing by the house and stopped on impulse. I wanted to meet you, actually."

"You did?"

"Yeah." He gets up and walks to the mantel, handling and looking at the knick-knacks – a small ceramic pig, a tiny bronze box. Then a picture in a wooden frame, which he brings to me. "This is Mac."

I take the picture. I've already looked at it but didn't know who it was. A cousin, I thought, or an uncle. Now I can see the resemblance between this man and the one in the picture in Jill's desk, only he has longer hair and no beard. "He's so young."

"Nineteen in that picture. Hiking in Peru. When he graduated from high school, he worked a year and then travelled the world for, like, two years? Had all these amazing adventures. Saw everything there was to see, met Jill's mom on the plane ride home, and the way he always said it was that he never looked back."

So it does happen. People meet in unexpected ways in unexpected places, and it can be true and lasting love. It was like that with Christopher. Unexpected and true, anyway. Lasting is something else and I don't know what, exactly, because I've never seen a relationship that did that.

In my next letter to Alex, I'll tell him this story of Mac and Robin, and maybe he'll see that people can meet on a plane or on a train and share a real connection. Never looking back, that's important, too, when you need to think about the future.

The door opens; Jill drops her book bag onto the floor. When she sees Dylan, she pulls her earphones out and lets them dangle around her neck. "What are you doing here?"

That's not how I'd greet my boyfriend. Even if the relationship was complicated. "Always look happy to see your man," my mother says, "even if you aren't. Make him feel like a king, and he'll treat you like a queen."

Jill strides over to me to take the photo of her father from my hand.

Dylan and I watch her place it on the mantel, exactly where it was. Then he gets up and goes to her and, to her back, asks, "Do you have time for coffee or something before work?"

"I'm off tonight." Her voice is softer than I've ever heard it. Small, sad.

"So...yes?" Dylan says.

Something's happening between them. I feel like I should get up and act like I have something to do, but it's too late now.

Jill nods, still facing the mantel. She raises one of her hands to wipe at her face, then Dylan takes it. Their fingers intertwine – at first cautiously, it seems. Then Jill's hand tightens around his, and Dylan turns her body to him and puts his other arm around her and holds her, pressing her hand, still in his, to his chest. It's so tender and gentle, the way he enfolds her.

Maybe my mom got treated like a queen by some of her boyfriends, but I never saw any of them hold her like this.

Jill

Dylan and I skip coffee. Instead, we go straight to his house and into his room, leaving the blinds open a little so that we can see the snow that's started to fall. We undress each other. I press my nose to his skin and inhale him, imagine I'm smelling muscle and bone and blood vessels and soul, all of the Dylan I've known in this way for two years now, and who's known me.

Afterwards, we fall asleep for a while. I wake up first and stare at him – his beautiful face and compact body – running my hand over the slightly olive skin he gets from his Greek mom. My fingers find each rib, careful not to tickle. Feeling for who he is, who we are together, for myself.

"I love you," I whisper, so quietly, not even close to his ear.

A slow smile materializes on his lips, his eyes still closed. "I knew it."

"You're supposed to be asleep!"

"I knew someday you'd actually say it." He opens his eyes and rolls over to face me, serious now.

"I've said it a lot." Of course I love him. I wouldn't be here now if I didn't. Love was always part of the many, many, many discussions about sex I've had with both my mom and my dad. In their efforts to raise me to have neither an over- nor underinflated sense of guilt and weirdness about sex, they *may* have overdone it in the discussion department. Anyway, I love Dylan. I do. And of course I've said it.

"You have not. You totally have not. E-mail and texting and 'love ya' don't count."

"Yes, they do."

"I say 'love ya' to my dude friends."

"Because you love them."

"Jill. Not the way I love you."

I turn the other way and pull his arm around me like a blanket. Despite all the love lectures and even though I just said it to Dylan, sometimes I'm not sure I know what it really means to say "I love you". These days with Dylan – when we're together – it's more friendly and cosy than romantic and exciting, but it still soothes me. Isn't that more caring about myself, though, than loving him? Shouldn't love have at least a little to do with the other person, separate from yourself? But how can you see anything or anyone in the world apart from yourself? I mean, everything we experience is subjective, since we have no way of experiencing it other than through our eyes. And I get to thinking that love is just a word we use to describe what boils down to a selfish and temporary state of happiness.

I'm not trying to be a cynic. I seriously wonder about this. Because after my dad died, I thought a lot about what a pathetic job I'd done of loving him, and I couldn't figure out why I was so bad at it or what made it so hard. Then I thought maybe I didn't *really* love him until he was gone. And that has made me wonder whether love is impossible until it's too late.

Except I know love is possible, because I know my dad loved me and loved my mom. What I don't understand is how he learned to do that so well and what I'm going to do now that he's not here to show me. Maybe I can't do it. Maybe I don't have whatever it is it takes.

"You okay?" Dylan asks.

"Yeah."

"What are you thinking about?"

I stay quiet a moment longer. This is my chance to say what I'm feeling and thinking and missing about my dad, a conversation Dylan's been trying to get me to have for almost a year. Not that we haven't talked about it some – when we're talking at all – if you count me saying "yes" and "no" and "I don't know" and "Can we please talk about something else?" Dylan doesn't.

"Mandy," I answer. She's so easy to fall back on, even though I keep telling myself that I'm going to give her a chance or at least learn to tolerate her for two more months.

"Oh." He scoots away from me a little. "She seems okay."

"Aside from the lies and the fact that she ate all my peanut butter. What were you guys talking about? When you were looking at that picture?"

"I was telling her how your parents met."

I tuck my hands under Dylan's back to warm them up. "I wish you wouldn't talk about him like that. I mean with her."

He sighs, then asks, "What lies?"

"The baby is a girl."

"Ah."

"And due in seven weeks, not three."

"Hmm."

"Yeah."

"Goes to show doctors aren't always right, I guess." He stretches across me to look at the time on his phone. "We should get dressed."

I get up and collect my clothes from the floor. There's no point in going on and on about Mandy and ruining what's been an otherwise nice afternoon. Being with Dylan like this feels so natural. I never think about the fact that I'm naked – how my flab might look, or about the stray hairs on my thighs that I missed when shaving. It's like we're an old married couple.

I catch myself in the mirror on his door and say, "Hey. Where might a girl put a tattoo that she didn't want her mother to ever, ever, ever see for as long as she lived?"

Zipping his jeans, Dylan comes over to stand behind me. He touches my pelvic bone. "Here?"

"Too sexy. The tattoo...it would be something to remember my dad by. So I don't want it in a tarty place."

He traces his fingers on my back. "You're going to honour your dad with something he hated?"

True, Dad did always warn me against getting a tattoo. He'd gotten one when he was eighteen, right before his trip around the world, as a kind of send-off for himself. He claimed to wish he hadn't. I thought it was cool, though. And the permanence of it is the point. You can't un-take a trip around the world. Your father can't un-die.

"It's not like he's ever going to know."

Dylan looks at me in the mirror. "You don't think he's up there watching?"

I used to. But right now, I've never felt a sense of gone as absolutely as I feel it for him. I shake my head.

"You could put it where your bra would hide it. On your back. But then *you* wouldn't be able to see it, either."

I like that idea. Unless I wind up in the hospital or something, my mom's not going to see it. And I don't want to go around looking at it every second, constantly being reminded. It will be enough to know it's there, as much a part of me as a mole, or a scar.

"I'm going to do it."

Dylan doesn't seem too sure. "Maybe you should think about it for a while. Like a year."

"You love tattoos on girls."

"True. Tattoos are rock. But that's what I'm saying. Indestructible. Be sure."

"There's laser removal." I step away from the mirror and finish dressing.

"I've heard that hurts like a mofo. And doesn't always work, and leaves a mark, too."

He's right. That's why my dad didn't remove his. Also because he was cheap, and busy, and his tattoo – the planet Earth as seen from space, on his shoulder – was kind of big. I don't know. Maybe I won't get a tattoo.

"I don't think doctors would be *that* wrong about the due date," I say.

"What?"

"Mandy. She could be innocently clueless, or she could be trying to take advantage. I don't trust her is all I'm saying." I sit on the edge of the bed to lace my boots. "My dad wouldn't have liked her. And that's why I don't want you talking to her about him."

Dylan watches me for a few seconds, then sits on the bed next to me, quiet.

I finish with my boots. "Pick me up for school tomorrow?"

"Sure."

I get up. He doesn't move. "What?" I say.

He gives me the saddest look. It's almost too much, but I stay strong, holding his eyes with mine. "Say it, Dylan."

"I know he wasn't my dad or anything. But I miss him, too."

Mandy

Normally when Robin gets home after being out, she comes straight to me, wherever I am in the house, and asks me how I'm feeling. She asks how the baby is doing and what I ate and if I got any exercise and whether I read any of the books she got for me about taking care of yourself and the emotional things about giving birth. Sometimes we sit at the big wooden table in the kitchen and have a snack together, like organic muffins that don't have much flavour or cheese that Robin's careful to make sure I'm allowed to eat.

I like how she talks to me. We have conversations. My mother never had conversations with me. My mother told me things, and I told her things back. Like she would say, "Mandy, don't stay in the bath so long. It's a waste of water. Your grandmother used to say only floozies spend that much time in the bath." Or I would say, "I need you to sign this paper so I can take driver's ed." No, what was the point, and did I think I was going to have my own car while I was in high school? Did I think she was going to let me use hers? Like that. Not really conversations.

Robin talks to me about how she's going to change her schedule when the baby comes, and asks if I think the baby should go to preschool to get socialized or if it's better to have a full-time stay-at-home mother? "It depends on the mother" is what I said when she asked. She laughed, and that's another thing I like about Robin. She thinks I'm funny, but it's not like she's laughing at me.

None of the normal things happen today. Today she sets her shoulder bag down in the entryway and barely looks at me on the couch. "Hi, Mandy" is all she says before walking heavily up the stairs.

More than an hour later, she still hasn't come down. I'm hungry. I could make myself a sandwich, but usually she cooks something. I start upstairs. If I phrase it like, *I was thinking I could cook dinner tonight*, she'll probably realize what time it is and say, *Oh no, honey. I'm coming down now.*

Her door is cracked only a tiny bit, and her room is dark. Through the crack I can see her legs on the bed and hear her crying. Not like the big sobbing you do when something tragic and unexpected happens. It's the quiet kind of crying that can go for hours, when over and over again you try to stop, try to tell yourself it's going to be okay, but another part of yourself can't stop thinking about the thing that's breaking your heart.

Last time I went into someone's room while they were crying, I was told to get out. This time I go back downstairs and put a pot of water on to boil for the organic wholewheat macaroni-and-cheese mix Robin buys. She needs comfort food, I can tell. But she's still not down when Jill comes home and finds me in the kitchen, done eating, rinsing my bowl and putting it in the dishwasher.

"Hey," she says, looking at the pot on the stove. "Where's my mom?"

Jill never asks how I am. She didn't even say goodbye when she left earlier with Dylan, who at least said, "It was nice to meet you."

"Upstairs."

She picks up some macaroni out of the pot with her fingers and puts it into her mouth. She has no sense of hygiene. I could remind her I'm very susceptible to infection right now, but instead I say, "Maybe you should go up and see her."

I wonder if either of them knows about the time they spend crying in their separate rooms.

Jill wipes her fingers on her black jeans, leaving a faint orange smear. "Why?" Then she closes her eyes for two or three seconds, and her face goes from her usual annoyed expression to one that is so sad. "Shit." The first time she says it is tired. The second time, her eyes now open, is mad. "Shit!" She slams the lid onto the pot.

"What's wrong?"

And the way she stares at me, defiant, it's like she doesn't want to say. She folds her arms in front of her, clutching each elbow with the opposite hand. "Twenty-five years. Twenty-five years they would have been married, today. Thirty-three years if you count when they met and the years they lived together. Can you imagine seeing someone basically every day for thirty-three years and then one of those days..." She shakes her head and pinches her mouth together.

There's so much anger in her eyes. I want to remind her that only a few hours ago Dylan was holding her like she was the most special thing in the world. Maybe that would make her feel better. I step back towards the dishwasher and close the door. The chances of me saying the right thing are not good. Still, I have to try, because I can't pretend she didn't just tell me about something important and awful.

"At least they had those thirty-three years." It's the wrong thing; Jill's eyes go hard. "A lot of people never find real love," I say to explain what I mean. "Or they find it, and it gets away before they experience any happiness." I only want her to understand how lucky she and Robin are to have ever had Mac. Lucky that she had a father like that as long as she did.

She takes two quick steps towards me. Her face is centimetres from mine; I can smell the cheese sauce on her breath. "You don't get to talk about this."

My mother says that when another girl steps up to you, just smile and let her have the last word. My mother says it's usually jealousy or her wanting something you have. But I can't think of one thing I have that Jill, who has everything, could want. And I can't smile when we're talking about a tragedy.

"I only meant—"

"What did I just say?"

I put my hands on my belly.

"You," she continues, "aren't family." She lets go of her elbows. Her hands shake. "To me you're just an incubator for the one thing that might possibly make my mom happy."

She turns, her boots squeaking on the tiles. As she leaves the kitchen, I think about what I could say. Those aren't last words I want her to have. *I'm sorry*, I could say. Or, *Why are you so mad at me when I didn't do anything?* It doesn't matter. She's already up the stairs.

It was July.

The cornfields outside of town had come up green and tall like always, oceans of them. You would drive into the farmlands and think that the whole earth was made of these fields. I rode in the back of Kent's pickup because my mother liked to be alone with him in the cab. I didn't mind. The warm, moist air flowed over and around me as I watched the road unfurl behind us.

We'd left the city to go to the Riverbrook County Fair. Kent had an idea to maybe buy a horse. I don't know why, and I don't know where in Council Bluffs you'd put a horse, but Kent had a lot of ideas he didn't think through. My mother said not to contradict your man. "Men are fragile," she said. "They need a cheerleader, not a negative Nelly."

When we got to the fair, Kent and my mother looked at the brochure and went off to the livestock show. Kent gave me twenty dollars and said to meet them back at the truck by sundown. They didn't want me to come with them. I mean, they didn't say that in so many words, but it was obvious, so I went in the opposite direction.

I saw him by the sideshows. I was looking for a booth where I could get roasted corn and lemonade, and I saw him.

He walked slow, wearing sandals, his shirt off and tucked

into the back of the waistband of his jeans, a string of blue beads around his neck. It was his profile I saw because he was with his friends and had his face turned towards one of them, laughing. A big laugh, the kind that makes everyone look to see what's so funny, and when I looked to see what was so funny he was tucking his shoulder-length hair behind one ear. I stopped walking right in front of them and stared.

One of his friends saw me staring and asked, "What's the matter? You never saw Indians before?"

I didn't answer, because I was still looking at him, waiting to see what he'd do next, waiting for him to look at me. When he did, his smile got bigger at first, then it went down, and his expression grew serious. He felt it, too, the air between us, the invisible lines that something or someone had drawn to connect us. That's the way I remember it.

He spoke first. "Hi."

"Hi."

The friend who'd first caught me staring looked at him and then at me and watched us watching each other and said, "Always it's the white girls."

"Shut up, Freddy."

One of his other friends elbowed Freddy. "Come on." And to the boy I still stared at said, "See you later, Christopher, yeah? Or maybe never again?"

"You wanna walk around?" Christopher asked me, but we were already moving forwards together, leaving his friends behind.

All day we walked and talked. I never talked so much to anyone. I told him about my father and about how it was for me at school but even with that I liked the school year better than summer because I could be out of the apartment. Everything I said to him was real. My real thoughts, my real feelings. He listened. He listened so well that I almost told him about Kent, but I didn't want to ruin our day.

He bought me a snow cone. He tried to win me something at the booth where you throw darts at balloons, but couldn't. When we were walking away, a man in a baseball cap who'd been watching him said, "The balloons are underinflated and the darts are dull. You shoulda just thrown as hard as you could. Accuracy don't matter."

If someone had said something like that to Kent, he would have gotten embarrassed, then mad, and told the guy to mind his business and maybe a fight would start. Christopher only laughed and said, "Next time," then held my hand and we kept walking.

On the Ferris wheel he put his arm around me, and I rested my head there between his shoulder and his chest, the way I'd always imagined I would in a situation like that.

We watched people go by beneath us, and every time our car neared the top the world would get quiet, the music and crowds fading. When we got off the Ferris wheel, he said that there should be a Tunnel of Love. "At the state fair they have one," he said, "but I never had anyone to ride through it with. Now I do and there isn't one."

We went through the haunted house instead, and in front of a dangling glow-in-the-dark skeleton he kissed me.

Outside the fair gates we made a path through the cornfield until we found a clearing. He spread his shirt on the ground and lay back, and I lay next to him. It wasn't like with Kent, just the night before and always, fast and anxious and him reminding me not to make any noise so my mother wouldn't hear. When Christopher touched me, it was like none of that had ever happened.

He took off my sundress and kissed me up and down and moved on top of me, so careful and slow, and I felt everything my mother says you're supposed to feel, what I never felt before. After, Christopher took off his necklace and put it on me.

"Where do you live?" he asked, running his hand over the swell of my hip, smooth brown skin on white skin.

"Omaha." If you live in Council Bluffs, you should always say "Omaha" when people ask where you live, my mother says.

"That's a hundred miles. I don't have a car."

"Do you have a horse?" I could picture him on a wild pony with no saddle, his hair streaming behind him as he rode into the city and swept me up to sit in front of him and gallop me away.

He laughed his big laugh. "No. I don't live in a tepee, either."

"I didn't think that."

We were on our backs, watching the tops of the corn shiver in the wind.

"You're the prettiest girl I've ever seen. Those eyes." He rolled over onto his elbow. "Stay here. We can live in the corn."

I smiled. "Okay." And he laughed a smaller laugh.

In the time since we first lay down, the sky had gone from blue to pink to purple. "I have to go." I sat up and pulled my dress over my head.

He kissed my hand. My arm. My shoulder.

"Don't forget me," I said.

He told me the name of the town where he lived, the reservation. "Just ask for Christopher B. Everyone knows me." He walked me almost to the parking lot, and then I told him he should go find his friends. I didn't want Kent or my mother to see us. "Don't forget me, either," he said, and our hands separated, then our fingertips very last.

I went running towards the truck, gravel getting between my feet and my sandals. The necklace bounced against my collarbone. Kent stood outside the truck cab, impatient and getting ready to yell at me. I didn't care.

I know it all sounds like a fantasy. But that's how it was, and those are the things we said. It's true. It's mostly true.

And Jill should understand that, even if she can't imagine it, there was at least that one day when I mattered.

Jill

Dylan and I sit in his car in the school parking lot as snow piles up on the windshield, gradually reducing the area of visibility until all we can see are the very tops of the heads of all the people going to class. *Trudging* to class, I should say, like prisoners of war off to the work camp to haul rocks with their frozen fingers, under the beady yet watchful eyes of corrupt guards.

Generally, I don't have a problem with school. I mean, you get through it, and it's what you've been doing nearly your whole life, and there are people who make you laugh and all of that. And of course I'm not anti-learning. I like learning. Education is pretty much the number one value around the MacSweeney home, only Dad didn't think it had to come from school, necessarily. For him it came from living in the world, trying new things, paying attention. And school can be such torture sometimes, seriously, when you just don't want to be there and everyone is in your face with all their usual bullshit, not picking up on a single of your *please go away now* cues.

I admit: I liked school a lot better before, when it didn't seem that everyone knew all about my personal life and felt sorry for me. I was never late; I always participated.

"I don't want to go in." I put my left foot up on the dash and start doodling on my sneaker – a string of hearts. I can't stop thinking about my parents' anniversary yesterday and what Mandy said: "At least they had those thirty-three years." What kind of a thing is that to say? How would she feel if she just found out she had terminal cancer and someone said, "At least you had a good eighteen years"?

"Aren't you, like, one cut away from suspension?"

Dylan. Such a rational thinker.

"That was last year. They gave me a clean slate in September, and I've only cut twice since then." I attempt to turn the hearts into skulls. If the day after my parents' anniversary feels this bad, I can't imagine what the anniversary of the accident will be like. Another cut day to ration.

Dylan pulls down his visor mirror. "Do you have any eyeliner on you?"

"No, sorry. You'll have to go natural."

When my dad first met Dylan, they made small talk, and

Dad showed Dylan his DVD collection and acted totally normal all around. As soon as the door closed behind Dylan, my dad turned to me and said, "Why the hell does a boy need to wear eyeliner?"

My dad was a walking mass of apparent contradictions. So much of my parents' life together was what you'd expect from any good liberal household, and as far as I know they always voted Democrat. But also his world travels made him a hard-core patriot. He truly believed the United States is the best place to live, and American is the best way to be. And part of being American is respecting all people's right to be whatever they want to be and at the same time respecting your own right to bitch about it, as long as you're educated and can reason your way through your bitching.

"They did it when you were in high school, too," I reminded him. "Hello, KISS?"

"Not around the house!"

"How do you know? At least Dylan doesn't wear platform heels."

It was funny. My dad was funny. Every day I reported the Quotable Dad to Dylan and, when I had them, my friends. And it feels good to laugh now at Dylan's request for make-up, until I think about how there will never be any new Quotable Dad quotes. All over again, a loss. He would have been the best cranky old man. Now he doesn't get to be that, and I don't get to tease him, and the part of me that loved to do that and was so good at it is as gone as he is.

I toss my pen on the floor mat and take my foot off the dash so I can lay my head in Dylan's lap. "Dyl." I ignore the emergency brake digging into my ribs and nuzzle my face into his thigh. He runs his fingers through my hair, plays with my eyebrow ring.

"I know." He kisses my ear. "But I think we should go to class."

A startling thing happens at lunch. Laurel comes up to me while I'm in the cafeteria line and almost smiles. "Hey," she says.

"Hi."

As the line inches up, she inches with me. "Cinders warned me not to do this, but I'm doing it because I miss you. She does, too, but won't admit it."

A lump gathers in my throat. I force it down. "Warned you against doing what?"

"*Talking* to you, Jill."

I do my absolute best not to stare at her in order to take in that face I love, with its wide cheekbones and brown eyes that are always looking for the most fun kinds of trouble. Instead, I sneak glances. She's got part of her long hair in two little side braids sort of swooping along the crown. "That looks good," I say, pointing to them.

"Thanks." We inch. "Are you eating with Dylan? I don't see him."

"He wanted to work on something in the chem lab."

"Come sit with us." And she walks away, having made her statement, which is an invitation and a command all in one, as only Laurel can issue.

When I come out of line with my taco soup, Cinders and Laurel and a few others are waiting at their table. It's a long walk. All I want to do is find a dark closet where I can eat without the judgmental-yet-pitying stares of all the people I've pissed off or put off. But I'm pretty sure this is my final, final chance with them.

Cinders doesn't exactly acknowledge me when I sit down, though she does scoot her bag slightly to the left to make more room for my tray while continuing her conversation with Gianni, the Italian exchange student, who I guess is sort of the new me. At least in terms of filling seats and looking cute, which I always did well.

"So." Laurel is making efforts. "I got into Boulder. I mean, everyone gets into Boulder, so it's not like this big accomplishment, but I guess I was a little worried about my grades."

"That's good. Good job. It's what you wanted."

She nods. "Are you still..."

Cinders stops talking to Gianni and tunes in to listen for updates about my college plans.

"Yep. Still planning to take a couple of years off." *Don't sound defensive, Jill. Don't sound defensive.* "Mom's still not happy about it."

"Your dad didn't go to college, right?" Cinders just says it – "your dad" – so in my face, as if my problem talking about him wasn't the key reason my friends and I haven't been talking about *anything.*

I take a breath, let it out. "No. He took some business classes after he started his company, but, no."

"And he was a big success," Laurel says.

"Right?" Oh so subtly moving away from the topic of my father, I say, "I'm going to go eventually, I think. I'm just not going to go *now.*" I need to be away from here for a while. I need to get out from under homework and classrooms and have room to breathe and think and figure out what I want to do, and who I am now that I don't have him and pretty soon won't have my mother, either.

Cinders shrugs, Laurel nods, and the conversation moves on to Gianni's host family and its strange bathing habits. I eat my taco soup and try to grow accustomed to the idea of possibly having friends again.

* * *

Ravi is setting up a sting operation at work.

That's what he calls it. Apparently, there are some bold and prolific shoplifters hitting up all the Margins stores in our region, and they're a menace to society, to hear Ravi tell it. So he's come to our store to look for "vulnerabilities". As we do a walk-through together, he's completely professional, even a little bit cold. He'd planned to be doing this with Annalee, but she wound up getting stuck with a manager trainee that the RM had dumped on her with no warning.

So it's Ravi Desai and his assailant, strolling down the how-to aisle.

"I'm working on a lone-gunman theory," Ravi is saying. "Corporate thinks it's a team, but I'm not too sure."

"You think one person jacked thousands of dollars' worth of merch in a two-week period?" Sounds unlikely.

"Sure." He stops in front of a display of travel books – we've turned the corner – and puts his hand on his hip, the bottom of his suit jacket hitching up behind his hand the way it does on every single suited detective on TV. You'd think he practised it in a mirror or something. "Let's say you wanted to steal a few of these. What would you do?"

"I wouldn't."

"I'm trying to get you to think like a criminal. To help me see if I'm missing anything obvious. Seriously, what would you do?" A customer walks by and Ravi has to squeeze in close to let her pass. When he does, something peculiar happens – for a fraction of a moment I see myself as a little kid, in my kitchen, standing on a stepladder. Then the image is gone, leaving the faintest whiff of I don't know what, homesickness or nostalgia, an ache that doesn't quite hurt.

Ravi steps back. I stare at him, bewildered.

"Well?" he asks.

"Well what?"

"What would you do?"

I try to think like a criminal instead of someone who's losing it. "Okay. Easy." I've caught enough shoplifters in my day to know the basic MO. "I pick it up, flip through it as if reading, but really I'd be looking for the anti-theft device so I could take it out. Of course, I'd be wearing a big coat or holding a roomy purse or a bag from another store. I'd stroll along and let the book casually drop into the bag, then be on my merry way."

"And if a sales associate walks by?"

"Act innocent."

Ravi seems disappointed that my criminal mind is not better developed. "Not very original."

The bruise on his face is nearly gone, but it's still visible enough that I reach to touch my own cheek in sympathy and guilt. Ravi gives me a searching look, and I scratch the side of my nose.

I pick up one of the paperbacks to get us back where we were. "In real life, I wouldn't bother with swiping something like this, though. Fourteen bucks. Unless I actually *needed* to know how to get around Honduras but didn't have the money to buy this, there'd be no point in taking it. I'd be after the art books. Some of those are worth over a hundred. I'd turn around and sell them online. Even at half price, that's cash money – scrilla – in my pocket, yo." I throw a gang sign to lighten the mood.

"Right." Ravi taps one finger against his chin, thinking. From his chest pocket he takes a little notepad and jots something down before flipping it shut.

"What? What did you just write down?"

"Nothing."

"Nothing. That's helpful." I want to stand close to him again, see if I get another random snapshot of my childhood, another twinge of whatever that was that went through me like a current just minutes ago. But there's no good excuse for invading his personal space, so instead I ask, "What's with the suits, anyway?"

He touches his lapel with his slender hand, looks down. "I figure it helps people take me seriously. When I go around the stores, you know, I don't want them to think I'm some kid fresh out of high school telling them what to do."

"Even though you basically are."

"You wouldn't think that, though, looking at me." He pauses. "Right? I mean, did you think that?"

"No, but I *did* think you were a creepy stalker, remember?"

"Oh yeah." He starts walking backwards, leading me to the self-help section. "What about someone in a wheelchair?"

"What about them?"

"Think how fast a shoplifter could get away in a wheelchair or one of those scooterlike gizmos."

Gizmo. My dad used that word all the time. "Where's the gizmo for the DVR?" Meaning the remote. "Have you seen my gizmo?" Meaning his cell phone. "Jill, will you put the gizmo back in my car?" Meaning the GPS. I almost always knew exactly which gizmo he meant, even if he didn't provide much context.

"Even if the thief misses a security tag in one of the books," Ravi continues, "by the time the alarm goes off and the employees rush to the exit—"

"Yeah, we all know how they 'rush'—"

"He's long gone on his Zipr Roo or Jazzy."

"Halfway to Tijuana with a retrospective of the Dutch masters."

He stops walking and laughs. I made a joke. I made someone laugh, and not at the expense of anyone else. Not a real person, anyway. When was the last time I did that?

Ravi's smile is a bit goofy. If I picture him without the suit, in jeans and a T-shirt, I can almost see the nineteen-year-old he actually is.

"Well," I say, "we can't go around profiling our disabled customers. PR nightmare for Corporate if anyone figures it out."

"I know. I'm just saying keep your eyes peeled. Evil wears many disguises."

Annalee's voice comes over the PA. "All booksellers to the tills. All booksellers to the tills."

Ravi puts his hand out, like *after you,* and he smiles again, and I smile back and remember I never looked up the tennis page in the yearbook like he asked me to.

Varsity tennis. Ravi's on the team, with his big hair and glasses and the rounder face. But what he wanted me to see is squeezed into the lower corner of the page in ballpoint pen and neat printing:

Jill
It was nice sitting near you in Schiff's. You seem

really smart and funny. Of course that's only my guess from a distance. Maybe you're stupid and dull! Ha-ha! Not possible. Too bad we didn't get a chance to talk much. Okay, at all. But I hope we'll run into each other sometime. I bet we will.

Ravi J. Desai

(the quiet guy who just loaned you a pen so you could sign Amy Diaz's yearbook)

Mandy

It's hard to sleep. I don't know if that's because of being in a new place and a different bed or because of being so pregnant. Robin says I should sleep on my left side. She told me why, but I forget. I try that and wind up on my back and then worry it's not going to be good for the baby, so I turn onto my side again, but I'm not used to it. Before, I always slept on my stomach with my hands tucked under me, like I did when I was a little girl.

Every morning that I've woken up here and opened my eyes to see the branches of the tree by my window and feel the soft edge of the blanket, I've stopped to say *thank you*. I don't know who to. The ceiling, the sky, the world that I'm a part of now, luck. It's lucky that I saw Robin's post when I did, and lucky that she wrote back when I wrote to her, even though I had so many rules. How does it work, I wonder – that kind of luck that would bring two people together at the right moment? Three people. Four if you count Jill.

It's the same kind of luck that made me see Christopher at the fair and made him see me.

Whatever it is, wherever it comes from, I'd never had it before then. Always it's been the other kind of luck – when you're in the wrong place at the wrong time with the wrong people. I don't want the baby to have that kind. I want her to be born into this kind.

I get up and dressed, checking the bottom drawer, under my bras and things that don't fit me any more, to make sure Kent's watch is still there. Every morning and every night, I check. Even though I don't think I have to worry about Robin and Jill snooping that way, it makes me feel better to be sure. I should start moving the watch around, too, to different places, just in case. It used to be that when Kent was in a good mood, he'd talk to me about his gambling strategy. That if you're smart, you hedge your bets. If you bet on something crazy, you always make sure there's also a sure thing, or as close to a sure thing as you can get, in case the crazy bet doesn't go like you hoped. The watch is my sure thing.

Downstairs, Robin's in the kitchen, tuning in a music station on the radio instead of the news she listens to on weekday mornings. Jill is still asleep, or at least still in her room. Sun reflects off the snowfall from last night and lights up the kitchen and living room, showing off how warm and clean the house is. It's like a house in the kind of catalogue that's full of down quilts and cotton pyjamas.

Robin seems happier now than she has the last two days. When she sees me standing in the kitchen doorway, she smiles and waves me in with the whisk in her hand. "I'm making crêpes. Do you like crêpes?"

I've never had a crêpe. I'm not positive what it is, exactly, even though I've seen it on menus before. "Yes."

There's a glass of orange juice already on the table for me next to all my vitamins, and a blue-and-white checked napkin folded up. The big wooden table, every time I see it, looks like a picture from a magazine. Not because of the table but how Robin does it, like with the checked napkin this morning, or the fruit bowl that always has real fruit in it, or sometimes a sweater hanging over one of the chairs. It just makes you feel good. She knows how to make a home even out of a table. Not everyone can do that.

"Is every Saturday like this?" I ask.

She cracks an egg against the rim of the mixing bowl. Even an egg and a bowl in her hands looks like home. "What do you mean?"

When someone lives a certain kind of life all the time, it's hard to describe to them what it looks and feels like to someone who lives a certain other kind of life. On Saturdays in Council Bluffs, Kent and my mother were usually in a bad mood from drinking too much Friday night or staying out too late or losing money gambling. A lot of times I would be trying to forget that Kent had visited my room after my mother was asleep. And there could be a lot of cleaning to do before they came out wanting coffee or aspirin. Sometimes it didn't smell very good; they were always trying to quit smoking and only lasting a few days here and there.

My mother usually had a long list of things she had to do that she could only do on Saturdays because of her job, which she was angry to have in the first place because Kent had promised her she wouldn't have to work any more, that he would take care of things. But he didn't, so on Saturdays my mother did errands like any working housewife, even though they weren't married. Grocery store, bank, nails and hair. Kent sometimes did nice things, like bring me doughnuts or give me fifty dollars to go shopping if he'd had a good night at the casinos. Usually not.

At Robin's table I drink my juice and say finally, "I don't know."

She beats the eggs, adds flour and milk, not measuring anything. "Is Jill up?" She holds the whisk in front of her face and studies the way the batter drips.

"No."

"Let's get her up. These are best hot and fresh."

When she doesn't move from the counter, I realize she means I should get Jill up. Jill, who said I'm just an incubator. "I think she'll like it better if you go."

Robin laughs, slicing ham into thin strips. "Oh, don't let Jill scare you. She's exactly like her father – all bark and no bite. Knock on the door nice and hard and say 'crêpes'. She'll come out."

Upstairs I stand outside Jill's door and listen. Maybe she's already up and about to come out and I won't have to do anything. After a minute of nothing but silence, I knock on the door twice. "Crêpes!" Then I turn and go down the stairs as fast as I can in my condition.

When I get to the bottom, the baby moves. Not like a kick. More like a roll.

All of a sudden I see her. I see her at five years old, coming down these stairs sideways, one step at a time, holding on to the railing with both small hands. She's wearing pink pyjamas, the kind with feet built in, and she has Christopher's dark hair and my light eyes. She calls out Robin's name – she calls her "Robin".

But reality is she'll call her "Mommy". I didn't think about that before.

Where will I be in five years? How far away from here, and from her?

These are questions I maybe should have thought about harder a few months ago.

All through breakfast Jill reads a comic book. Trying to make conversation to show her I'm not mad about what she said to me, and showing Robin I'm not scared, I say, "I used to like *Sailor Moon*. That was the only comic I read."

Jill gives me a look of disdain. She and I haven't been in the same room since she yelled at me on Thursday night. "This isn't freaking poser-ass magical-schoolgirl *anime*. It's a graphic novel. It won awards."

"Jill," Robin says, but she's not really upset. She's reading, too, one of her magazines.

"What's that about?" I ask Robin.

"Hmm?" She looks up. "Alternative transportation models going forwards into a post-oil age."

"Oh."

It's good that my daughter will be with smart people. My mother says it's better to be pretty than smart, but I don't know. Lately I've been trying, in my head, to put things in the opposite order of what my mother says. Being nice would come first. Then smart. Pretty is last. Or, why can't you be all of them? If you're pretty, does that mean you can't also be smart and nice? I think Robin is all three. Jill is two out of three. Maybe she's nice, too, just not to me. I don't care. I only care that she's nice to my daughter, her sister. So I need to make sure not to say or do anything else that will make her mad.

When I go to the fridge for milk, I say, "Can I get anything for anyone while I'm up?"

Robin says no thanks. Jill doesn't acknowledge that I talked. I guess she needs more time.

Dear Alex,

I know you probably only just got my last letter and haven't had time to write back. Or maybe you haven't even gotten that yet because you could still be travelling. You could be on a train right now.

Well, I am settling in here. The family I'm giving the baby to is very nice. It's a mother and daughter. There is no father. And I know that's not perfect, but this family acts like a family with a father. By that I mean there's a ghost of a father still here. He died not that long ago, and you can tell they'll never forget him, never ever stop missing him. Not like my family, which I bet has already forgotten about me.

I do wish they would talk about him more, but

it seems like it makes them sad.

For a second today I had the thought that I would like to keep the baby. Robin, the lady who is adopting, sat down with me this week to talk about emotions and psychology and all of that, and she's constantly telling me it's normal to have mixed feelings right now. I've never really had any, though, until today. They were short. Anyway, it's an open adoption and I can visit the baby if that's how we decide to do it. It's not set up legally that way, but we trust each other.

Sometimes I see the future and it's like I'm a blank. I mean I know what I'll look like, that I'll exist. But I don't know who I'll be or who will be with me. At least I know who I'm not and who won't be with me. I won't be my mother, or with someone like her boyfriend. That is a guarantee.

Do you know who you'll be in the future? And who you'll be with?

Yours,
Mandy (from the train)

It's only a first draft. When Robin and I were e-mailing back at the beginning of the year, I got used to writing my letters out in my school notebook first, then typing them, then checking them against books, then retyping them. The mail doesn't go out again until Monday, so I have plenty of time to change it. I fold the paper and put it inside one of the magazines Jill brought me on my first day here, which I've already looked at but like to look at again. Magazines – and TV, too – help me think about who I might want to be.

The house is quiet. Jill went out after breakfast, and Robin is in her office downstairs. I'm sitting on the bed with pillows propped up behind me so I can see not only the tree outside my window but the next house and the one after that.

I look back at the week.

I got here and Robin didn't change her mind.

I saw the doctor and the truth came out and Robin didn't change her mind.

I fought with Jill, but Robin said not to worry, and it seems like things with Jill could stay like they are and it won't make Robin change her mind.

I could start to believe that she never will. That this is actually going to happen. That this could be my sure thing.

Jill

Dylan comes over to study on Sunday, and it's almost like old times. Like we never broke up and got back together and broke up again, or fought, or went through whatever it is we went through. Me being angry and sad. Him trying to make me feel better. Me saying "But I don't want to feel better" and asking to be left alone. Then there was the Grady thing.

To make a point, I let Dylan see me leaving school last June with this fifth-year senior, Grady, who'd always been after me. Grady drove me to his house and, as soon as the door closed behind us, pushed me up against it and proceeded to kiss and grope, and I stood there in my own little petrified forest of detachment, not responding, until he pulled back and asked, "What?"

"I'm grieving."

"I know. Before your dad died, there's no way you would've gotten into my car."

And we ended up on opposite ends of the couch while he played Xbox and I texted Dylan a hundred apologies.

Over the summer we got back together, technically, but the whole time I could tell he was still mad at me, and I was still sad, and neither of us was enjoying any of it. Meanwhile, Laurel and Cinders tried to be there for me. I mean, they more than tried. They really were there, like, *all the time*. E-mailing sympathy notes and sending Facebook gifts and constantly taking me out for coffee. Dragging me to parties to keep my mind off things. Dropping by the house to "check in" and see how I was "holding up". Dylan was doing all this, too, plus talking talking talking about it. Wanting me to "express my grief". Telling me over and over that he was there to listen. Hugging me all the time, until I couldn't stand the feel of his hand on my back. Looking at me with soul-bruisingly sad eyes that said, *How is Jill ever going to get through this?*

It was all too much.

Fourth of July weekend, Dylan and Laurel and Cinders took me to Confluence Park and sat me down by the water and told me they were worried. It had been three months and I needed to talk about it. I needed to cry. It was time to lean on my friends, not shut them out. Each of them took a turn telling me what was wrong about how I was handling the whole deal. An intervention, basically.

It wasn't as if I hadn't cried. I just chose to do it privately. In fact, I'd been crying all weekend.

My dad loved the Fourth of July. It was the perfect holiday for him, combining patriotism, world history, and grilled meats. So he'd get the flag out of the garage, where it had been properly folded and stored since Memorial Day, and I'd help him put it up. I always acted like it was this big pain. The year before he died, we got in a fight about it because I wouldn't get out of bed at the crack of dawn to help him like I'd done every year of my life until then. I just wanted to sleep. He came into my room and pulled the sheet off me, raised the blind. I should have gotten up. But I pulled the sheet back over my head, and he said, "Jilly, let's go. It's a good day to be an American." I could have said, "Give me five minutes." I could have said, "Coffee first." Instead, I muttered something completely rude. I think it was, "Eff America," and the room got quiet and when I tossed the sheet back, finally, he was gone, without so much as a reminder to try a little tenderness, because this went way beyond my usual bad manners.

But then when I went outside in my pyjamas, he was there on the porch, with the flag, like he knew I'd come out, feeling like shit. And instead of yelling at me for being rude and maybe treasonous, he said, "Here, take this corner."

While Laurel and Cinders and Dylan were telling me to express myself, all I could think was that I'd trade them all for Dad, but how could I express *that*? There are so many pieces to grief. Sad pieces, angry pieces, guilty pieces, pieces of regret, and pieces that are a certain kind of pain that doesn't even have a word.

And that's when I expressed myself by saying, "Leave me the hell alone." They did.

Then Dylan and I got back together once more, when senior year started. September always feels like this clean slate, an optimistic time. It was fine until the holidays, when I started having more memories of me being an insensitive jerkface to my dad: suddenly deciding to be a vegetarian the very moment he was carving the Thanksgiving turkey. Changing back to an omnivore two days later. Getting up halfway through our annual viewing of *The Bishop's Wife*, even though I knew how much it meant to him, saying I was tired, then him catching me later that night playing The Sims on my mom's computer. Stupid, childish crap like that.

I don't know why I had to be like that. Not only that time but a lot of times. It's as if once you hit high school, you're programmed, like a robot, to be an asshole to your parents. Why couldn't I have simply helped him with the flag the first time he asked? I don't know why. I don't know why I do half the things I do.

And when you can't stand yourself, you don't want people around who are constantly saying how much they love you, because you know you don't deserve it. So I pushed Dylan away again until he came back for me, God knows why, on Thursday.

Now, here we are, three days later, doing homework, and I'm not totally sure we should be back together. All that same stuff is still there, still un-talked about. Just older.

The Black Keys rock from my laptop, and we're sitting side by side on my bed, surrounded by books and red liquorice laces. Dylan shifts, exposing the corner of my sophomore yearbook, which he pulls out from under the covers and opens up. "Hey now. Our misspent youth."

"Oh yeah. I found that when I was cleaning my room this morning."

He glances around at the mess. "You were cleaning your room this morning?"

"Sort of." I think about what Ravi wrote. That I seemed smart and funny. What about nice? Did I seem nice? I take the yearbook from Dylan and flip to my class picture. "Am I nice?" I ask him.

"Nice?"

"Yeah, Dylan. Nice." I jab at my smiling sophomore face. "As in not mean. Am I or was I or have I ever been?"

He stares at my photo. "You're definitely not fake-nice, which is good."

"Way to dodge the question. Forget it." I slam the yearbook shut and toss it aside.

"Jill. Come on. I guess I don't really remember. You're you. You don't have to be nicey-nice to be a good person."

"But it helps."

I wonder what he'd think about my goodness as a person if he knew about my moment with Mandy the other day and my incubator comment. The truth is I'm ashamed of it. Mandy may be annoying, but she didn't do anything other than get caught in my path at the wrong time. And the way she's been avoiding me has got me wondering: Am I *scary*? I mean, I know I've always been grumpy and to the point, like Dad, but Dad was never *scary*. What I wish Dylan could tell me is if I'm a different person now, a worse one. Or if this is who I am, have always been, and I'm only now noticing it.

I wonder if Dylan truly doesn't remember or doesn't want to say.

We get back to homework, and after about ten minutes Mandy starts walking up and down the hall in this really conspicuous, distracting way until I hiss at Dylan, "Close the door."

He laughs. "Is this you trying to be nice?"

I put my head back and groan. Mandy walks by again, refusing to turn her head and glance at us the way any normal person walking by a room full of people would.

"Mandy," I say out of exasperation. She stops and looks around as if my voice could be coming from any one of a hundred places in the house. "Um, in here."

"Yes?" She stands in the doorway. Her long, full hair – which she spends, like, an hour on every morning – is piled up on top of her head and held by a hairslide. No one over the age of twelve should have a hairslide on the top of her head. Plus, she always wears these horrifying flowered dresses that make her look like she travelled here from another, uglier era. At the same time she does manage to be pretty in a golden, wholesome way that even bad clothes and hairstyles can't mask.

"Are you okay?" I ask.

"I'm fine."

I pick up a liquorice lace and tear off a bite. "Because it seems like you want something. The way you keep strolling by."

Dylan writes in his notebook, *Try nice*, and angles it towards me.

"Robin said I should walk."

"In the hall?"

"It's icy out."

Dylan shoves his notebook into my lap and asks Mandy if she wants a liquorice lace.

"She's not supposed to have too much sugar," I say.

"Just one." Mandy steps into the room and takes one from the big cylinder of them while smiling at Dylan. "I don't want to interrupt."

"We need a break, anyway," he says.

We do? I write, shoving the notebook back, but he ignores it.

"You can sit if you want," Dylan continues, actually getting up off the bed, relocating a pile of my clothes from the futon chair to the floor, and helping Mandy lower herself onto it before he flops back down next to me.

I try nice, a little tenderness, to make her feel welcome. "Are you warm enough? Do you want a blanket?"

She rubs her hand over her gigantic belly. "I'm hot. The baby is like a little furnace inside."

Dylan rolls onto his stomach and inches over to the edge of the bed, resting his head on his folded arms. "What else does it feel like?"

Mandy chews her liquorice lace slowly, eyes blank. "What do you mean?"

"You know. What does it feel like to have a baby in there? Is it weird? Or awesome? Or what?"

I nudge him with my foot. "Dylan..."

"What?" He lifts his head briefly to address me. "It's not like I'm ever going to get any first-hand experience. I just want to know. I think it's cool, what you ladies can do with your bodies."

"Maybe she doesn't want to talk about it."

He looks back at Mandy. "Do you not want to talk about it?"

"It's okay. It's hard to describe," she says. "The main thing is it's an honour. To have made life out of love."

Gag.

But Dylan is totally into it. "Yeah, so what's the story with that? The dad is okay with you giving up the baby?"

Mandy blinks. "Of course."

"Of course?" I repeat, now interested. "You say that like it's no big deal."

She turns her stare on me. "He wants what's best."

"So," Dylan says, "he signed a thing saying he gives up all rights or whatever? To never see it or have it know who the dad is? I don't know if I could do that. I mean, I'm pretty sure I couldn't."

In all the conversations Dylan and I have had about this whole situation, he's never mentioned anything like this. I haven't really thought about it, either, the dad. We wait for Mandy's reply, but her stare has gone all distant and unfocused. "It's not like that" is all she'll say.

"Not like what?" I ask. "What does that mean?"

She wriggles on the futon, helpless as a turtle on its back. Dylan jumps up and holds out his hands. "Here." She takes him by the forearms and, after a scary second during which it looks as if he's going to fall down with her, they get her into a standing position.

"I'm going to lie down for a while."

"Okay," Dylan says. "See ya."

"Notice how she ignored my last question?" I say when she's gone.

"It's probably totally emotional for her. Thinking about the father and stuff." He's already back to his homework. "Anyway, Jill, she's here and this is happening. You gotta let go."

I know he's right. But I don't know how letting go works. And you could say the fact that he's gotten back together with me three times even though there's still something not quite right between us proves that he doesn't, either.

"I'm trying."

Mandy

YOU'RE PROBABLY GETTING UNCOMFORTABLE AT THIS STAGE OF YOUR PREGNANCY, YET EAGER TO MEET YOUR BABY IN PERSON! A LOT OF FIRST-TIME MOTHERS START TO WORRY AT THIS POINT THAT THEIR BABY WILL NOT FIT THROUGH THEIR BIRTH CANAL! YOUR HEALTH-CARE PROVIDER CAN HELP YOU DETERMINE WHETHER OR NOT YOUR BABY IS TOO BIG TO FIT THROUGH YOUR PELVIS. OTHER WOMEN WORRY THAT THEIR BABY COULD FALL OUT...

I close the book. Robin shouldn't make me read these things. In the old days there were no books about being pregnant, and women did it anyway and for generations we were all born, so what's the point? My great-grandmother was born in the middle of a dust storm in South Dakota that killed all the crops and half the livestock. We're strong. At least on my mother's side of the family. I don't know about my father's.

We have another appointment with Dr. Yee this week, and I'm *not* going to ask her if the baby will fit through my pelvis. She'd only give me one of those looks like I'm stupid.

It's been exactly two weeks since I got here. By now my mother must be wondering how I am. I dreamed about her last night, that she was holding my baby and telling me at last I'd done something right. In real life she wanted me to get rid of it, but in my dream her eyes were so full of love and pride that I woke up aching for her.

The house is quiet; Jill's at school, and Robin has a meeting with the city. A few flakes of snow blow by the living-room window every now and then. I wonder if it's snowing in Omaha. My mother hates winter. She'd like to move somewhere like Florida or Arizona and be warm all the time. Kent says it's too expensive. Maybe when he retires, he used to say, and Social Security can pay for it, or after he makes his fortune. After his luck changes.

I stand by the window and stare out until my back hurts. Normally I don't feel lonely here, but today I do. I can't get the dream out of my head, the eyes of my mother and how she touched the baby's downy head with so much tenderness.

Every day or so I pick up the cordless phone next to Jill's father's chair and imagine punching in the number at the apartment in Council Bluffs. It's an impulse that lasts minutes, and then I walk around the room or go upstairs to lie down or see if there's anything new and interesting in Jill's room, and the impulse goes away. Today it's stronger, the ache I woke up with like hunger.

Sometimes you want to hear your own mother's voice.

I sit in Mac's chair and put my feet up on the ottoman and hold the phone, running my fingers over the smooth silver buttons. My mother and Kent should both be at work at this time of day. I could just hear her voice on the answering machine; I don't even have to leave a message.

She answers on the second ring.

I should hang up, I know. I know. She repeats her hello, impatient, and asks who it is in that commanding way that still has power over me.

"It's Amanda."

My mother is quiet.

"Your daughter," I add. "Mandy?"

"I didn't think I'd hear from you again."

Her voice. It's low and hoarse, the way a voice gets when a person has had a cold, but hers has always been that way. Her boyfriends always say it's one of the sexiest things about her. They like her voice and the fact that she's small, like me. They like that they could pick her right up off the floor. They also like her hair, which she keeps long and blonde. If money is tight, she'll touch up her roots before

163

she buys groceries. Men don't like women with short hair or grey hair, she'll say. But Jill's hair isn't that long, and she has Dylan. Robin's hair is as short as a man's *and* grey, and I think she looks beautiful.

"How are you?" I ask.

"Great."

She's started smoking again. The flick of her lighter, the draw of breath.

"Is it snowing there?" I ask.

"It won't quit."

I wish she could see me here, sitting in this leather chair. Living with crêpes and people who own shelves and shelves of books, and the way Robin calls me every day when she's out, just to say hi and ask how I'm doing. I'd told my mother I found a family for the baby, a perfect family that wanted me to come live with them, but nothing else, and she didn't ask. Now I want to tell her everything.

"When you were pregnant with me did you worry I was going to fall out? Or that I wouldn't fit through?" I want to know one thing, any one thing, about what she felt when she was carrying me. If she had the same kind of fear and excitement and growing sense of attachment that I'm having.

"Don't be silly," she says. "Is that why you called? To ask me that?"

"Partly."

"What's the other part? I don't have money, and if I did I have better things to spend it on than a baby I told you not to have."

Already it's hard to remember what the apartment looks like. When I try to picture it, all I see is her, ashing her cigarette into one of the diet pop cans that are always nearby. The image of her blocks out everything else, like the furniture and the colour of the rooms and where the windows are.

"I don't want any money. I'm calling to tell you I'm all right."

She pauses. "I don't care, Mandy. You walked out on me. You think you can do so much better? I don't care."

The leather of the chair's arm is worn soft, looks faded. Mac must have run his hand over it a million times, the way I am now. "Okay. You can tell Kent I'm all right. If he's worried."

She laughs her small, hoarse laugh. "Don't you wonder why I'm home when I should be at work? I'm packing up to leave. Almost the second you were gone, Kent gave me the heave-ho. I've got my things here in garbage bags, lined up by the door."

"Where will you go?"

"You don't care. A friend from work is putting me up."

A man friend, probably.

165

"Tell me this, Amanda," she says. "Does your perfect family know they're getting themselves an Indian baby, born to a high school dropout?"

"Yes," I say quickly.

"That had better be the truth. Knowing you, it's not. And you'd be surprised how even the nicest people get ugly when it comes to these things, so if it doesn't work out don't come looking for me to take care of you."

The phone is getting warm against my cheek. "Maybe it won't be Indian."

She takes another drag on her cigarette, then says, "I knew it," and I imagine her shaking her head, as if she's so sure when it comes to who I am. "I knew you had to be lying when you said that was your first time."

It was my first real time. "Maybe it will be white. Like Kent."

There's a long pause, and I'm glad there are more than five hundred miles between us.

"What are you saying? Mandy?"

My hand shakes as I take the phone away from my ear and press the red button that ends the call. Mac's chair is in the perfect position for looking out the big living-room window. The snow has stopped, and the mailman is coming up the walk. Here the day is normal, just like yesterday was and tomorrow will be. I work on erasing the conversation with my mother, and all that's left is the same ache that I woke up with, the ache that was for the mother in my dream.

I try my letter to Alex again, copying it over onto a sheet of the nice stationery from Jill's drawer.

Dear Alex,

I don't have much to do these days while I wait for the baby. Writing to you helps pass the time, and the truth is I don't have anyone else's address. I hope it's okay. You can write me back but you don't have to.

One of the books I've been reading says the baby is probably five pounds now. It won't change much in the coming weeks except to get bigger and bigger. I can't wait to see what she looks like. Did I tell you I'm having a girl?

After she's born and I'm recovered, I have to figure out where I'll live. I don't think I'll stay here in Denver. The baby should have her own life, and I don't want her to be confused about who her mother is. I think it's important for children to have a good, stable environment and not have to *worry what's going to happen from day to day.*

If you could live anywhere, where would it be?

Sincerely,

Mandy Madison (from the train)

I seal and address and stamp the envelope and put on my coat to walk to the mailbox.

The snow here is different from the snow in Omaha. More powdery, dry and crunchy under your feet. And the air is not quite so cold, and it's not windy; it doesn't hurt your lungs to breathe in.

All the houses on this street are like Robin's: no saggy porches, no peeling paint, no old cars crammed into driveways. They all have shovelled walks. Juniper bushes are tied up for the season so the snow doesn't break them. The air smells fresh. This is the kind of life I want – a neat life, where people pay attention to details.

When I saw Robin's post on the Love Grows website, I could tell she was a person from this kind of life.

I'm happy for my baby, for the life she'll have.

What I don't know is how to have this life for myself.

Jill

It's the third time in about a week I've had lunch with Laurel and Cinders. They're warming up to me again. It feels mostly good, though there's definitely this sense that it's their trial period with me; they can still cancel their order at any time and send me back to wherever it is I came from, and none of us are getting so committed that it will hurt if that happens. We keep conversation as trivial as possible. I eat with them only if they invite me. They choose what and where we eat. Like today, Cinders craves Greek breakfast, so we head off campus to a place where she can get some scrambled eggs with gyro mystery meat.

What makes today different is that Dylan is with us. Things aren't as awkward between them and him – not perfect, either. He defended me all through my worst behaviour, and it got a little tiresome for Laurel and Cinders. But it's the first day of March and there are hints of spring in the air and we have Greek food. All good things.

Until the subject of Mandy comes up.

Of course it makes sense that Dylan assumed Cinders and Laurel knew about Mandy. When you're getting reacquainted with people who were, in a previous life, your best friends, naturally you'd tell them about the most earth-shaking, life-changing event to occur since, you know, the sudden death of your father. Only I hadn't, because of the whole experimental nature of the dynamic here. And ever since last week when he was over studying, Dylan has taken this acute interest in Mandy and her doings around the house and the crazy stuff she says. The peculiarities that are Mandy – the ones that drive me crazy – amuse and intrigue him.

Therefore it's not so surprising to me when he picks up a chunk of souvlaki and says, "I bet Mandy's never had Greek food. We should bring her here."

"Who's Mandy?" Cinders asks.

Dylan, across from me, chews slowly and raises his eyebrows.

"Um," I say.

Where do I begin?

"Mandy is this girl who's living at...well, she's staying with us. With my mom. She's sort of like...a relative? You know? Like a distant, distant relative."

Laurel frowns. "I thought you didn't have any family left. I mean after your dad...I thought you and your mom were the whole family tree."

"Reeeally distant."

"From another country, or what?" Cinders asks.

"Nebraska," Dylan says.

Shut up. I try to communicate it with my eyes – subtly, so Cinders won't notice.

"Just tell them, Jill."

Now Laurel is losing patience, too. "Tell us what?"

I wave my coffee cup at the waitress. I don't want to share the whole saga of Baby Girl MacSweeney with them. It's embarrassing. It feels like evidence of a failure – on my part, at being a good daughter. And a sign that my mom is losing her mind, not coping with her grief.

"Well..."

Laurel holds up her hand. "You know what, Jill? If you don't want to tell us, don't. It's fine. You can just keep on living in your Balloon of Jill and float on over our heads. It's no big deal."

Dylan nudges my foot with his under the table.

"Can I get a refill first? Please? The waitress is totally ignoring me on purpose." I lift my cup again, to no avail. I set it down and put my hands around it, concentrating on a slice of mushroom on the edge of Dylan's plate. "All right.

Mandy isn't a relative. Mandy is an eighteen-year-old stranger who is large with child and occupying our guest room."

"Aaaand…" Dylan prompts me.

"*And* my mom is adopting her baby."

Cinders blinks. "That's…unexpected."

"Uh, yeah."

"She's not really a stranger," Dylan says. "I mean, she's been there two weeks. You're getting to know her."

"And what a treat that has been."

"What's wrong with her?" Laurel asks.

Before I can list the Things That Are Wrong with Mandy, Dylan jumps in. "Nothing is wrong with her. She's just different from us."

Cinders says, "Isn't your mom a little old to be taking on a baby?"

"Yes!" Hey, maybe this telling thing isn't so bad; finally I'm getting some sympathy. It all spills out. "I think it's a huge mistake. And my mom didn't even get a lawyer… There's no contract, no nothing. Just a flimsy e-mail agreement! My dad wouldn't—" I stop myself. Dylan glances at me.

Cinders is gratifyingly appalled by the whole thing, and for the rest of lunch she and Laurel ask questions and express disbelief, like, on top of dealing with my dad's death, now *this*. It's great, really, and energizing, except when Dylan keeps defending Mandy and my mom. But it's three against one and eventually he stops and by the time we get back to school I'm high on righteous indignation and the feeling that, once again, I'm a part of something, and I'm right.

I carry that energy through my shift at Margins, where there is lots of excitement because, while I was at school, Ravi got his man.

Ron fills me in. "Harmless middle-aged man on crutches comes into the store. He talks me into letting him keep his backpack, right, because how else is he going to get his purchases up to the register? I'm an idiot."

So Ravi was on the money with his theory about sneaky people acting disabled. I guess the rest: "He loads up his backpack with art books and other expensive crap? If anyone stops him, he can say, 'I was going to pay. I am but a helpless man on crutches.'"

"Right. And it's not the first time. Oh no. Ravi's been trailing him from store to store. The guy's been hitting every Margins in our region since before Christmas, but no one could ever quite catch him in the act. The guy's a one-man cottage industry of stolen merch." The cops came, he tells me; it was this whole scene.

"Where's Annalee?" I ask.

"She took Ravi out to celebrate. She'll be back soon." He looks at his watch. "Actually I thought she'd be back by now. They left nearly two hours ago." Ron smiles. "Think something's going on between those two?"

"What? No." I say it as if the very idea is nonsense, but for the next hour I find myself obsessed with wondering what Ravi and Annalee could possibly be up to all this time, and the comments she made when she first met him. I try to add up in my head the number of times he's been in the store since that night. Five? Six? Dude works fast. Anyway, *we're* the ones who had a bonding experience first. Okay, so that experience involved injury to Ravi's face, and me apparently ignoring him for an entire year of Ms. Schiff's computer science class, but the point is we have history.

When Annalee finally shows up, Ravi is right behind her, and they are happy, happy, happy. I'm trapped in the customer service booth in the middle of the store, watching them be happy from a distance. Annalee has that look on her face, that energy you get when you have a new crush. Or when you get good news, or there's a fun trip coming up or even just the weekend. Like despite all the b.s. that goes on day after day, life has some zip to it after all.

I don't know when I felt that last. I highly doubt I look

the way Annalee looks now when I'm with Dylan. Definitely not lately; we've been off and on for so long. Did I feel that way for at least a few hours when we got back together? I can't remember if I *ever* felt that way. I must have, before.

I don't know.

Annalee comes over to the customer service booth. "Hey, Jill." She toys with the store keys she wears on a black leather cord around her neck. "I'm going to buy a frap for Ravi. I'll be on in about fifteen, and then you can take your break, okay?"

Fifteen? I know our barista isn't the fastest in the West, but how long does it take to make a frap?

"Sure."

And off they go to the cafe area, laughing it up.

"Nice takedown," I say. Way too loud. Even Ron, clear across at the register, looks up.

Ravi turns around and says, "Thanks, Jill," and Annalee walks with a noticeable bounce in her step.

Do you remember if I ever looked like that? I want to call after him. *Like I had something to look forward to?*

I'm still hanging on to the remnants of Laurel and Cinders's reaction to the Mandy situation when I get home and find Mom in her office, working and listening to Neil Young, a cup of tea beside her keyboard. The desk lamp casts a halo of light around her. It's a lonely scene. I shouldn't go in and do what I'm about to do. The timing is wrong. There's probably not a right time, though, which in the moment seems like reason enough to proceed.

I come in close, lean on the back of her chair. "What is that? Same thing you've been working on all month?"

She takes the glasses from the end of her nose and puts them on top of her head. "Yes. The feasibility study for RTD. They want to extend the light rail, and I'm trying to help them figure out how to do that without upsetting residents along the corridor here." She hovers her fingers over a map on one of the two monitors she has set up.

Sometimes I forget my mom has this whole other life, where she's great and competent and well paid for the consulting work she does with transportation-engineering firms and the city. She's so smart at work stuff.

Then I see, taped to the other monitor, ultrasound pictures of Mandy's baby. There are two: one doesn't look like much, but the other one is a close-up of her face. Her hand is up by her mouth, her puffy little eyes shut, the outline of her nose clear. "Mom..." I say, unable to take my eyes off the picture of this person, this person who's on her way into our family.

"Yes?"

Let it go, Jill. Let. It. Go. "Never mind." I almost touch her shoulders, almost lean over and kiss the top of her head. What I want more than anything in this moment is to have faith, the way she does, that everything's going to be okay.

"What, Jill?" She spins her chair around; my arms drop. She touches the mole on her jaw. "You've been wanting to say something all week. I can tell, and it's made me nervous. Spill it or let me get back to work."

I grasp my fingers together, stuck. I have to ask. "Do you have something from Mandy about the father? Like a thing where he signed over his parental rights or something?"

Instantly she's beyond irritated. "Why are you asking me this?"

Just as instantly, I manage to find that self-righteousness that was so sharp and fresh at lunch today. "Because you've never said anything, and I would think it's kind of important. God. Sorry for caring."

Mom speaks slowly. "Jill. I have been trying to involve you in this from the beginning. You practically put your hands over your ears every time I brought it up. Now you have questions?" She turns back to her computer. "Trust I've got it taken care of, and by all means don't let it bother you."

Her back is rigid, and though she's moving the mouse around and typing figures into her map, I don't buy that she's paying any attention to her work.

"Well it does bother me. It bothers me. I'm sorry for how I was before." She spins her chair to face me again. I take a deep breath and continue. "It didn't seem real. I didn't believe it was going to happen. Now that Mandy's here, I'm just saying what if in five years, after we're all attached to this thing, some dude comes knocking on the door and is all, 'That's my baby, give it over.'"

Mom picks up her mug of tea and gazes into it. Less irritated. More contemplative. "'This thing'? You say that it wasn't real *before*, but you still don't see the baby as a human being who's going to be in our lives for...ever. Since you're so concerned about 'this thing', I'll tell you. Mandy did her best to contact the father, but she couldn't. It was difficult because she..." Mom sighs, and her voice goes from serious to sounding *what-the-hell?*-ish. "She didn't know his last name or live in the same town. She only saw him once."

"It was a one-night stand?"

"It was a one-night stand."

After that bullshit Mandy was saying last week about the baby being "made from love." *Love!*

"I didn't want you to hold it against her," Mom says. "Or the baby. So now you know."

Now I know.

"Here's another shocking revelation, Mom: that doesn't

make me feel any better. Dad would have asked more questions." I blurt it. Stupidly. Meanly.

Chair spins back. Clicking of mouse. Entering of figures – traffic counts, GPS coordinates. "Well, he's not here now, is he?"

As if either of us needed reminding. I try to sound less accusing this time. "I'm merely saying, the guy could turn up—"

"I *know*, Jill." She turns around again, and her face – her face so much like mine, no matter what Mandy says about us looking nothing alike – is full of outrage, yet so alive. "The father could show up, Mandy could change her mind. The baby could be born deaf or blind. I could die tomorrow. I know. I know! You think I don't know, after the year we've had, that anything could happen? That no matter what precautions you take, how smart you are, how much you prepare and plan, anything could happen."

My eyes burn. I don't know why she had to say that she could die tomorrow. Why did she have to say that part?

I'd miss her so much. It's a jagged thing in my throat, how much I'd miss her, how much I miss her now, how much I want us to be able to find each other now that we don't have Dad as a bridge between us.

I want to say it. *I'd miss you*. My vocal cords are paralysed.

"You want to shut life out, Jill, that's your choice. Push

everyone away. Refuse change." She laughs a little and throws her hands up. "You used to not give a damn about anything, but that was because you were *brave*, not cynical. You used to have so much courage. Dad and I would lie awake at night worrying about the trouble you'd get into because of your courage."

They did? I had courage?

Mom continues, "I don't know how you got so scared."

She tosses it off, unthinking. We stare at each other. How can she say that? She does know. She does! I swallow, finally finding my voice. "I don't know how you didn't."

What I mean is, *Tell me how*. Tell me how to keep being the way I was. But she's still defending herself. "I have to believe..." She jabs at her collarbone. Her voice cracks. "I have to believe something surprisingly good can still happen."

I nod and retreat to the living room, where I sit in Dad's club chair and put my feet up on the ottoman, trying to understand Mom the way he understood her.

"Your mom doesn't listen to sense," he used to say.

"Your mom does what she does, damn the torpedoes," he used to say.

"Your mom's a nut," he used to say. "I'm just along for the ride."

I mean, I get it. I sort of get it. She's not just doing this because she wants a baby, though I think she really does. She's doing this to say a big eff you to fate, or God, or luck, or whatever it is that took Dad away from us. *I dare you,* she's saying. *I dare you.*

Mandy

What I've noticed is that certain people can make you feel like a fraction of yourself. As big as my body is now, after talking to my mother yesterday, my soul could squeeze down into almost nothing. It could live in a matchbox. It could slip between the cushions of this leather couch where I spend almost all my time now, while I wait – incubate – for five more weeks.

I reach into my dress pocket and close my fingers around the watch. Today I need it with me, close, to remind myself that I can decide what I want. Nothing is settled yet. And no matter what happens, I'll never have to go back to my mother.

I wish she couldn't make me feel like that. It's hard to know *what* I should feel about her. She gave birth to me, and even though she lived her life mostly like someone who didn't have children I always had food and clothes and somewhere to live because of her. I have her eyes and her small hands. She never wanted me, though. If she'd done what I'm doing, instead of keeping me, everything about my life would have been different. But then I wouldn't be me. It's impossible to think of myself as anyone else.

And I know when I make this choice, I'm giving something to my daughter but also taking something away. The something I'm taking away is me. She won't be able to look at Robin and see her own eyes or her own hands. Maybe in eighteen years she'll be sitting here on this exact couch having the same thoughts about me that I'm having about my mother. I don't want it to be like that, but I don't know how to make it not be.

When my mother told me Kent is making her move out, I thought, *Good.* A thing in myself I don't like was glad it happened to her. Like I was the reason Kent let us stay there, like he chose me instead of her. Even though I never wanted him to. But out of the two of them, Kent is the one who paid more attention to me, I think, and that counts for something? Or, I don't know. That wasn't caring attention. Not how it's supposed to be. The way things were with Kent is complicated, and all mixed up in my mind. Sometimes he did nice things, like remember the kind of pop I like, and drive me to school if I slept too late for the bus. Sometimes.

He pretended I wasn't pregnant.

I told him before I told my mother, before I showed. It was a Saturday and she was out. Kent was sitting in the living room watching TV, with his computer in his lap. Maybe doing billings and things for his business, or maybe looking up what truck he wanted to buy next, or playing poker online, I don't know. I came in and stood near the TV, waiting for him to say, "What is it?" but he never did, so I sat in the chair and watched the TV awhile. During a commercial he asked me to get him a can of pop, so I did. When I handed it to him, he didn't look up or say "thank you". I could see the top of his head, the little bald spot under the grey-brown. His thick neck, his big upper arms.

"I have to tell you something," I said.

"What."

You should pay attention while I'm telling you this, I thought. You're going to want to see my face.

"I'm pregnant."

His hands stopped moving on the laptop for a few seconds. Then they started again.

"No, you're not."

"Yes. I am."

He folded his laptop shut, got up, and took his keys and cell phone from the coffee table. "It's got nothing to do with me." And he left. After that, we never talked about it again, and my mother never said anything about it in front of him. I don't know if he told her not to talk about it to him or if she just decided not to. Once in a while I'd catch him staring at me, staring at my stomach, but mostly whenever I came into a room, he left it. And never came into mine at night again.

Sometimes I missed it.

That's what I mean when I say it's all mixed up. I hated him, I hated it. But after I told him I was pregnant and he left me alone, and I told my mother I was pregnant and she was mad, I would sometimes lie in bed at night and wonder, *Does it matter any more to either of them that I exist? Do I exist?* I would run my hand down my arm to make sure I was still there. Sometimes I would stay in my room during dinner time to see if either of them came to get me. Sometimes my mom would, but not always, and never Kent. Other times I would go walking after school and stay out until my feet hurt too much to keep going, and wonder if they would yell at me for being late and worrying them. They never did. Days and days and days could go by when all they did was look through me. All I wanted to know was that they saw me. That I was seen by someone. That feeling of disappearing can be worst of all.

One night when I touched my arm, I started to doubt I was really there. I pinched the skin. I dragged a fingernail across my collarbone until it stung. I got up and looked in the mirror. I didn't know if I could believe what I saw, that I was there, that I was me. I touched the mirror where my face was. I put my cheek to it and breathed on it until my breath condensed on the glass. But I still wasn't sure. The only sure sign I had that I existed was the ripple of life inside me.

That was the night I decided I would leave.

I've gotten used to the way Robin's footsteps sound on the stairs – *clip-clip-clip* – whereas Jill's are more *clomp-clomp-clomp*.

"I'm headed to a client meeting," Robin says. "Need anything? I could swing by the store on my way home."

I turn so I can see her from the couch. Her head is down, one hand deep in her bag as she pauses on the bottom stair. This morning when we had breakfast together, like we always do, she had on yoga pants and a sweatshirt. Now she's wearing dark brown slacks with pinstripes, a white top, and a burgundy blazer. A real career woman. "You look nice."

"Thanks, sweetie." She withdraws her hand, keys found, and continues towards the door. "Call if you think of anything you need."

What I need is to not be alone, where that disappearing feeling might come back.

"Maybe I could go with you."

"To my meeting? *I* don't even want to go to my meeting."

It takes a lot of concentration to not beg her. *Please, please, don't leave me here alone.* Normally the TV is enough to keep me from thinking about Kent and my mother too much, but today I'm not that strong, even with the watch.

"I mean, I wonder if there's somewhere you could drop me off," I say, making my voice not break. "Like a mall or a movie theatre or anywhere?"

Robin presses something on her phone and looks at it. "I'm running..." Then she drops her arm and sees me. She sees me. "Of course. You must be desperate for a change of scenery. Come on, get your stuff. I'll warm up the car."

She leaves me at a big shopping centre that has an outside part and an inside part. Be careful walking and watch for icy spots if you decide to go to the outside part, she tells me, and that there are some cute stores there. Not to eat junk food. She gives me twenty dollars and her American Express card. "Get yourself a snack if you're hungry. And something special for yourself."

Something for myself?

She sees the expression on my face and smiles. "Just don't go crazy."

I spend a long time looking at the directory. The stores here are a mix of the same stores we have around Council Bluffs and Omaha, and places I've never heard of. There are two Starbucks, that's how big it is. At the closest one I get a hot chocolate and sit so I can rest my back and legs, which are already tired, and watch people go by. It seems like they're mostly wives. That's what they look like to me – women whose husbands make a lot of money, so they go out shopping, alone or with friends, and then have lunch in a restaurant and have a new purse every six months and their roots never show.

That's the kind of woman my mother always wanted to be. Every man she dated or lived with was supposed to be the one who could make it happen. Kent was it, she thought, the last one and the right one. Contractors can make a lot of money, as long as they work hard and do a good job and don't make their clients mad by not showing up or going over budget. As long as they don't think they have to have a brand-new truck they can't afford, every year. As long as they don't gamble or have to pay people off to not report them for using and underpaying illegal aliens for labour.

"Mind if I sit here?"

It's a pregnant woman, with two big bags and several small ones. That's the other kind of woman here at the mall: mothers. She's holding a coffee cup with a teabag string hanging over the side. The chair across from me is the only one left in the whole Starbucks. "Okay."

"Thanks." She lowers herself into it after setting her bags down. "What are you? Thirty weeks?"

I stare at her. "What?"

"I'm guessing you're thirty weeks. Along?"

"Thirty-five."

She leans over the table to get a better look at my belly. "I'll buy that." Her eyes narrow in a friendly way. She's pretty. "You're young. Your first?"

"Yes."

"Third," she says, patting her stomach, then grimacing. "Not sure what I was thinking."

I sip my hot chocolate which isn't so hot any more. I don't care. It's good and sweet and I'm having a regular conversation with someone who isn't Robin or Jill. "You don't like the other two?" I ask.

Her eyes widen. "What? God no, that's not what I meant. I love them. Of course! Being pregnant, though." She shakes her head. "Right?"

"Right."

She waits, smiling. No one has to tell me I'm not good at making conversation. At school I didn't have friends. There were two girls I had lunch with most days: Lucia Reynolds and DebAnn Forsyth-Miller. We were not friends. We were people to eat lunch with. Lucia always had earphones in. I don't think she listened to music as much as people thought, because even though she acted like she couldn't hear anything, if DebAnn or I actually talked about something and Lucia had an opinion, suddenly she could hear us. DebAnn wore a long, beige puffy coat – every day, even when it was hot, and she'd been wearing it since ninth grade. If you bumped into her in the hallway, she wouldn't feel it.

Lucia had earphones, and DebAnn had her coat. I had something, too. I don't know what it was, but it made me as invisible as they were, at school like I was at home. Until the baby started to show.

I miss school. I'm not a dropout – at least, not the way my mother makes it sound. I would have graduated this June, finally, after getting messed up from missing sixth grade when I was supposed to have it, which was my mother's fault. Her boyfriend that year was a truck driver. Leo. It was temporary – he had a plan to drive his truck for a year and save every penny, then start a business. The business would be selling little supplies and things for truckers, like televisions and coffee-makers and blenders that all ran on twelve-volt batteries. For the plan to work, he couldn't have housing expenses for one year. So we went with him and lived in the cab of his truck. After the first few thousand miles, Leo and my mother fought a lot. The cab was cramped. Sometimes we went a week without a shower. And I was absent for all of sixth grade.

When I took the tests to see if I could go straight to junior high, I didn't do too well. My mother said I did bad on purpose to make her feel guilty about Leo, who broke up with us and never started his business.

The woman across from me now looks like the kind who had lots of friends in sixth grade.

"So you must be excited," she says, dunking her teabag up and down. Her hair is brown and bobbed, and you can tell her clothes aren't cheap, even though they're plain. I imagine us meeting here once a week.

"I'm giving this one up," I say.

Her dunking suddenly stops. The teabag drips, suspended above the steaming water. Then she starts dunking again. "Good for you, I guess. Personally, I couldn't do it."

"You could. If you knew it was the best thing."

Her eyes narrow again, different this time. "Just wait. When you go through hell to give birth to your baby and then it's over and you finally have it – wait, boy or girl? Do you know?"

"Girl." Christopher's skin. My eyes.

"When you finally have *her* in your arms and hear that helpless little cry, you know you'd give your life for her and you wouldn't let anyone prise her from your cold, dead hands. You'll see."

She flicks a packet of sweetener between her fingers. Her face is smooth and worry-free, as if she's only making friendly conversation.

"Where are they now?" I ask.

"Hmm?"

"If you're so attached to your children, where are they now?"

The flicking stops. Her mouth hardens. "One's at kindergarten, and the other is with the nanny." She rips open the packet and dumps it into her tea. "Obviously you're missing my point."

I stand and let my purse accidentally knock over my cup. What's left of my hot chocolate spreads out over the small table, and she can't stop some of it from running over the edge and onto her lap. "Shit!" she says, grabbing for napkins.

"I hope you don't use that language in front of your children."

* * *

Outside it's cold but sunny. It feels good, and I walk up and down the streets of the outside part of the mall, and I wonder: If you don't grow up to be a wife or a mother, what are you? A person alone, always wanting to be one thing or the other or both? My mother was never a wife, and that's what she wanted more than anything. She didn't want to be a mother, and she wasn't one. Where does that leave her? A husband makes you a wife, and a child makes you a mother. Robin, she has everything and is everything, because she had Mac and she has Jill and also her job. What if there isn't anyone to make you something?

A lot of times when I look at the world and everyone in it, I feel like they all know something I don't. I'm not dumb; I can see how it works. But it's like double Dutch jump rope. In grade school I would watch the ropes fly and see girl after girl jump in and either get it right or get tangled in the ropes and laugh. I'd stand there with my hands ready and my body going back and forth, trying to get the rhythm and the right moment, and Ms. Trimble, the PE teacher, would say, "Come on, Mandy, everyone's waiting," and I couldn't do it. I couldn't figure out how to get in.

That's how life feels to me. Everyone is doing it; everyone knows how. To live and be who they are and find a place, find a moment. I'm still waiting.

193

Jill

"You need to stop obsessing about her."

Dylan and I are back at the pho place, only two weeks since the day I hid in his car.

"Having actual concerns is not obsessing. She's living in our house. Bearing the child my mom wants. My sister. It's kind of a big deal." A largish blob of chilli sauce shoots into my broth from the bottle I've been squeezing – too hard, apparently. My conversation with Mom last night still bothers me, so much, but I haven't told Dylan about it. Maybe he'll agree with her, say I'm too closed off to life, a coward. Which isn't something I need to hear; it's not like I know how to do anything about it.

"It's going to be okay. Your mom is rock."

"My mom is *not* rock, Dyl." Fearless and indestructible aren't the same thing. He should have seen her on the day of the anniversary. He should see the way she still looks at Dad's chair. "There's this guy at work—" As soon as that much comes out of my mouth, I freeze, unexpectedly shy about saying Ravi's name.

Dylan shovels noodles into his mouth with chopsticks and widens his eyes at me, nodding, as if to say, *Go on...*

"Just this annoying loss control guy."

"Loss control?"

"Theft prevention. Theft by employees or customers or whatever. Can I finish?"

"Continue."

"So, he's this annoying guy, this loss control dude from Corporate who, for some reason, is always hanging out at our store. He completely thinks he's a super-spy. I mean, he did catch this major thief, but he takes it all so seriously." I'm talking into my bowl of broth, pushing bean sprouts and mint leaves around, and my face feels hot. "It's lame."

I don't know why I'm saying he's annoying. Dylan's not the jealous type, so there's no need to make Ravi into a non-threat by going on and on the way I am, no reason not to mention that Ravi went to our school, signed my yearbook sophomore year, and said he bet we'd meet again. It's actually kind of a great story. Only I don't want to tell it. It feels personal, so mine.

Dylan steals one of my beef strips. "Anyone who takes anything seriously is 'lame', according to you."

Mom's words come back: *Cynical. No courage.* "He wears these stupid suits."

"Oh no. Not *suits.*"

Dylan's been arguing with me all day. This morning I merely suggested that he park on the other side of the school lot from where he usually does, because the sun had melted the ice over there, and he said, "No, thanks," and parked in his favourite, icy spot. Then in English I made a point about Anne Brontë being a more interesting Brontë than Emily and why did high schoolers around the country always have to read *Jane Eyre*, anyway, when there were other Brontës? And Dylan said, in front of the class, that *Jane Eyre* is awesome and why shouldn't everyone have to read it? As if he's even read any Anne or Charlotte. Now he's defending Ravi, a stranger.

"Anyway. Yes, he's an annoying suit-wearer, but he *is* good at what he does, and I thought I could hire him. As, like, a private investigator."

Dylan sets down his chopsticks and squints at me. "To investigate what?"

"What do you think? Mandy."

He makes a church and steeple out of his hands and points the steeple at me. "And you hope to accomplish... what, exactly? Pissing off your mother and making Mandy feel like crap?"

"They don't have to know. If Mandy hasn't done anything wrong, it won't matter."

"But what if you *do* find something out, Jill? Something you feel like you have to tell your mom?" He waits. Patiently. Will wait for ever while letting me stew in my own juices and think about the implications of my words and actions. I'd forgotten how good he is at that.

"Every single other person in the world uses a lawyer or social worker or has a contract or *something* before they go giving away their babies... Why won't Mandy?"

"Maybe not 'every single other person' does. You don't know. All kinds of people make all kinds of decisions that aren't by the book, and they have their reasons."

I set my chopsticks on the edge of my bowl. One rolls off, and onto the table, and then off the table and onto the floor. The lady reading the paper at the register frowns at us.

"Your mom is smart, Jill," Dylan continues. "Give her some credit."

"You don't know her like I do. She totally rushed into this. She doesn't know enough about Mandy. She..." I press back tears with my palms, seeing spots and sunbursts. Mom's right: I'm scared. I'm scared something will go wrong. If I keep my eye on Mandy, maybe I can prevent that. Not everything has to be left to fate. "I'm the only one left to take care of her, Dylan. Me. I keep trying to think what my dad would do but I don't know, I don't know."

I feel Dylan's fingertips on my elbow and uncover my eyes, blinking a few times.

"I think it's gonna work out," he says.

"You think."

"Yeah. I have a feeling."

"Gee, how can I argue with that? It should completely put my mind at ease." I pull my elbows back and get out my wallet. "I owe you from last time."

"Promise me you won't hire this work guy, or anyone, to investigate Mandy behind your mom's back. If you're that worried, talk to your mom and let her decide."

I slide the bill towards me. "How much is it?"

"Jill. Say okay. Say you won't do anything stupid."

"Okay." I put cash on the table. "I won't do anything stupid."

As if he heard all my accusations about being a relentless suit-wearer, Ravi isn't wearing one tonight. Instead, he's got on dark-rinse jeans and a palest yellow T-shirt with a black cardigan. The yellow sets off his dark skin, and a thought floats through my mind before I can stop it: I bet his neck smells like a cinnamon graham cracker, the kind my third-grade teacher used to pass out at recess.

It's the strangest thing, the way my senses play strange tricks when I'm around him. I think of baked goods, I think of childhood. I feel like I'm seeing the world – or glimpses of it – through the eyes of the smiling sophomore Jill, the courageous Jill, the excited-about-life-and-possibility Jill. But because I'm not her, because I'm me and because the idea of being excited about life is, let's face it, a little bit scary in light of what life has given me in the recent past, I greet him with "How come you're always here?" instead of *Hi, how are you?* "There *are* five other stores in our region, you know."

He spins a rack of greeting cards, picking out one and opening it. "Mm-hmm."

A customer – one of our regulars, a middle-aged lady with giant glasses – comes up to the register with a paperback by this author who's got a new book out every other month, and she's always the first to buy a copy. If we don't have the book out *on* the release date, she harasses us. "You know he doesn't write these himself," I say, scanning the book and reaching under the counter for a bag.

"What?"

I tap the author's name on the front cover. "He doesn't write these."

She takes the book, turning it over. The entire back cover is a picture of the author, resting his chin on his hand

and attempting to smile devilishly. "Of course he does."

She's in love with him. I shouldn't shatter her this way, but I can't help myself. "He outlines them. He has his staff fill in the details." I've been dying to tell her this ever since I found out from one of the publisher's sales reps.

She runs her credit card through the machine, her kitty-cat charm bracelet jingling against the PIN pad. "How do you know?"

Ravi is nearby, still looking at cards. "I read it in the *New York Times*," I say. "It's not a secret." I've always wanted to say "I read it in the *New York Times*" to someone, about something. It sounds good, whether or not it's true.

"Did you, now?" She gives my brow ring and blue-streaked hair a meaningful look.

I slip the book into the bag, throw in a bookmark, smile. "Have a nice night."

Ravi sets a card on the counter. It's a birthday card with a drawing of a cute goldfish swimming towards a cake. I run it through and add the employee discount code. "We're not supposed to shop on the clock," I remind him.

"I'm not on the clock."

"Bag?"

"No, thanks."

He pays, then takes a pen from my pen jar to write in the card.

"Can you move down the counter? I don't want customers to think there's a line."

"The store is empty." Ravi looks at me and raises one eyebrow. One. The other goes down. At the same time one corner of his mouth goes up. It's perfect, the kind of thing you practise in the mirror because you've seen someone else do it and it's so cool you're dying to be able to do it yourself. I have to exert all my will to keep from smiling. Because smiling would be...bad?

"Whose birthday is it?" I try to see what he's writing, without being too obvious about it. I can only make out the words *fun week*.

"A friend's." He slides the card closer to him; I look away.

Annalee walks up from the back of the store. Ravi, hearing the unmistakable sound of her long skirt swishing, turns. They smile at each other. "Ready?" Annalee asks.

"Yep!"

To me, Annalee says, "I'm taking my dinner break early. We'll just be down at McGrath's. Ron is here, and Polly's running the cafe." She comes around behind the counter to get her coat. "Call if anything comes up."

"Maybe *you* should call *me* if anything 'comes up'," I mutter.

"What?"

"Nothing."

Ravi slips the card into its envelope and writes *Annalee* with a flourish. When he puts the pen back in the cup, our eyes meet. They're going on a date. A birthday date. I try to raise one brow at him exactly like he did at me. I have no idea if it works, but he looks away first. "There's a policy," I say.

Annalee hears me, nudging past to get her bag from under the register. "But you won't tell. Want us to bring you back anything?"

"I'm good," I say, as cheerily as possible. "Happy birthday."

I'll admit it: as I watch them leave, I feel a little jealous.

I'm the one who popped Ravi in the jaw. *I'm* the one who needs his help with Mandy. *I'm* the one whose yearbook he signed, the smart and funny one he wished he'd had a chance to get to know. It's hard not to think of him as mine. At least, more mine than Annalee's.

During closing, while Annalee counts out the drop safes, I make a call on my cell phone from the kids' section. Ravi's business card is in my apron pocket, where it's been since the night he came to apologize. I've kept reaching in and running my finger along the edge, working out what to say.

Since it's late, I expect to get his voicemail, but he picks up on the second ring.

"Ravi Desai."

"I thought you weren't on the clock. And what happened to R. J.?"

"Jill?"

He says it fast. He recognized my voice.

"Yeah. Um, sorry to bother you so late. I... It's not exactly work-related." I bend sideways so I can see down the aisle and to the front of the store. Annalee is printing out a register report, and the printer noise is loud. "Can we meet up sometime this week?"

We talk over each other.

Me: "I need your expertise..."

Him: "If this is about..."

About what?

"What?"

"I can't really talk right now," I say. "Do you think you could meet me at four tomorrow? For coffee? In Congress Park?"

"Sure." He doesn't even hesitate.

"See you then," I say, and click off my phone before he can say anything else and before I realize that I should have said "thank you".

I pick up a copy of *Pat the Bunny* from the floor and rub

the front before placing it back on a shelf. I spin the rack of Little Golden Books. I wipe what I hope is a smear of chocolate off the Frog and Toad mural. I finish my work and drive home, singing along to the radio.

Even though what I want to see him about is serious, even though he just went on a date with Annalee, even though I'm with Dylan, even though I'm apparently a coward who's scared of everything and most of all change, meeting Ravi for coffee feels like the first thing in eons that I've had to look forward to. It's almost like I have a date with my old self.

Mandy

Jill and Robin get in a fight because of me.

Robin met me at the north corner of the mall, inside, like she said she would. I saw her before she saw me, and I tried to look at her as if she were a stranger. Would I think she was a wife, or a mother? All I could see was Robin, who could be anything she wanted, being completely who she is.

She saw me and came over, smiling and unbuttoning her blazer. "It's warming up. Didn't you get yourself anything?" she asked. "Where are your bags?"

"I only got this." I pulled a small bag out of my purse and showed her the pale turquoise scarf I'd bought, with silver threads running through it. "It was twelve dollars."

Robin held it to my face. "That really is your colour. So gorgeous against your skin."

"It is? My mother always said I shouldn't wear too much

light blue." I curled my lower lip into my mouth and bit it. Normally I don't talk about my mother in front of Robin and Jill. It's better not to mention my family at all. There were questions Robin asked me back in January, when we were e-mailing our plans. I answered them all, but there's no reason to bring it up any more.

Robin was surprised, too. I could tell from how she drew the scarf through her hands a few times, watching me, until she said, "I think it matches your eyes perfectly," as if my mother's opinion didn't exist. "Is that all you bought?"

"You said not to go crazy."

"And you didn't." She put one arm around me and led me back towards the centre of the mall and more stores. "Now I'm saying we could go a little crazy. Mildly insane. I remember being that pregnant with Jill and feeling like a hippo, and so uncomfortable. There's a maternity store here somewhere..."

"It's okay. I have what I need."

"I know. Sometimes you should have something you don't need but that you want. It'll be fun. Jill never lets me shop with her any more."

I didn't really want new clothes any more than I needed them. I'd rather keep wearing dresses until I go back to my old size. I'll need clothes for my new life, and I thought maybe if I didn't spend too much of her money now, she'd help me then. I don't want to waste any of the watch money on clothes. But I wanted to make her happy. So we shopped and went out to a late lunch and came back to the house and took naps. After, Robin made me put on all the clothes again and walk around the house in different outfits.

I admit: it was fun for me, too.

It's another thing, like crêpes and reading on Saturdays, that's so different from how things were. Robin never says anything like she hopes I appreciate everything she's doing for me and I could show a little gratitude by doing something for her once in a while, in exchange. Kent would say that. Kent did say that, the two or three times he bought me clothes. When he made me walk around the house in outfits he bought, it wasn't because he was happy to see me happy.

Robin made popcorn for a late dinner, and we watched TV, and during one commercial I looked at her and smiled. I was about to say "thank you, thank you", and I wanted to let her know how it feels to be in her house, and if I thought I could make this kind of life for my baby, I would keep it. But I didn't want her to take it wrong, and I was trying to think of another way to say what I meant when Jill came home from work.

She had to scoot Robin's bag out of her way with her foot to get past the entryway. "What happened in here?"

There were bags and tissue paper everywhere, and stray popcorn kernels.

"Mandy got a makeover." Robin turned down the TV. "Show Jill your new look, Mandy."

I hauled myself into a standing position to show her: the navy blue long cardigan that Robin picked out, with rows of purple buttons down the front. It cost more than I've ever spent in one trip, let alone on one piece of clothing. Underneath you wear black leggings with a special supportive waistband for the baby. The whole outfit is warm and soft; the material doesn't feel like anything I've ever had on. Robin says that's because it's natural fibres. My mother always said wash-and-wear materials were best. "If I wanted to spend half my life waiting for my clothes to air dry, I would have stayed on the farm." But I think this is better.

"Did you use my straighteners?" Jill asked.

My hand went to my hair. I'd forgotten we did that. When I saw myself in the mirror with my hair like this, I could barely recognize who I was. My face wasn't so swallowed up.

"We borrowed it, yes," Robin said. "It was my idea."

Jill tripped on another bag, catching herself before she fell, but not before she swore. "Mom? Can I talk to you upstairs for a minute?"

That's when I knew I was in trouble.

Robin set the popcorn bowl down on the floor and stood. My mother would never do that. She'd say, "Anything you have to say to me you can say in front of Kent." Or, "I don't feel like getting up, Mandy. I'm tired, and I don't take orders from my daughter." But Robin, she saw the look on Jill's face and heard the tone of her voice and followed her right up the stairs, handing me the remote on the way. "Be right back, honey. You can change the channel."

I didn't. I left the volume down, too.

And now I'm down here, listening, while I start putting some of my new things back into bags. This is the kind of thing I expect to happen whenever it seems like things might turn out all right: someone will get mad; someone will get mad at *me*. You never get anything good without paying for it. I walk quietly in my socks to the bottom of the stairs. I hear voices but not what they're saying. Mostly I hear Jill because she's the loudest, but muffled. Pretty soon a door slams, and I waddle back to the living room, back to the couch.

I hear Robin's footsteps on the stairs; then she's in the room with me and has that look a person gets when they've been fighting with somebody. Tired, disappointed.

"Maybe you shouldn't have bought me all this stuff. It cost a lot." I pick up a grey shirt Robin called a charcoal tunic from the cushion next to me and fold it into a perfect square. There are tears pushing up, even though I know not to cry in front of people. It was a good day. Nearly perfect. Now I'm paying for it.

Robin comes closer and runs her hand over my smooth hair before sitting next to me. "I don't want you to worry about that. We have plenty of money." She takes the folded tunic and places it on top of the stack I've been making.

I wish Christopher could see me right this second. The way Robin touched my hair. The way I belong. I take a mental picture and send it to him in my head. A moment in time when I feel loved, to go with the other moment I felt it, the one that he gave me.

"What is it, then?" I ask. "Why is Jill so mad?"

"Oh. Jill isn't mad. Well, she is. Or she thinks she is." Robin looks at the club chair, Mac's, the one they never sit in, then at me, and her eyes are full of tears, and she doesn't even try to make them stop. "Mostly, she isn't mad. She's sad."

Dear Alex,

I think by now you must be back home and have gotten my letters. This time I'm enclosing a self-addressed stamped envelope. I know sometimes you have the idea to write to someone or call them, but it's too much trouble to look up an address and a phone number, especially these days when we do everything on the computer. I do have an e-mail address that I don't use very much. Someone I used to know, his name was Kent, was on the computer all the time, practically addicted to it. I don't want to miss out on important things because of needing to check something on the computer all the time. Also, I think handwritten letters are more personal. My hand is on this pen writing on this paper, and when you get this paper, you'll know I touched it, and you'll touch it, and it's a connection.

Well, not to sound so serious. It sure is different being here from living my old life back in Omaha! Did I tell you that I used to be an administrative assistant? It was only about twelve hours a week, for my mother's boyfriend's construction company. A little bit of filing and answering the phone and things. When I leave here, I might look for that kind of a job again.

In my last letter I know I said that my future is a blank. I didn't want you to think I'm dumb, that I haven't thought about it at all. I have some money. Or I will have. I would never have left Omaha without a plan, including a plan for if I decide giving up my baby is the wrong thing. Not that I would, but you always need a plan. One of my mother's boyfriends, not the one with the construction company, liked to say motivational quotes. "Failure to plan is planning to fail." And things like that.

So you can use the envelope in here to write to me. All you need is a piece of paper and a pen or pencil. I bet you have that around somewhere.

Yours truly,
Mandy (from the train)

Jill

On Wednesday, Dylan wants to eat lunch with some guys from his geometry class who are starting a band – The Substitution Postulates. They've asked him to play bass.

"But you don't know how to play bass."

"So?"

We're at my locker, where I'm hunting for a scarf I know I had in here at one point this winter. Dylan's behind me, his hand on my hip. I lean back into him. "You'd seriously rather watch a bunch of guys chew with their mouths open than hang out with me? We could drive to your house."

"Nice try, MacSweeney." He kisses my neck and moves his hand from my hip to the less sexy shoulder zone.

I finally find the scarf under piles of books and papers, and shove everything back in to close the door, barely, and turn to Dylan. "I really need to talk, though. Can't you have band camp some other time?"

He takes his hand off me and pulls his hood up. "I love it when you belittle my interests."

"You don't play bass! And you won't believe what Mandy pulled yesterday. My mom—"

"Jill?" He takes my arms, looks into my eyes. "I'm going to lunch now. You can tell me about it after school."

"But—"

"Remember when we first started going out and you had these things called friends? And sometimes you'd do stuff with them instead of with me, and we both survived it?"

It does sound vaguely familiar.

He drops his arms and continues. "You're back with Laurel and Cinders. Eat with them."

I don't want to eat with Laurel and Cinders. I know they'll sympathize and agree that the situation with Mandy is total insanity, but in fact I don't want to sit around and bitch about Mandy. I only brought it up with Dylan because lately I'm not sure what else to talk to him about. It's either that or my dad. Who's the person I really want to talk to right now. So I might as well let Dylan go.

"Okay." I step back so that he's free of me. "Have fun."

I attempt to do homework in the library during lunch. My mind keeps drifting to my coffee plan with Ravi. Once we made the plan last night, I felt so great. So. Great. Then the second I walked in the door at home and saw Mandy and all the bags all over the floor, I was down again. It's just all so out of control. Life, I mean. The way it flies off in all these different directions without your permission.

Still, it's been so long since I hung out with someone new, the prospect of it is keeping my day going. New things. Instead of doing homework, I open a fresh document on my laptop and try to make a list of every new thing I've done since my dad died so that I can prove to my mom, to myself, that I'm not scared. That I have courage. That I'm not pushing away life and change and whatever else.

Only I can't think of anything. I open my calendar page and review the last ten and a half months for signs that I lived a life. Here's what I find: school stuff that automatically imports to all the students, notes on when to change my oil, and reminders about Mom's and Dylan's birthdays. That's it. And I don't think I got either of them a present. I see I didn't bother putting Mandy's arrival date or due date in; I do that now. I also put my coffee meet-up with Ravi in today's box.

I click and scroll into the future.

Graduation, an oil change, and a tyre rotation. No wonder I'm so excited about a stupid coffee plan.

And, I'm moving after graduation, or so I keep telling

people and myself. That's something. That's bold and new. I type *Move out* into a random day in July. See, I'm not scared of change, of life. Under *event details*, I put *See the world. Like Dad.* The words are fiction. I have no concrete plans for seeing the world and don't know how I'd come up with them without his advice, and when I picture myself moving out, it doesn't feel like a bold adventure. It feels like running away. Because all I can see is the part where I leave, not the part where I arrive.

But if I don't leave, and I haven't applied to any colleges, then I truly won't have anything to look forward to and may never arrive anywhere.

I rest my weary head on the fake-wood desk of my study carrel. It smells like hand sanitizer. The school's gone crazy with that stuff. My dad would say germs are good for you, germs make you stronger, germs help evolution along, and haven't you noticed it's the obsessive hand washers who are always getting sick?

I can hear his voice inside me. I know what he would say not only about germaphobia but also about Dylan being in a band ("Dylan's a good kid, but joining a band is just asking for a heroin addiction"), my mad self-defence skills against Ravi ("You should have kicked him in the head while he was down... What is he, anyway, Pakistani?"), Mom's haircut ("I never liked short hair on women, but your mom looks damn cute"), and the school librarian's ART CAN'T HURT YOU T-shirt ("I'm all for free speech, but has she ever seen a Steven Seagal movie?").

What I don't know, what I need to know, is what he would say about my future. Travel. Staying with Dylan or not. College. Mandy and this baby and it becoming part of us – part of him, in a way, too. How I'll do at being a sister. What his face would look like when he saw the ultrasound portrait.

The only voice I hear inside me about any of that is mine, asking:

What, Jill? What is it? What do you want?

I don't know.

I'm ten minutes early to the coffee shop, which I don't want Ravi to take as a sign I'm oh so eager to see him. It's just that Dylan forgot he had an old detention to serve after school, so he had to bail on me – again – and when I got home, Mandy was moping around in one of her new outfits and her straightened hair, stopping at every window to stare out as if waiting for someone to come save her.

"How was school?" she asked me. Well, she kind of asked the kitchen window while I made a cheese sandwich. She totally sounded like a mom.

"Fine." Great. Fantastic.

Then she limply half-closed the curtain with one hand and rubbed her stomach with the other. Everything she does is like that. Limp. Weak. Non-committal. "I think I miss it."

"Miss what?" I asked, more out of impatience at her being so lethargic than out of caring to know.

"School."

Mandy at school. Now, there's a picture. "Then you must have forgotten how much it sucks." I folded my bread over the cheese and took a bite.

"Maybe if I'd finished, I'd..." She stopped then and turned back to the window.

"You didn't finish?" New news to me. I figured my mother knows, and it's one more thing she didn't want to tell me in her ongoing and futile efforts to keep me from having a bad impression of Mandy.

"It wasn't my choice."

Right, I thought. Because you're so helpless. Yet you're smart enough to have my PhD-holding mother wrapped around your finger and buying you a new wardrobe.

I finished my sandwich up in my room while getting ready to meet Ravi. I hadn't intended to change clothes as if this were anything special, but I saw my purple sweater hanging over my chair and thought, *Why not?* I feel good in it.

He comes in, seven minutes early, which is nearly as bad as ten. He's wearing the suit pants, but instead of a shirt and tie with a jacket, he's got on a lilac V-neck sweater and a white puffer vest. Very preppy. A ripple of relief passes through me, and I realize I was worried he'd forget or blow it off. Or turn up with Annalee or be late or some other weird thing.

"Ravi," I call from my table near the window, where I'm sitting with my au lait.

"We match," he says when he gets to me, pointing to my sweater.

"Not really," I mumble. "Plum and lilac are—"

"In the same colour family."

I let it go. "What do you want?" I ask, looking towards the menu board.

"You invited me."

"No. I mean, what do you want to *drink*? I'll buy."

"I got it," he says.

"No, I'm buying."

"I don't let girls pay for my drinks."

"Well, then, you're stupid. I said I'd get it." Now I'm standing, pulling his arm downwards so he'll sit. Maybe I pull it a little too hard. He falls into his chair, rubbing his arm. "To thank you for your time," I add.

He looks at me like I'm of unsound mind. "You're...

welcome. Americano. Please."

I really need to start acting normal around him.

When I get back to the table with his drink, I'm all business. I figure I'll start with Mandy, and then maybe we can talk about other stuff once I've relaxed a little and have stopped calling him stupid and hurting his arm. "Okay. So. I guess I'll start at the beginning. And feel free to say—"

"Wait."

"What?"

There's the searching look again, like I know something, when in fact I know nothing.

"Don't make me ask because it's getting embarrassing."

The yearbook! "Tennis club. I read it."

"And?"

And I've been trying to picture you, trying to remember Schiff's classroom and where you were, and who I was, and if I was nice, and courageous, and seemed like I had stuff to look forward to. "My memory's really bad."

"Oh." Ravi nods towards his coffee cup. "But isn't it kind of funny? Small world and everything? That two years later you'd be elbowing me in the face, which would lead us right here to this very coffee shop."

"It is." God. My mom is so right. I'm scared of everything. Ravi's offering me a wide-open door into a real conversation, so of course I change the subject before that can happen.

"Anyway, feel free to say no and that this isn't your thing. I'm only asking, and it's kind of a half-baked idea anyway, and if you don't want to get into it, that's okay, and I won't hold it against you."

"So...this isn't about what I wrote in the yearbook? Or anything like that?"

"Oh. No."

"All right." He's shifted gears again, the way he does, back into his work persona.

"You may want to take notes."

From his vest pocket he takes his little flip notebook with a spiral-bound top, the one I knew he'd have on him, and a pen, which he clicks with confidence. "Go."

I tell him everything I know about Mandy: why she's living with us, where she came from, how my mom found her or she found my mom, and why I'm worried. "It's not that my mom is stupid or naive or anything. And she really does want a baby. She and my dad used to talk about it... being foster parents or something, since they had room in the house and were still relatively young and healthy and could afford it. They're the kind of people who think it's your job to give back to society if you can. You wouldn't think my dad was like that, to look at him – or *talk* to him – but underneath his Tough Guy act, he was a real bleeding heart and—"

"Wait," Ravi interrupts, holding his pen in the air.

"Sorry. I'm getting off track."

"No, just – your dad. Was?"

I realize I've failed to mention that my father, a prominent figure in this tale, is dead.

The first thing I think is *I haven't said it aloud in so long.* But as I'm staring at Ravi, who is ever the professional, pen poised to write down whatever I say next, it strikes me: I've never said it, period. I've never had to. Everyone simply knows. When I told Dylan, I said, "He was in an accident. A bad one." And Dylan said, "Did he...I mean, he's alive, right?" And I said, "No." Then everyone else kind of found out.

Here's the opportunity again. For a real conversation, a real connection, something new and something old. Ravi knew me before, which makes it sort of safe and familiar. And also he doesn't know me, which makes it safer still. If this goes wrong, if it hurts too much, if I'm the way I am and wind up driving him away, no big loss.

Also, it's practice. Someday I'll be somewhere and meet strangers who will become friends, and if I want them to know this thing about me, this very important thing, I'll have to say it.

As soon as I begin to shape the words in my mind, I feel myself coming apart. All I can do is keep my eyes on his, and my lips sealed.

He turns his notepad to a fresh page. Slides it across the small table to me. Then the pen. "I know you don't remember me," he says softly. "But, pathetic as this may sound, in my mind we've always been friends. I mean, we signed each other's yearbooks. Friends do that. So pretend we are."

I pick up the pen. I could use a friend, even a pretend one.

I close my eyes and draw in a deep breath.

In all the conversations I've had or avoided having with Dylan and my friends, with my mom, in the dark corners of my own injured heart, I've never been this scared.

My dad died, I write. *Almost a year ago. Car accident.* My hand is shaking; my eyes sting and fill. I add *Not his fault* before pushing the notebook and pen back across the table, wiping a hand across my cheeks.

As he reads, my impulse is to reach out, grab the notebook, run outside, dump it in the trash, bury it in the snow, throw it under the wheels of a passing car – something, something, so I can go back fifteen seconds when this part of me was still shut away and private. Then I look at Ravi's face again, and the normally white white whites of his eyes are pink. This causes major disruption to my ability to control the flow of my own tears. I see myself when I look at him right now: he's reflecting my sadness, my broken heart, back to me.

He takes the pen, writes, and slides it over. You'd think it's something epic from the way it levels my heart. It isn't.

I'm really sorry, Jill.

Four little words.

I put one hand over the notebook to cover it. I put the other over my mouth, saying through my fingers, "Be right back."

In the bathroom I shake with tears. I'm still holding the notebook somehow. It's not only Ravi's words. It was his eyes, how in them I could see him seriously feeling my pain, close to crying, himself. That touches me like nothing else has and I don't know why. It's not like Dylan didn't cry. But he *knew* my dad; he'd lost something, too. It's been like that with everyone – my mom, my friends, friends of our family. Ravi is sad for no other reason than he knows I'm sad. Sad for me. For *me*. Me, who's the kind of person who can't remember an obviously nice guy who thought of me as a friend. It's completely sincere, what he wrote. And it's not lame. At all.

I tear off the sheet we've written on and put in my pocket. I scrub my face with rough paper towels until it's the same shade of red all over, not just around my eyes.

When I make it back out and sit down, Ravi asks, "Are you okay?"

"Yeah." I hand him the notebook, our page gone.

Say "thank you", Jill. Say "thank you".

"Thank you."

And he's perfect. He doesn't say *Are you sure you're okay?* or *I really am sorry, I meant it* or *Do you want me to tell Annalee you need the night off?* or anything. He hears the tone of my voice and makes himself all business again, pen to paper, ready for action. "What do you need?"

I need a friend. A new friend, who hasn't already been damaged by me beyond repair. One little blow to the face; we can get past that.

"I want to find out everything I can about Mandy."

Mandy

I'm waiting for my toast. The bread Robin likes me to eat is dry and hard; if I don't butter it when it's hot, right out of the toaster, it turns into cardboard. So I have to stand here with my plate and the butter and knife ready. Honestly, I don't think white bread is going to hurt the baby, but I do it for Robin. We have another doctor's appointment tomorrow – two weeks since the last one – and I want it to be better this time, I want to do good and not get any strange looks from Dr. Yee.

I feel like I'd do almost anything for Robin.

But my feelings are always confused. Sometimes I think maybe I'm going to give up my baby and maybe I'm not. Other times I'm very sure. One thing I know is I needed the watch in my pocket and the space to think without my mother's voice in my ear and her face in my face, telling me over and over the same things about how no man will ever want me if I have a baby or if he knows I gave birth, even if I give up the baby. After all, look at her, she said. It took her for ever to find someone like Kent because no man like him in his right mind wants to take care of another man's child. There are plenty of other women out there, women without kids.

"That's why I have to do the things I do, Amanda. That's why I have to do all the things I do, and go along with married men and some of the crazies we've had, because this rent is not going to pay itself. I make myself special. I keep myself up. I'm different from these women who only want to go to have careers and take care of themselves and be with men who will be their 'partners'."

She didn't need a "partner", she said. "If I wanted a partner, I'd be in a three-legged race." She needed a man. And so did I, and how was I going to get one dragging around a baby? Especially an Indian baby.

I said, "But you work. It's not like you don't have to work."

She said, "Thanks for the newsflash."

She said I don't know anything about how the real world works. She said what she makes at her job is not even a third, not even a fourth, of what she needs to keep up her lifestyle, and if I thought we could take care of ourselves without Kent, I was welcome to try it. Did I want to be on welfare? Did I want to live in public housing? Did I want to be like all the other cows shopping at the dented-can grocery store and getting my STDs treated at the free clinic?

She said, "Because that's the track your train is on, Mandy. Without Kent, that's the picture."

At first the e-mail I sent to Robin on New Year's was mostly so I could get away from my mother's talking long enough to breathe. I didn't really think that much about the giving-away-the-baby part, how doing that would take away the evidence of the only true and beautiful thing that's ever happened to me. If that's what this baby turns out to be. Or it could also be evidence of something else, someone else, and I don't want to think about that.

Now that I'm here, it's different. I'm changing. It's just like when I felt my body changing in the first few months of pregnancy, only this time what's changing is something even deeper in me. Robin is special. This house is special. I'm more sure all the time. Even Jill, who hates me, has something she doesn't even know she has, and I can tell she'll make a mark in the world. And that's probably because of Robin, who could raise another daughter who'd make a mark. Who would matter. Even if the only person she mattered to was Robin, it would be more than I had. The funny thing is, being here also makes me think maybe, maybe I could do it. Maybe I could be a mother.

The doorbell rings at the same time my toast pops up. I ignore the bell and butter my bread and put a layer of the no-sugar jam I'm getting used to, and sit at the kitchen table to eat it.

"Hello?" a voice calls. A male voice from inside the house, and at first I freeze, scared, until the voice repeats "Hello?" and I recognize it as Dylan's.

"In the kitchen."

"Oh, hey, Mandy." He stands in the doorway, his hands in his coat pockets. "I let myself in. They keep a key in the mailbox... You probably know that. Hope you don't mind. I didn't think anyone was home."

"It's okay. Jill's at work."

"Yeah, I know. I left my history book over here the other day, and this is the night I promised myself I'd catch up on all my homework. So...I'll just –" he takes one hand out of his pocket, pointing up – "run upstairs and get it?"

"Okay." He's not wearing any eyeliner today, but a few of his fingernails are painted dark purple.

He pauses at the bottom of the stairs. I can see half his body through the doorway. "Need anything while I'm up there? I'm sure stairs are no fun for you at this point."

"No, thank you."

"Hey," he says, leaning backwards while gripping the rail. "You look nice. I like your hair that way."

"Thank you." I smile. He really is so much nicer than Jill. How they get along, I don't know. "Would you like some toast?"

"Um, sure."

While he's upstairs I put two slices in for him and check my reflection on the toaster. Him saying that he likes my hair, that I look nice, those are the first compliments I've had from a man – or someone close to being a man – in months. And aside from Christopher, boys my age don't usually notice me. Not in a good way. They might say something about my body or what they'd like to do with it, but that's more of an insult than a compliment, if you think about it.

"Got it," Dylan says, coming down the stairs with the book. He stays just on the other side of the kitchen doorway, as if he's afraid to step all the way in.

"Sit down. Your toast is almost done."

He comes in and takes off his coat, putting it on the back of one of the chairs before sitting. I get down a plate for him and, when the toast is up, put butter and jam the way I like and pour him a glass of milk.

"Thanks, Mom," he says, grinning, as I put it all on the table.

Mom. "I like doing things for people."

"Sorry, I didn't mean to make it sound like...here, you sit

down, too." He uses his foot to pull one of the chairs out. "How's everything going? In there?" He points to my belly. "It's the coolest thing. A whole new human being right inside you. You must feel like God or something."

He's sweet. Sincere. Like the last time it was only the two of us talking, I feel comfortable. The way it would feel with a brother, I guess, or a friend. "No," I say. "I don't think about it like that. It's normal. Women get pregnant every day."

"Good point." He's finished his first piece of toast in three bites.

"Do you want any more?"

"No, thanks. This is perfect."

I get up to tie the wire twist tie around the bag so the bread doesn't dry out more than it already is. "Everything tastes better when someone else fixes it for you."

"True." He brushes crumbs off his shirt. "So...is Jill being nicer to you?"

The bread, the milk, the jam all go back into the refrigerator. I have to answer carefully. "Robin says she's that way because she misses Mac."

Dylan lets out a big breath, tilts his neck to stare at the ceiling. "God, yeah. So much." He tilts his head forwards again. "Don't take it personally. She treated me like crap for a while there, too."

"She did? But you're her boyfriend."

"Right?" Now he's relaxed in his chair, curling his hands up and putting them in his jeans pockets. "I don't know how it feels to lose a parent. I try not to judge. I try to just be there for her, but she doesn't always want me there, and I don't know when she does and when she doesn't, so it gets...whatever. Anyway."

"I don't know what it's like to lose a parent, either. Unless you count never having a father in the first place."

He's silent, and I feel him watching me while I sponge down the counter where the jam knife left a sticky spot.

"My mother got pregnant with me from a married man," I say, "and she told him, and he gave her a lot of money to go away and never come back."

The money ran out. One time she went back to him to ask for more. She took me with her. I was four or five, and I remember it, or I think I do. Maybe I only remember it from her telling me about it so many times. We walked from the bus stop to his house, and my mother told me, "It's a mansion, Amanda. You'll see. And when he gets a look at you, it'll be yours, too. Ours."

Dylan's voice calls me back. "Wow."

Only at this mansion, which was really just a big house, the man who answered the door had never heard of the man who was my father.

"From the minute I...developed," I tell Dylan, embarrassed, "she always told me how not to have a baby and how it's the worst thing that can happen and how I had my whole life in front of me and not to ruin it with a baby. The way she ruined hers." Maybe my father had moved two owners ago, the man at the door said. "With me."

Dylan makes a noise, air rushing from lungs. "Your *mom* said that to you? Like, to your face?"

I rinse the sponge, squeeze out the excess water, set it by the tap to dry. When I turn around to answer him, "Yes, she said that to my face and not just once," he's leaning on his elbows resting his face on his fists, watching me. Looking like he can't believe anyone on the face of the earth would say a thing like that to her own daughter. No one has ever looked at me like that before, not like pity but like they're truly sorry you've been hurt.

Now I know what people mean when they say they have a lump in their throat.

"I should probably lie down now. Robin wants me to be sure to get all the rest I need."

He gets up. "Okay. Thanks for the toast."

"Don't forget your history book."

"Right," he says, picking it up. He puts on his coat, and I walk him to the door. He pulls a green ski cap on and looks at me, and there's a feeling between us. Not like the kind of feeling I had with Christopher. Not romantic. Not sparks. It's more like the kind of feeling I have with Robin.

He holds his arms open. "Hug?"

I stare. What if Jill walked in right now? Or Robin? Would I get kicked out? He doesn't wait for me to say yes. He leans in and puts his arms around me. It's not long and, because of my stomach, it's not that close. When he's done, I want to say something, but I'm not sure what.

"She gave up a lot" is what comes out. "My mother."

"Still," he says, with a shake of his head. "I mean, she *got* a lot, too."

I can't think what my mother got that would make what she gave up worth it. When I look at him, wondering, I realize he means me.

Jill

Tenderness. When Dad and I used to tell each other to try a little tenderness, we meant calm down, be soft, stop having to be right, give a person the benefit of the doubt for a change. We never talked about what it's like to be on the receiving end of it. How it leaves you the other kind of tender – raw, bruised. In certain cases it might leave you bewildered and stumbling, a person who's been crouched in the dark, afraid someone will turn on the lights and find you, and then it happens and in some ways it's not so scary after all and in others, well, holy shit.

Last night, after seeing Ravi, I got through my shift by shutting down, because I couldn't keep feeling what I was feeling and also do my job. Thank God that Mandy and my mom were in their rooms when I got home. I slugged some NyQuil and slept in my clothes. It's hard to get up and go to school and be me, be Jill MacSweeney, in the same way I was yesterday. I feel exposed, like Ravi has found some unlocked door inside me and now anything can get in.

So I compensate. And maybe I go overboard. In need of extra armour, I do the major smoky eye. The black jeans, the black boots, the black hoodie – hood up. Leather cuff. All my rings. Hair straightened and waxed to a perfect edge. When Dylan comes by to pick me up, I get in his car and hold my backpack on my lap.

"Wow," he says. "That look is rock."

Indestructible.

"Yep."

"Everything okay?"

"Yep."

"You sure about that?"

I check myself in the side mirror. Sunglasses: on. "I'm fine. Let's go."

On the way he tells me some story about Mandy and her terrible mother and toast. I know I should be paying attention. Only my brain is occupied getting everything that Ravi loosed back on lockdown.

"...and what's she going to do after the baby is born?" Dylan is asking as we turn into the school lot.

Oh, that. Mandy. Whatever, who cares. "I don't know."

"Isn't the point of an open adoption that she'll have contact with the kid and stuff?"

"I guess."

He pulls into his spot. "So you've lost interest."

"No," I say, impatient.

"Two days ago you were planning to call a PI on her ass, Jill." He turns off the ignition; we get out. "Don't tell me you actually listened to me and talked to your mom about it."

"Ha." I tighten the strings around my hood, adjust my sunglasses, and survey the parking lot. I feel like I could get in a fight right now. I feel like I could slash a tyre. "I'm tired of thinking about it is all."

Dylan doesn't notice that I'm bent on destruction and in no way interested in Mandy at the moment. "After talking to her yesterday...man. I feel sorry for her," he says. "Seriously. She may be giving up the baby so it has a mother, but she kind of needs one herself."

I kick a chunk of ice off the wheel well of Dylan's car with my boot, and then kick it again so it skids across the lot and breaks up. "One what?"

"A mother. She's the one who needs a mother."

I call in sick to work, from school. I never do that unless I'm actually sick, which is rare. Annalee asks me if I want tomorrow night off, also, because Polly is looking for more hours this week to pay for a car repair. Fine. When Dylan drops me off at home, I lie to him, too, and tell him I'm sick and getting straight into bed and he should leave and not kiss me goodbye or anything because he might catch it. It, my phantom illness.

Mom has left me a note on the kitchen counter – she and Mandy are at the doctor's.

Dad's CD collection is organized strictly by the first name of the artist. Nothing fancy. It's easy to find Otis, right between Neil Young and Paul McCartney. I haven't fired up the components since way before Dad died. He refused to get on board with music downloads and digital storage; rebuilding his collection from vinyl to CD was as far as he was willing to go. He'd never rip anything to his computer or listen on an MP3 player – albums were meant to be heard whole, he said, not chopped up and portioned out like hors d'oeuvres. Albums are meals. For him it was all about the component system and the giant speakers on either side of the fireplace. Between which I now lay, on the floor, the remote in my hand.

The horns start in, then the little strum of an electric guitar.

That's all it takes; I'm gone. Otis and a box of tissues and me.

Weary me.

Unsurprisingly, considering I've got the volume as high as it will go without distorting, I don't hear Mom and Mandy get home. They find me listening to "Try a Little Tenderness" for the twenty-first time, surrounded by wadded-up tissues, still in my sunglasses and with my hood up. I don't love my mom seeing me like this, but it's definitely the last thing I want to be doing in front of Mandy. I scramble up, turn off the CD player, amass my snot rags, and toss them into the fireplace.

Any normal person would look away and make up something about needing to excuse herself. Mandy, being Mandy, stands like a deer in the headlights and takes it all in as if she's watching one of her shows.

I want to tell her to go away and leave us alone. But you can't listen to Otis for an hour straight and then yell at someone. And you definitely can't do it when your mother is starting to cry, too, and coming at you with open arms.

Ravi calls after dinner. I'm in my room, trying my best to concentrate on homework. Though I've been ignoring texts from Dylan all night, I lunge for the phone when I see it's Ravi. *Hey, hi, where are you, when can we talk again?* And it scares me, because then I think, *No. You're going to lash out. Maybe not now, but you will, because you always do, and then he'll hate you.*

Bravely, I answer. "This is Jill."

"Jill. Ravi."

We're both doing this big act: professionals, co-workers. "Hello."

"How are you feeling?" And I fear he means *feelings* feeling, about which I'm far too exhausted to talk. Then he clarifies: "I was by the store a little while ago, and Annalee said you were sick."

"Oh yeah. Not too bad. Kind of stuffed up." From hours of weeping.

"Sounds like it. So you probably don't want to meet up to go over some of the results of my research into your situation." He talks as if our phones might be tapped, in his Grown-Up Ravi voice, the one that makes him sound like a distant, uninterested uncle. It's comforting, in a way, to know that just because we had a moment yesterday doesn't mean every conversation has to turn into an emotional root canal. Maybe I won't ruin this after all.

"You already have results?" I ask.

"Well, nothing specific. We could talk about it right now, or if you have video chat…"

He's pretending he only wants to go over "results" of my "situation"; I'm pretending to believe him. When what it feels like is that we want to see each other.

But I hate video chat. It's so hard to get the laptop screen at a flattering angle, and the colours are weird; I don't need Ravi seeing me all beige and busted.

"No, we can meet. This may shock you, but...I'm not actually sick."

"Ah."

"Don't rat on me to Annalee."

It's awkward saying her name, and Ravi replies, "I wouldn't," a bit too quickly.

We make plans to meet for coffee, where we met before, and I put myself back together so that when I go downstairs to tell Mom I'm headed out, she can see that I'm fine, absolutely fine, and no one need worry about me, despite the fact that only hours earlier I was in a sorrowful heap on the floor.

Mom is unconvinced. "Where are you going?" She and Mandy are at the kitchen table, the laptop open and a notepad nearby.

"Meeting a friend for coffee."

"Why don't you stay in? It's been a long day already, and the snow is really coming down." Understatement, re the long day. "You can help us decide which birthing class to take."

"Fun. But no."

"You could do the class with us," Mandy says. She's smiling, wearing one of her new outfits, happy as a clam. "In case something happens and Robin can't be there."

"I'll *be* there," Mom insists. "Of course, that doesn't mean you can't be there, too, Jill."

Even in a world in which I accept that Mandy's baby will be in our lives for ever, I cannot conjure up an image of me in a hospital room with her and my mother, shouting out breathing instructions and fetching ice chips or doing whatever else needs doing in a baby-having scenario. I try to be polite. "Thank you so much. Don't plan on it."

Yet I have a twinge of jealousy, seeing them there, cosy, looking at birthing websites like they're planning a wedding or something. *It's your choice, Jill.* As Mom said, she's been trying to include me from the beginning, but I wouldn't have it. Instead, I'm about to go discuss Mandy as if she's a criminal. Except, okay, that's not *really* why I'm going out on a cold night to see Ravi.

Mom gets up to give me a kiss. "All right. Don't be late. One hour, then home to bed, okay? Since you're not working, you might as well get some sleep."

I worried that when I saw him, I'd get nervous, freak out about yesterday, start crying again, or want to turn around and run. But when I walk in and spot him already at a table, what I feel is relief. Nearly joy. I want to blurt out, *Thank you for being my friend,* which would be so awkward and crazy and not me. When I get to the table, there's a weird second where he stands and it's like, should we hug? Then we don't, and sit down. Ravi is suitless again, in jeans and a sweater with a moth hole near the collar, so real, normal, nineteen. Tonight he's even wearing his glasses, like he has on in his senior yearbook portrait.

I watch him as he opens what he calls the "Mandy dossier" and flips through it with elegant hands. *Let's not talk about Mandy,* I want to say. *Let's talk about tennis club and Otis Redding and movies and books. Let's walk in the snow, sink up to our knees in it, get cold and come back for hot coffee.* That's the kind of stuff you do with new friends you want to know better. I'm remembering how this works. How life doesn't have to be only anxiety about what's gone wrong or could go wrong, and complaints about the world around you. How a person you're excited about can remind you there's stuff going on beyond routine oil changes and homework. Stuff that matters. Stuff to look forward to.

So I say, "Whatcha got?"

"Based on what you've told me, I've identified a number of red flags."

Red flags. The opposite of stuff to look forward to. "Like what kinds of red flags?"

"This is a start based on generalities. Every red flag could be explained away, potentially. We're looking at a set of circumstances. Simply...laying out information."

"Right."

Ravi sips his Americano and glances up from the dossier to catch my eye. "Like I said, all of this could be nothing."

"Okay. Just tell me."

"You said that Mandy lied about her due date?" he asks.

"The baby is due later than she originally told my mom. But my mom thinks that's just because Mandy had a bad doctor."

Ravi taps his pen against the folder. "You also said it all happened fast, back at the beginning of the year. Like, instant match."

"Yeah. Mandy saw my mom's post on some weirdly unofficial adoption board and e-mailed her, basically saying, 'Hey, you're perfect, you can have my baby.' That's weird, right? For such a big decision?"

He makes an "mmm" noise and a non-committal shoulder move.

"You don't think that's totally nuts?"

Ravi runs his hand over his notes. His fingers are long and graceful, gentle-looking, trustworthy. "Haven't you ever had a gut feeling about something? Like your mom did about Mandy? Something you categorically *know*, whether or not it makes rational sense?"

No, I think. Normally my mother is the one who does things by impulse and gut feeling. Normally I'm in total control of my actions and emotions. "Not really," I say, even though I might be starting to understand it.

His cell phone beeps, and I nearly jump out of my skin. He checks it, oblivious to my reaction, and texts something before putting it back in his jacket pocket. "So let's say, for the sake of argument, that both Mandy and your mom experienced this gut knowledge, this sense of destiny about the baby."

"Okay. But what about money? When my dad died, my mom got a pretty big insurance settlement. Could Mandy have found out about that?"

"Possibly. Does she ask for money?"

"I don't know. I have this feeling there's a lot my mom doesn't tell me. And my mom is so..." I almost say "dumb", but my mom is not dumb. That's not it. *Trusting* is what she is. And somehow I've come to see trusting as dumb. "I mean, I'm sure all the doctor's visits cost a fortune, and my mom is paying out of pocket for Mandy's baby stuff. And the other day she gave her AmEx to Mandy and left her alone at the mall for like three hours. We had a big fight about it."

I don't even know if I was mad about that. I think I kind of wished it could have been me shopping with my mom.

Ravi takes notes. "And what happened? Did Mandy use it for something she wasn't supposed to?"

"No. I mean, maybe? She got a bunch of clothes, but my mom made it sound like it was all her idea, not Mandy's. Like she had to practically force Mandy to get even that much. But who knows? I doubt my mom even checked her statement afterwards."

"See if you can find that out." He looks at his watch and closes the dossier. "Of course, what's most problematic is what you told me about Mandy not wanting any lawyers or social workers or agencies involved. That right there is your biggest flag."

Is he getting ready to leave already? "And biggest potential disaster."

"No legal recourse for your mom if Mandy decides to take off."

"I know. That's my nightmare."

His phone beeps again. Somehow I know it's Annalee. He ignores it this time. "Do you think I could meet Mandy? Talk to her? Subtly, I mean. Without her knowing I'm trying to find stuff out."

"Oh. You could, I don't know, come over to my house for dinner or something?" In the far, far reaches of my memory, I must have, at some point, known how to invite friends over.

He gets up, gathers his stuff. "Better if I can meet her in a more neutral environment, kind of incidentally."

"Yeah." I point to his cup. "You didn't finish."

Ravi looks down at me with that half-smile. He nudges my shoulder with his elbow. "Next time we'll stay longer."

Something inside me opens further. Another door. A window. I can almost hear the creaking hinges. I blink back tears. "Without your suit you could almost be a normal nineteen-year-old."

"I am a normal nineteen-year-old."

"So you claim."

He laughs, a lilting laugh. "See you later, Jill."

"Bye, Ravi."

I watch him head outside; snow floats and swirls in the lamplight as he dashes to his car. For long minutes after he pulls away I stare at the spot where his car was parked, probing and poking at this feeling, at once familiar and foreign. Expectant, hopeful. After I've successfully slashed and burned a huge swathe of acreage around me, just in case anyone tried to come near, Ravi has forged across, and I let him. *How did he do it?* I wonder. *How did I?*

Mandy

When Jill gets home after school on Friday, the first thing I hear after the door closing is her calling my name. Usually I'm right there in the living room. Today I feel sad, the kind of sad that makes me want to be alone. To hide. Until now I haven't spent much time in this room, my room, other than when I'm sleeping. It's not that I don't like it. It's classic and comfortable, like the rest of the house. The walls are painted light orange – the colour of summer sunsets on postcards – with cream trim and the same dark hardwood floor Robin has through most of the house. There's a rug made of different blocks of colour and everything on the bed is bright white. I've never slept on a bed this comfortable. The first night, I tried to get under this thick cover, and Robin said no, it's a feather bed; you sleep on top of it, not under it.

Cheerful. The whole room is cheerful.

What I feel is that I don't belong in it. When I'm here, it feels too much like home, and I don't mean like home felt back in Council Bluffs, at Kent's. I mean *home* home. An idea of home you carry with you your whole life, only you don't know it until you're there. I know I can't stay, and that's why I don't like to spend too much time in here, feeling home the way I'm learning it's supposed to be felt. Every day I feel it more, and every day the sadness of knowing that it will end gets worse and today it's the worst so far.

"Mandy?" Jill is outside my door now. Usually when she says my name, it's with a combination of question mark and exclamation point and is followed by a complaint or request. Like: "Mandy! Can you not use my hairdryer without asking?" "Mandy! Did you put the peanut butter back in the fridge? It goes in the fridge, you know. It's not the kind filled with all that sugar and trans-fat crap."

She really is attached to her peanut butter.

This time she's saying my name in an almost friendly way, with a gentle kind of question mark.

It takes me a while to get to the door; by the time I open it, I half expect her to have given up. She's still there, as close to smiling at me as I've ever seen. "Hi."

"Hey. Are you doing anything right now?"

Maybe she's going to ask me for a favour or tell me I did something wrong and I need to fix it. "Kind of."

She looks past me into the room. "Really? What?"

"I'm supposed to rest."

There's a long pause. Jill puts her hands into her sweatshirt pockets and nods slowly, then takes a deep breath. "I'm off work tonight. It's Friday. Mom is at a meeting and Dylan has stupid band practice, which is a joke, since he doesn't play an instrument or sing, but anyway I figured you must be going slightly crazy around here and might want to get out for some coffee."

It feels like a trick. Why would she suddenly want to spend time with me? "I'm not supposed to drink coffee."

"You can get decaf. Or herb tea."

"I don't like tea."

"Mandy, okay." She takes her hands from her pockets to hold them up and make air quotes. " 'Going out to coffee' doesn't necessarily literally involve drinking a hot caffeinated beverage. It's just something to do. You can have water. You can have a soda. You can get a brownie or a bagel or a muffin or a sandwich or a pretzel or a piece of cake. Whatever."

Maybe Robin talked to her and told her she has to be nice to me. "You don't have to," I say. "I know you don't really want me here. It's not for that much longer. You don't have to be nice."

A certain expression lands on her face. One I've never

seen before other than maybe a little bit yesterday when we got home and found her crying, but she had on sunglasses then so it was hard to tell. The expression is not hard, not trying to show that she doesn't care or is separate from me and Robin. I think what I'm seeing is the real Jill.

"My mom doesn't even know about this," she says, and I believe her. Then her expression changes back to the usual. "It's totally my idea. I mean, you've been here almost three weeks, and you and me barely know each other. Come on."

I wouldn't mind going out to be distracted from sadness awhile. "Can I go dressed like this? Is it nice enough?" I have on my new black maternity leggings and a sort of half dress, half sweater.

"This is Denver," Jill says. "You can wear your good Wranglers to the opera."

"I didn't do my hair or make-up."

"You look gorgeous."

I touch my hair. My mother would never leave the house like this. "Are you just saying that?"

Jill puts one hand on each of my shoulders and stares me in the face. It's a little scary. "You're beautiful, okay? I promise."

* * *

251

At the coffee shop, Jill orders herself a latte and buys us a big piece of chocolate cake to share. "I won't tell my mom about all the sugar," she says. "Anyway, it's Friday. Fridays don't count."

We sit at a table near the big front window.

"I like people-watching," Jill says.

"Me too."

A light snow is falling, but it isn't too cold. You can begin to imagine that spring will be here soon. The snow is pretty, the way the small flakes float down and seem to disappear moments before they would land. There's music playing, a kind of music I've never heard that's not too jazzy or too rock. It's quiet; it feels good.

"This is a nice neighbourhood," I say. We're in a part of town I haven't seen before. I guess most of Denver is made of parts I haven't seen before. I wonder what else is in this city that I could discover. Could I fit in here, be a part of it? If I came to a place like this without Jill, I wonder if I could feel like I belonged.

"It's all right. A lot of overeducated white people and hipster coffee shops."

"Like where you live."

"No, where we live it's more – okay, yeah. There are more wire-rim glasses per square mile here, though."

She seems nervous. I worry she regrets bringing me out.

What are we supposed to talk about?

"Did it hurt?" I ask. "The eyebrow ring?"

"A little. That stuff always hurts."

"Why do you do it, then?"

"Because..." She touches the ring with her index finger, resting her hand against the side of her face, and turns her head to look out the window. The way the street light hits her face you can see how pretty she is, and how pretty she'd be without the hair dye and dark eyeliner. She turns back. "You know what? I'm going to get a tattoo. That will *really* hurt."

"My mother always said only whores and soldiers have tattoos."

Jill jerks her head back and coughs out a laugh. "Thanks."

"I'm only saying what my mother says. I don't think that."

"What is she, like, eighty?"

"No. She has strong opinions."

Jill takes a big forkful of cake. "With opinions like that, I don't think I'd listen to anything that comes out of your mother's mouth."

The baby kicks, and kicks hard, like she's angry. So hard I bend over and touch my stomach and gasp. Jill swallows her cake and asks, "Are you okay?"

"I think so. I—" The baby kicks again.

Jill gets up and comes around to my side of the table. "Seriously, are you sure? Because if you're anywhere near going into labour, let's call my mom right now."

"No, she's only kicking. Here, feel." I take Jill's hand. We've never touched before. Her skin is cool and dry and rough around the cuticles. I put her hand on my stomach, firm.

"Oh my God," Jill says. Her face has that real expression again. "Is that her foot?"

"Maybe. Or her elbow or knee."

Jill laughs and looks up at me, eyes sparkly. "She's, like, doing a whole routine in there."

"Yeah. This is her active time of day. Usually you're at work."

"That's...wow." She stays crouched down by me, feeling everything that's happening inside me.

The cafe door opens, letting in a gust of cold air. A man walks in, tall and young, in a ski parka and purple knit cap. His skin is almost the colour of Christopher's but a tiny bit more brown. I notice him before Jill does, because she's still putting her hands all over my belly. He looks at us, at Jill, really, and his lips spread into a smile and his eyes go soft.

"Jill," he says.

"Hey," Jill stands up. "I know you."

"Yes, you do."

"This is Mandy," she says, as if I'm somebody. "Mandy, this is...oh, crap, I'm totally blanking on your name."

"Clark," he says to Jill. "It's been a while." He reaches his long arm down and across the table, offering his hand to me. "Mandy, nice to meet you."

"Your hand is cold," I say, shaking it.

"Well, it is snowing."

We all laugh.

"Go get coffee and sit with us." Jill pulls an extra chair to our table, and Clark goes to the counter to order. He's the opposite of Dylan – tall, clean-cut, grown-up.

"Did you date him?" I ask Jill.

"What?" She glances over her shoulder at Clark and lowers her voice. "What makes you say that?"

"The way he looked at you when he came in."

She prods the cake with her fork, eyes down. "I think I would have remembered his name if we went out, Mandy. I'm not that much of a tart, even if I do want a tattoo."

Clark takes long steps to us and sits down. He pulls off his cap and runs his hand through his neat black hair. Naturally black, not dyed, like Dylan's. "So," he says to me, "having a baby, huh?"

"Astute observation there, Clark," Jill says, emphasizing his name in a funny way.

"Yes. In almost exactly four weeks. Jill's mom is adopting it."

Jill looks at me. "Her. Not it. Do you always go around telling strangers about the plan?"

"Her. It's not a secret," I say to Clark. "I'm not embarrassed. I know I'm making the right choice."

"Really?" Jill asks. "You never have a moment of doubt?"

Yes, I think. Of course. The closer it gets, the more moments of doubt I have. Those are only emotions, though, not reality. My mother made decisions based on emotions. Fear, usually. Of being alone or not having a good place to live or that this will be the last man who wants her. She didn't think things through and look down the road and see how what she felt was right today might not be what she thought it was, all the things that could go wrong.

"No," I say. "Have you met Jill's mother?" I ask Clark.

He shakes his head. "Not yet."

"When you do, you'll understand how I know what I know."

Clark looks at Jill. "That's a nice compliment for your mom."

"Yeah," Jill says. "It is."

We all talk and people-watch. What I notice is how different Jill is with Clark here. She's not so scary. She doesn't seem so much like she's mad at someone. Like she hates life. And Clark asks me questions about me and the baby and my plans for the future. Making real conversation. I answer without giving too much information. I enjoy this, the same way I enjoyed talking to Dylan. Except Clark is a little different. And anyone can see he likes Jill. He keeps looking at her for reactions, and asking her if she wants more coffee, and sitting closer to her than he needs to. It makes me think of how Christopher looked at me, and how maybe someday, when I'm not so pregnant and I figure out who I'll be, someone could look at me like that again.

It's nice to end the day with a sense of possibility instead of sadness.

Jill

Saturday morning breakfast at our favourite diner is the first chance in days that Dylan and I have had to really talk, and you'd think I'd have a lot to say, that I'd want to tell him about last night. Okay, not the part about how I felt when Ravi walked in the door at almost the same second I felt the baby kick, but the rest of it. How I actually had a good time with Mandy.

Dylan is barely alive, slumped in the booth and holding his cup of coffee level with his nose, lowering it every few seconds to take a sip.

"You look like crap," I say, finally.

"Thanks."

"How late did you stay up?"

"Um…all night?"

"I guess band practice takes a long time when none of you know how to play or sing or write." I should have known that starting the conversation this way would not set a good tone. The waitress sets down my Greek scramble. "I didn't know you were in a band," she says to Dylan. She's our regular, Babette, who isn't all that young but pierced and tatted head to toe, and a local music scenester. "What are you guys called? Where do you play? Are you in it, too?" she asks me.

"No," I answer, laughing a little. More at the ridiculousness of the idea that she would have heard of them than the idea of me being in the band.

"The Potato Rebellion," Dylan says.

Babette laughs. "Love it."

"What happened to The Postulates or whatever?"

"New direction."

"Right," I say, spreading jam on my sourdough toast. After Babette moves on, I spear some home fries with my fork and wave them in front of Dylan's face. "Rebel against this, sucker."

He doesn't react. "And what did *you* do last night?"

"I took Mandy out for coffee. Showed her the time of her life."

Dylan's eyes narrow. "Oh, did you now. Funny, because last time we talked, I seem to remember that you hated Mandy and thought she was out to ruin your mom's life."

"I never said I hated her." I don't think. "Anyway, maybe

I changed my mind. Maybe I'm giving her a chance."

"You changed your mind. I see."

"I felt the baby. I—" He stares; I eat another bite of potatoes. *My friend Ravi was there. And I felt life. Not just in Mandy but in me.* "We had fun, that's all."

He sits up straighter. "I'm sure this newfound interest in Mandy has absolutely nothing to do with what you were telling me the other day about getting that guy at work to help you smoke her out. I'm sure you're not, like, luring her into some evil trap you're setting just to prove you're right."

That's the Jill he believes in. The Jill he's been putting up with. The Jill I seem to instantly become again now. And, I mean, he's right. That *is* why I took Mandy out. But when I got home, I didn't even care any more about any of that. I went to sleep thinking my dad would probably love Mandy as much as Mom does. Dylan takes my silence for guilt, which is only half right.

"She's a nice girl, Jill. You know? Maybe give her a break."

I shake hot sauce onto my eggs.

"Do you even know anything about her life? And what she's been through?" He's sincerely scolding me, big-time, as if he and Mandy are best friends. "Her mom is this world-class bitch."

I stop mid-chew. "What do you know about it?"

"I talked to Mandy when I went to your house to pick up my history book. It came up. I told you."

"No, you didn't." Did he?

"I did! I totally did!" He puts his fork down. "You don't listen to me. Seriously, Jill, not to make a thing out of it, but I feel like you haven't listened to me since..."

Our eyes meet.

"I'm just saying," he continues, "that, for example, you could think about me once in a while. In addition to thinking about yourself."

In classic Jill style, I turn on him in my hurt. "Is this about the band? I'm sorry, but the whole time I've known you, you have not expressed a single iota of interest in being in a band, so it's hard to take seriously."

"You don't have to take it seriously. I don't take it seriously. It's for fun. It's something fun and new to do to get out of the rut."

"The rut? Thanks."

"The Rut, capital R. Not the rut of *you*, or of you and me. The Rut of life. We're all in it from, like, the day we're born. It's good to mix it up a little."

I push my plate away. "Very philosophical of you."

He scrunches up his napkin and tosses it onto the table. For a couple of seconds, I'm pretty sure he's going to get up and walk out, and I feel ready. I almost want it, can almost picture him gone, and with him the Jill I'm sick of, and then I could start over. He doesn't move, though, which shouldn't surprise me. Dramatic exits are not Dylan. He leans back against the booth and pinches the bridge of his nose, squinting. "I missed you, Jill. While you've been going through your thing. Like crazy I've missed you, and when you hid in my car that day, I was so freaking happy, even though I pretended not to be. But now I remember we didn't always get along that great."

So he's noticed.

"That's part of the Jill-Dylan charm?" I say weakly.

Dylan nods, a lie of a nod, his eyes fixed on his coffee cup.

The barista says hi when I walk in, and points to Ravi at a table by the window. "He's over there."

We're officially regulars. It's our place. And it's the first time I've had that other than with Dylan.

"*Clark?*" I ask, joining him. "Really? Why is every boy in the world obsessed with Superman?" We don't have much time before my shift. There's a coffee shop closer to work, of course, and one *at* work, but we have this unspoken understanding that it's best not to have these meetings too close to Margins. Too close to Annalee. Annalee is the most unspoken part of all.

"Superman?" He runs his hand down his tie. It's one I haven't seen before – kind of a rose-and-navy-striped thing. No glasses. This Ravi makes me feel different from the way the jeans-sweater-glasses Ravi does. A little on edge.

"Clark," I say. "Clark Kent? Aka the Man of Steel?"

"Huh. I was thinking of William Clark. As in Lewis and Clark." He gazes at me. "The explorers?"

"Yes, I'm familiar, but that's..." Then I catch something in his eyes, around his mouth. Ravi has made a joke. "You were not thinking of Lewis and Clark."

"No, I was not."

"You were thinking of Superman."

"Totally thinking of Superman," he says with a conclusive nod.

"Well, I hope you like it, because you're stuck with it for the duration of this whole Mandy thing. By the way, iced coffee is not coffee. Just so you know."

He rattles his ice at me. "I'll file that information away under J, for *Jill Is Wrong*."

We're flirting. Nothing serious, just the way friends do. I was always good at that, since seventh grade, when I discovered my sense of humour and figured out how to use it. Maybe that's what Ravi saw that made him write that I

263

seemed smart and funny, that he wished we could have talked more. These days I'm more likely to clear a hallway or hear someone say "ouch" after I make a "joke". I want to go back to this. This is better; this is energizing and doesn't leave me feeling like an asshole.

I'm thinking of my comeback when Ravi says, "Hey." And I know whatever is next is not going to be about Mandy and not going to be flirting. No more joking around.

"Hey what?"

He opens his mouth.

"Don't ask me how I am," I blurt. "Please?" I want to keep feeling good. Just because the lights are on doesn't mean I have to look.

He closes his mouth.

I brush a crumb off our table, something left by a previous customer, and keep brushing well after it's gone. "Sorry, Ravi," I say, unable to look at him.

"Let me ask you a different question, then."

"Okay."

"You know how I said I've always thought of you as a friend, and maybe you could pretend that we are?"

I nod. I'll never forget that.

"Are you..." He's squishing his straw wrapper into a tiny ball with long fingers. "I mean, I know it started because you only wanted help with Mandy. But I think it would be good, or what I'm saying that I want to know...sorry." He leaves the wrapper alone. "Is this pretend?"

I put my hands in my jacket pockets and shake my head. "No."

"So... if we're not just pretending, and we really are friends, I can ask you how you are. Right?"

"I guess that is how it works. Technically."

"I thought so." He folds his arms over the table. "Jill?"

"Yes, Ravi?" I look at him and make efforts at a smile, trying to find the humour in the moment but only feeling raw as a burn, like if someone brushed against me right now, I'd yell out in pain.

"How are you?"

I close my eyes. Make myself think about it before answering. "I'm okay. I mean, you know. I don't know. Kind of weird." I laugh. I shouldn't be laughing.

"Weird how?"

"Weird like the whole last year has been a mistake. Or a dream. The way I've handled it. Like...I've messed up my 'grieving process' or whatever. And I can't go back and do it right."

My eyes, now open, maintain contact with his.

"I don't think there's a right way to do it. It's hard enough that your dad died. Don't criticize yourself for how you've dealt with it."

I blink. "Okay."

"You're doing great," he says.

"I am?"

"You're doing your best."

I really am. As short as it falls, I really, really am. And I love him for saying that.

"Do you want to talk about Mandy?" Ravi pulls out his notebook.

"I guess." I shift in my seat, get focused. "What did you think? She's not normal, right?"

"She does seem pretty awkward," he concedes. "And young. How old did you say she was?"

"Eighteen."

"She comes off younger."

"I know. I just figured that was part of being from Corn Country, and being small, and not being all that bright. I'm already feeling bad about last night," I confess. "The lying about who you are and all that. She really had a good time, you know? She kept talking about it on the way home, how neat the coffee shop was and how nice you were and everything. And when I felt the baby..." *and looked up at you, everything seemed possible again.*

"You don't have to do this. We can forget the whole thing."

"But what about the red flags?"

"They could all be explained away." He puts his pen down, closes his notebook. "I only want to help you. If you want me to try to check Mandy out further, I will. If you don't want me to, I won't."

I toy with the cardboard sleeve on my coffee cup. I don't even know any more what I want, if I started this to protect my mom or because I didn't have anywhere else to put my anger, or if it was all an excuse to bring Ravi closer, and if that was it, why can't I just admit it?

"Are you going to the store tonight?" I ask. There's frustration in my voice, which surprises us both.

"I'm on duty, but I have some follow-up to do at a couple of the other stores. I'll probably stop by, though."

"To see Annalee." It comes out of its own free will, is what it feels like. It's not what I mean to say. It's not where I mean to go.

"To work," he says, flipping some pages in his notebook, something for him to look at. "To thwart evil."

"And see Annalee." *God. Shut up, Jill. If you don't want to be this person, then stop. Fucking. Being her.* "Isn't she kind of old for you?"

Ravi flinches. "She's seven years older."

Why isn't he saying it doesn't matter, because they're not dating? Why isn't he flirty again and making a comment on the two-year age gap between *us*? That's what I want him to say, I realize. That's where I want the conversation to go.

"Old. You're only nineteen." I try for a smile, try to make it playful.

He pauses, and I can tell he's straining with all his might to read my tone and get it right. It's awkward. It's painful. We turned a bad corner; I want to take it all back. "We both like *Doctor Who*," he says. Which I'm sure he thought would be a safe answer.

What he's about to find out is that no one is safe with me when I'm this mad at myself. "I mean, that's fine if your whole ambition is to work at Margins the rest of your life, dating the staff and living with your parents. Great goals."

We stare at each other, both stunned. Ravi looks injured, and I've hurt myself, too. After this great moment of trust and connection and letting us be friends, I had to go and do what I do.

"So, um," he says, quiet and self-conscious, the way I imagine he was back in Schiff's, "take some time to think, and tell me what you want to do." Louder, more confident, he adds, "About Mandy, I mean. You'll figure it out, Jill. You're a smart girl." He stands, pointing to my cup. "All finished?"

"Yep."

He takes it with the rest of our trash. "See you." And he's gone.

Yeah. I'm so smart.

Mandy

I'm standing outside Jill's bedroom door with a cup of coffee. The coffee is for her. Robin showed me how to make it the way she likes: with a lot of half-and-half and a little bit of brown sugar. "She also likes it when I throw some cinnamon into the grinder with the beans, but we're out." Robin pulled her robe around her body and said, "Remind me again why you're taking coffee to Jill? Don't let her boss you around."

"I'm not. But it's Saturday morning, and she hasn't been down yet. Maybe she'd like coffee in bed. I have to go upstairs anyway."

The truth is that one of the three times I got up to pee in the night, I heard a sound coming from Jill's room. A gasping. At first I thought she had Dylan in there with her, but when I stopped to listen as hard as I could, I knew what it was. Crying. The kind of crying that takes over your whole body and makes your head hurt and your ribs sore. You think you might throw up. You try to bury your face into blankets or pillows to keep from being heard, but when you do that you can't breathe, you start to choke. So you pull away and gulp in air, then try to hide your face again, quickly. That's the sound I heard.

It made my own lungs empty out for a second, hearing her. My body remembered what it was to cry like that. I went back to bed and pictured myself in my room in Council Bluffs, six months ago, gulping air and clenching layers of blankets in my fists. No one in the world should have to feel like that. Not even Jill.

It's been one week since we went out together and she felt the baby. She's almost ignored me since. It's like it never happened. I've tried not to feel hurt. It's hard.

"Jill?" I ask, tapping lightly on her door.

"Go away, Mandy."

"I have coffee."

There's no reply.

"For you," I add. "Your mom showed me how."

After a few seconds the door opens a crack, and Jill's forearm snakes out. I pull the mug just out of her reach. She opens the door wider and looks out. "Are you going to let me drink it or what?" Her eyes are puffy. There's a pimple near the corner of her mouth. She's wearing regular clothes, like she slept in them all night.

"Can I come in?"

"Mandy," she says, squeezing her eyes shut. I can tell she's trying not to blow up at me. I want to say the right thing that's going to make her see me as somebody who sincerely feels bad for her. Because that's what I am.

"I heard you crying last night."

She opens her eyes. "I don't want to talk about it."

"Me neither. I thought this would help." I extend the mug. "That's all."

She takes it. "Why do you want to come in?"

Because I'm lonely, I think. Why does anyone ever want to be with another person? "I thought maybe you're lonely," I say.

Jill touches her mouth. Her eyes shift away. "Not really. But okay." She pushes the door all the way open and gets back in bed. I look at the futon chair. Without someone to help me, I don't think I can sit in it, let alone get up.

"Here," Jill says, reaching to flip back a corner of the blanket at the bottom of the bed. "Sit against the wall. Put your feet under."

I do what she says and watch her sip her coffee. "How is it?"

"Pretty good."

"We're out of cinnamon."

She watches me over the rim of the mug.

"I mean, *you're* out," I say. My feet feel under the blanket for the warmest spot, and I accidentally brush against her foot. "Sorry," I say, jerking mine back.

"Don't worry about it." Jill draws herself up to sit cross-legged. "So what are you up to today?"

"Same as always." I smile. "Nothing."

"What would you be doing today if you were back in Omaha or Iowa or wherever?"

"Same."

"I mean, like, if you weren't pregnant. Say you were back home and this" – she waves her hand towards my belly – "had never happened. What was your life like before? I mean, did you have a job or were you living at home or what?"

Jill's never asked me this many questions, been this interested in my life. Probably it's because she doesn't want to talk about herself or why she's sad. Maybe if I talk about me, she'll talk about her.

"I lived at home with my mother and her boyfriend. Sometimes I worked for his company, helping him with billing or entering stuff on the computer." Kent liked it when I came to his office and sat behind the front desk. Contracting customers liked to see a pretty girl, he said. Half the time he forgot to pay me. But he would take me out to lunch. If we ran into anyone he knew, he'd always say,

"This is Mandy." He never explained that my mother was his girlfriend.

"What about for fun? I mean, going out with friends and stuff?"

I finger the edge of the quilt. "My two best friends, DebAnn and Lucia, sometimes we'd all go out." I imagine going to a movie with them, sitting in the theatre with DebAnn's coat taking up an extra seat and Lucia with her earphones in, staring straight ahead. DebAnn and I did spend a Saturday together, once, when I gave her twenty dollars to take pictures of me with her digital camera so I'd have something to send Robin. "Do you have friends?" I ask Jill. I only want to change the subject away from me.

Jill laughs. "God, Mandy."

"Sorry, I didn't mean it like – I just never see anyone here. And all those people signed your yearbook."

"When did you see my yearbook?"

I pat the blanket where it rests on my belly. "I think maybe your mom showed me?"

"The answer about friends is: not really. There's Dylan, and the people at work. I used to have a couple of good friends and a lot of what you'd call friendly acquaintances. The friendly acquaintances disappeared when my life got tragic, and the good ones sort of got tired of being treated crappily." She looks at her mug. "So it's not just you I'm an ass to. I'm sure that makes you feel tons better."

"It does." Maybe not tons. But some.

"We've patched things up, I guess, but...I don't even know if any of us like each other any more."

"What about Clark?"

"Who? Oh." Jill nods. "Yes, there's Clark."

Her face goes complicated, and maybe she's had enough of me. "Well, I'm hungry." I work my feet out from under the covers. "I think I'll go down to eat."

"Wait." Jill sits up straighter. "Can I ask you something?"

I look at her, waiting.

"How come you didn't get an abortion?"

She's probably been wanting to ask me that since the first day at the train station. That's the question I feel, or have felt, whenever she'd look at me with that mix of anger and disgust. Why didn't I get an abortion. Why can't I just make it, and me, disappear.

"I almost did. My mother wanted me to."

She took me to the doctor to have it done. We planned it for weeks. I didn't argue, because arguing with my mother never changes anything. Then the morning of it, after Kent left for work, pretending he didn't know where we were going, we got in my mother's car and I closed the door behind me and stared up at our apartment building, in our apartment community, with its broad range of amenities. I knew when I got home after that, everything would go back to the way it always was. Me and DebAnn and Lucia alone at our table. Kent showing me off at work like I was his girlfriend and maybe starting to come back into my room at night. My mother not seeing me. It would be like the fair and the cornfield and Christopher had never happened. I'd have the memory and nothing else, and then eventually the memory wouldn't even be real. I knew this because that's how my memories of things that happened with Kent worked. Enough time would go by in between that I'd think, *Did that really happen? Did I dream it? Am I crazy?*

So when we got to the doctor, I told him I wanted to keep the baby. My mother yelled at me. The doctor told her to calm down, that it was my decision, there wasn't anything either of them could do if I was sure about what I wanted.

I didn't yell back at my mother. When I'm angry or scared or upset, I don't yell. I stay quiet. I've seen how she is, how she would get with Kent and with me and with other people, like if someone at the pharmacy got in the wrong line or asked too long a question, or if someone on the bus accidentally bumped her. I've watched her my whole life, the way people react to her. It doesn't actually help you get what you want, yelling and being like that. It only makes people think bad of you.

Sometimes it's more powerful to say nothing and keep still.

After I told the doctor I was having the baby and, yes, I was sure, there was nothing more to say and I let them yell about it.

"Why didn't you go through with it?" Jill asks.

I shrug and touch my belly. "I wanted my life to change." *I thought I could save this one*, I think, feeling her roll against my hand. *And maybe mine.*

Jill's brows go up. "Well, it's changing, all right."

"I know."

"One more question," Jill says.

"Yes?"

"I wonder...I mean, do you think she and I will get along?" She bends across her bed to tap one finger very gently on my belly. "Do you think she'll like me? A little bit?"

"Probably," I say.

Jill lies back down, her neck bent at what looks like an uncomfortable angle against her pillow. "Only probably?"

"Eventually. Liking someone takes time, it's the way it is with some people."

"Okay," she says. "I'll try to be patient."

Jill

On Sunday, I wake up after noon, and if I weren't starving, I would pull the covers back over my head and stay here in my death spiral of self-loathing. I'm not sure I've hit bottom yet; let's see how far I can go.

My phone shows four missed calls and eleven texts from Dylan in the last forty-eight hours, and two calls and one text from Ravi in the same time period. He hardly came into the store last week since our coffee date. I'm scared to listen to his voicemails or read the texts. I can imagine: the first one is a "call me" voicemail, the second is probably "I decided we can't be friends, because I realized whoever I thought you were sophomore year, you're not." The text would be: "Just wanted to let you know I quit Margins so that I never have to see you again."

I'm sure Dylan's are nice and concerned and practical, like wondering if we're riding to school together tomorrow.

Ever since the diner last Saturday, we've been being extra polite to each other, extra lifeless and rutlike.

I shove my blinking phone into my desk drawer and head downstairs.

Mom's at the table, working on her laptop. "She lives," she says to no one.

"Where's Mandy?"

"I convinced her to take a walk. It's lovely out, by the way. She only left a couple of minutes ago; I bet you could catch up to her if you got your shoes on fast."

"Trying to get rid of me?" I open the fridge and find half a leftover baked potato, on which I dump some shredded cheese before putting it into the microwave.

Still mousing and clicking, Mom asks, "What's with all the sleeping, Jill?"

"I'm on drugs."

She laughs a little. "You are not." She closes her laptop and feels for her mole, watching me mash up my lunch. After a hesitation, she says, "I'm worried about you."

It's hard for her to say that, I can tell. It scares her. Because this is where typical post-Dad Jill would say "Well don't" or "It's not your problem" and storm off, leaving her unsure how to react.

I add salt and pepper to my potato, mashing, stirring. The glimpses of a better self – with Ravi and Mandy over a week ago, when I felt the baby rolling and swimming and dancing... with Mandy yesterday morning when she brought me coffee and it occurred to me that being worthy of a sister's love would be a good thing – have been just that: glimpses. I can't catch her, that better Jill. I can't hold on.

Dad was my mirror, and without him I can't see myself.

The contents of my bowl become blurry. "Yeah. I had a hard week."

My constant inner dialogue about what a wretch I am has been distracting. I've locked my keys in my car once, and left the headlights on once, draining the battery. I got my work schedule wrong on Wednesday and received a panicked call from Annalee while I was fifteen miles away buying a new pair of sneakers. Yesterday after my conversation with Mandy, I went downstairs, ate cereal, and put the milk away in the cupboard instead of the fridge. Mom found it later while getting a snack.

She gets up now, and right when I'm thinking, *Great, my own mother can't stand my company,* she says, "Sit down. I'll be right back."

When she returns, she's got a big photo album in her hands and I know exactly what it is. She pushes her laptop aside to make space, and sets the album on the table. Sweeping a layer of dust off the grey cover with a napkin, she notes, "You used to look at this all the time."

That's not an exaggeration. I probably flipped through it every couple of weeks, imagining myself in his shoes, independent and free and in Peru, Argentina, the Netherlands, Morocco, becoming an adult.

"Mom, I can't."

The first page will be a map of South America. She opens to it and turns it slightly so that we can both get a good view. "You can."

I know what's on every page of that album. Used tickets from planes and trains. More maps. Postcards. Pages from his journal with his notes about the different stages of his trip. Receipts and a piece of paper money from each country he visited. There aren't a ton of pictures of my dad, since he was travelling alone, but there are some: him standing next to a llama, at a soccer game, behind some booth at a colourful street market.

"He would have loved helping you plan a trip," Mom says.

I haven't moved since she brought in the album.

"Maybe this will give you some ideas." She takes her hands off it and quietly slides her laptop back over. She pretends to be caught up in her work while I eat.

When I'm done, I pull the album closer and begin to turn the pages.

* * *

Later, I'm up in my room, catching up on my much-neglected homework, the door of my room closed. I hear someone on the stairs, and based on the slowness of the steps, I'd say it's Mandy. I know for certain when the bathwater starts running. She takes these long baths – warm, not hot, because apparently hot baths are a no-no for those with child, according to Mom. Personally I'm not one for sitting around in my own filth, but Mandy claims it helps her think. About what, I'm curious. Lately I wonder a lot about what she's thinking or feeling, and I have a zillion more questions about her life before she came here. If half the stuff she *says* is nutty, who knows what all goes on in her head, or what all she's been through.

The house phone rings. And rings and rings. I open my door. "Mom?"

No answer. The phone keeps ringing. I run down the stairs and hear my mom come in the back door. "Jill! Please get that! My hands are full."

"Can't the machine get it?" I call back.

"It could, but evidently it's not!"

When I get to the phone, near my dad's chair, I'm irritated and breathless and half my "Hello?" is lost in a sneeze.

"Amanda," this voice says, "where is the watch?"

I open my mouth to say, *Yo, wrong number,* but realize

Amanda is Mandy, and this person, who sounds very much like a mother, thinks I'm her.

"Amanda," she repeats. "Is that you?"

"Mm-hmm," I say.

"Kent came over today foaming at the mouth, claiming I stole his watch."

Hoping she'll continue talking, I keep my mouth shut and am soon rewarded.

"You got away with it, you really did. Until you called. Did you think I wouldn't get the number off caller ID and write it down? I can find you if I have to. Or tell Kent where you are. Not real bright, Mandy. But that's what I expect from you."

Wow. She's not even talking about *me*, and it still makes my stomach hurt. The quieter I stay, the screechier she gets. "Don't you have anything to say for yourself? Kent thinks I took the watch! He practically ransacked my new apartment trying to find it, and accused me of doing it out of jealousy. Over you! It was just lucky that Phil wasn't here..."

Mom comes into the living room, an onion in one hand and a questioning look on her face. I walk away with the cordless, holding a finger up, while Mandy's mother rages on.

"Amanda Kalinowski, you get that watch back here by

the end of the week or I will make trouble for you. I mean it." Even her pause is angry. "Don't you have anything to say?"

"Nope," I say, and hang up. My heart pounds as I put the cordless back in its cradle. I do my best to hide all symptoms of stress when I look at Mom, who asks, "Who was it?"

"No one. I mean a robocall." I put on a smarmy politician voice. "'Hi! This is John Q. Asshole and I'm your congressional blah blah blah!' You know how I like to talk back to the robots."

She shakes her head and goes back to the kitchen, and I turn the volume on the machine all the way down. The last thing Mom needs is to get a threatening message from Mandy's past. *What would Dad do?* He'd go straight to Mandy. He'd say, *Okay what's the deal with this watch, and what do we have to do to make your crazy mother leave us alone?* He wouldn't let it get out of hand.

Strengthened by the hour I spent looking at his photo album and by my determination to be the courageous person Mom says I once was, I go upstairs and slip into Mandy's room while she's still in the tub, and start searching. This watch must be some big deal. And of course there's just as good a chance that she didn't take it, and that this Kent person misplaced it or someone else took it or whatever, but when I think about it: if I were in Mandy's situation, I'd sure as hell wish I had more than a few dollars in my pocket, doing what she did. Collateral. So maybe she's not as out of it as I thought when it comes to real life.

The dresser drawers are sort of bare. All that's in there are the clothes she and my mom bought together. What did she do with all her flowered dresses and polyester cardigans? Under the bed, I find her suitcase and think about the day at the train station – almost a month ago, now. How I instantly didn't like her. Instantly wrote her off, had written her off even before she showed up. There's nothing in the suitcase or in the smaller duffel bag. Totally cleaned out.

I sit on the bed and look around, trying to think like Mandy. Not easy.

Then she walks in, swathed in a huge yellow towel, the ends of her hair dripping on her shoulders.

"Hi," I say.

"I don't have your straighteners."

"Close the door."

She does.

I try to channel my dad. How he'd be gruff but not scary. "What's the deal with the watch?"

She pulls her towel around her tighter, and her eyes shift around the room, landing on a stack of books on the nightstand. "What watch?"

The top book is the one my mom has always had in this

room, for guests. It's an anthology of poems. Underneath that is a Denver visitor's guide, also a standard item. And on the bottom is a Bible. Now, I know my mom would not have a Bible lying around. There's a big family Bible on one of the shelves in the living room that my dad got when Grandpa died, but as far as I know, that's it for religious texts in the MacSweeney home. I've never seen Mandy read anything thicker than *People*, let alone the Bible, but here it is by her bed.

I move the other two books aside and pick it up. It's light, lighter than it should be.

"Don't!" Mandy says, clutching her towel and looking towards the door.

"Mandy, calm down." I hold the Bible in my lap. "I'm on your side, okay?"

That comes out without any thought, and I know it's suddenly and absolutely true, an unexpected sense of loyalty based not on logic but instinct. Gut feeling.

She comes over and sits next to me, smelling like lavender and baby powder. "Did you tell your mother?"

"No."

I open up the Bible, and there's a hole the size and shape of a deck of cards cut into the pages. Lying in the hole, right under the first couple of lines of a psalm, is a little sandwich bag. I take it out, unzip it, and find:

An address label that's been torn off an envelope or magazine or something, with the name ALEX PEÑA on it.

Some neatly folded twenty-dollar bills – I don't know how many.

A key, like a house key, not a car key.

A cheap-looking necklace made of light blue beads.

An Iowa state ID card.

An expensive-looking gold watch. "Is this real?" It has to be, or else her mother wouldn't be so hysterical. I take it out and hold it up.

"Kent always said it was."

"Your mom just called here. They know it's missing."

Mandy blinks, takes the watch and holds it. "He never wore it. The only reason he cares about it is for poker. He pawns it and buys it back and pawns it and buys it back all the time."

"You gotta return it."

"But I need it."

"Mandy, let me tell you something about money. It's never been a problem for this family, okay? So don't worry about it. My mom will do the right thing if you need help. She always does."

While Mandy stares at the watch, I pull out her ID. Amanda Madison Kalinowski. In her picture, her eerie eyes stare out from behind her big hair. I waste all kinds of time checking out her height and weight and address and wondering why she's not smiling. She just looks kind of stunned. What grabs me is her birth date. Not because there's anything weird about her age – that checks out – but because her birthday is March 18. This Thursday.

"Hey," I say, "you're—"

"Jill?" Mom's voice sounds about halfway up the stairs.

I grab the watch out of Mandy's hand, stuff it and everything else back into the Bible, and put the Bible back under the stack. By the time Mom knocks on the door, I've got three hanks of Mandy's thick hair in my hands, pretending to be making a braid. "Yeah?" I call.

Mom opens the door, looking as surprised as I feel that I'm in here. "Oh. Jill, do you know where the soup pot is? The big one Dad used for chilli?"

I drop Mandy's hair and stand up.

"Let me come down and help you look."

Mandy

You have to go to the doctor a lot when you're pregnant. We're up to once a week now, and after one month and three appointments, Dr. Yee still doesn't like me. I don't think she believes anything I say even though I mostly tell the truth now.

"What did you have for breakfast, Mandy?" She gives me a little finger stick to check my blood sugar, plunging the lancet in quick and without much warning, as if it's not something that hurts.

"Wholewheat English muffin," Robin says, "with an egg and some soy sausage. Herb tea. Orange juice, but not too much."

It's true. That is what I ate, and since I knew I was coming to the doctor, I didn't also have any of the organic peanut clusters I usually have as breakfast dessert. The meter beeps. "Could be better, but not bad," Dr. Yee says.

She takes my blood pressure. "Okay. Could be better."

I'm under stress, I want to say. Of course it could be better.

She measures me and does the hand-held thing that monitors the baby's heart rate. It has a name – she told me last time, but I forgot. I wait for her to say "Could be better" again, but she pats my arm and smiles. "Everything's where it should be." Robin beams. Then Dr. Yee tells me to get dressed and that when she comes back, she wants to talk to us both. My heart beats a little faster than usual; from the sound of Dr. Yee's voice, it's like I'm about to get in trouble. Robin is happy, though, checking her phone every now and then because she has a meeting to get to after this. While I button up the soft new cardigan, she catches my eye and smiles more. "It's exciting, isn't it? How close we are."

"It is." Sitting with Jill on her bed Saturday morning, the hug from Dylan the week before that, meeting Jill's friend Clark, shopping with Robin, the way Jill promised not to tell about the watch and said she was on my side and would help me send it back with the right insurance and everything. It's true; we're all getting closer every day, and so much has happened.

"Just three or four weeks now," Robin adds.

Then I understand. She's talking about how close we are to the baby coming. How close the due date is. Not how close we are, not how we're practically a family. Dr. Yee comes back in. "Get comfortable," she says to me, pointing to a chair I could move to from the end of the exam table, where I'm sitting now.

"I am comfortable."

Dr. Yee sits in the chair and angles it so she can look at both me and Robin at the same time. "I wanted to talk to you about delivery day." Her voice is serious, her stare direct.

"Good," Robin says, nodding. "Me too. It's been a while. I'm sure things have changed since I gave birth to Jill."

"Oh, we'll go over all that. What I mean is..." She looks at the wall above my head. "Have you thought about who's going to be in the delivery room? Have you thought about the time period following the birth, the hours and days right after?"

"No," Robin says. "Well, of course, we'll figure it out."

"What I mean is," Dr. Yee says again, uncrossing and recrossing her legs, "I know you feel like your situation is unusual, but I've been through a few adoption births." Now she's speaking only to Robin, as if I'm not here. "Have you thought about things like whether you want Mandy to be allowed to hold the baby after she's born, or do you want the baby given directly to you? If you want to allow Mandy to breastfeed for a period of time?"

Allowed to hold the baby?

"What I'm asking is," Dr. Yee continues, still only to Robin, "have you decided when, exactly, the baby becomes yours? When *you* become the mother?"

Robin glances at me. Her eyes fall to my belly, then climb back to my face. "Well. We...there's a conversation, I know, to be had, but...what do most people do?"

Dr. Yee leans back, including me again. "Every situation is unique. I've seen birth mothers and adoptive parents choose from a range of options. Normally there's a social worker around, helping them make these decisions and helping them stick to them. I know you hadn't planned to go that route, but the hospital does have some social workers on staff, and if you like—"

"No," I say.

"Maybe we should think about it, Mandy," Robin says. Her voice is unsteady. "Just one meeting to talk it through."

"No." She can't do this to me now, when everything is going so well and Jill finally likes me and everything. I can't look at her. "You promised."

"We don't have to do what they say. It's still totally up to us."

Dr. Yee stands up. "You'll figure it out. I just wanted to bring it all up while there's still time to sort through your options." She smiles, like this is a regular appointment, like nothing has happened here that anyone has to worry about. "See you next week!"

In the car, Robin changes the station every sixty seconds and doesn't talk. She wants to, I can feel it, but she won't. I look out the window. It's a pretty day – blue sky, the last snowfall melted. People walking dogs, holding coffee cups, doing yard work in front of the nice old houses. Like a scene from TV.

Dr. Yee had talked to Robin like this was her decision. When I'm the one who is making this all happen.

Robin and Dr. Yee, they're on the same side. Everything works out for people like them. They've lived a life where things go according to plan. They had good childhoods and college and then a career. I bet everyone in their lives followed the rules of the system and the system gave them back an A+ and said, "Here is your perfect life." They don't know what it's like for the rest of us who don't have a system or don't know about the system or are forced to live with people who break all the rules, all of them, about what a responsible adult is, about paving the way for your child to wind up in a doctor's coat or to be needed at meetings that decide things for a whole city.

I know Robin's husband died, and that's not part of a perfect life. But everyone dies eventually. That happens no matter what.

Jill, she's on their side, too. Part of their life. She may be on my side about keeping the watch secret from Robin, but that's only because she loves her mother and knows it would upset her, and you protect people you love. That's how it should be. And it's easy for her to say money is never a problem and that Robin always does the right thing. What if we disagree about the right thing? The person with the money and the house and the good job gets to decide.

As we drive into Robin's neighbourhood – which, until fifteen minutes ago, I'd started to think of as my neighbourhood – the houses get nicer and trees tower over them, stretching their branches to protect the families inside. The cars driving down the street aren't rusty or too loud. Drivers stop at the stop signs. People keep their bird feeders filled so that little sparrows and chickadees can live through winter. All the people here have everything they need, and on top of that they have most of what they want. Still they want more.

What I know is this:

I'm the only one who's ever been on my side.

And this is my baby. My baby. Mine.

*   *   *

When Jill gets home from school, I ask if I can use her laptop while she's at work tonight. After a hesitation she agrees, if I let her log out of her e-mail and everything first.

Robin and I eat leftover soup in front of the TV and don't talk about what Dr. Yee said we should talk about. Or anything else. Usually we at least talk about her day at work and my day at home. Tonight is the first night when we don't say anything.

After dinner I go to my room and use Jill's computer to look on the Internet. Watches like Kent's are selling for about eight thousand dollars. It's not a fortune, I know that, but it's more than I've ever had at once, and it would be enough to get started. To get a small life started. I wouldn't have to live in a neighbourhood like this or have a car like Robin's, or even have a car at all. Just a little apartment. A crib. Diapers. A few toys and things, and then for eight thousand dollars' worth of time I could think about what to do when it runs out.

I look up different towns – places that wouldn't be too far to get to from here, since I don't have much time to get settled, but far enough away that no one would find me. Every few minutes the computer screen blurs so bad that I have to use a tissue to clear my eyes and blow my nose. This isn't what I wanted or planned and there's a part of me asking, *What are you doing, Mandy?* Another part answers back that I only ever wanted to do this if I could make all the decisions. There's not one single important thing in my life that I ever got to choose. Christopher, and this, which is part of that. Maybe. And I chose this for my reasons. I thought Robin understood. She promised we would do this my way; she promised it all along.

It's right here in my e-mail, in the account I set up just for talking to Robin, the one I always used from the library. I've saved everything including her post on the Love Grows website that first made me write to her:

DO YOU HAVE A HEART THAT NEEDS A HOME? I HAVE A HOME IN NEED OF A HEART.

Hello. I've never done anything like this before. Where should I start...

I'm a fifty-two-year-old professional woman living in a major urban area of the Intermountain West. I am successful in my business, own my home in a good neighbourhood and good school district outright, and have more than sufficient retirement savings.

That all sounds so formal. I should cut to the chase instead of dropping this bomb at the end of it all: my husband of nearly twenty-five years died suddenly this past April.

And she said even though she was still grieving, she felt hopeful about the future.

I will never marry again, but I'm not ready to call it quits on love. He and I talked for years about adopting a baby but foolishly never got the ball rolling, which is why I'm here at this site.

She wrote about her daughter, who was graduating and moving out soon, but didn't say Jill's name. She said love is something you do, and if no one is there to receive it, it's incomplete. She said it's like an electric current with nowhere to plug in. No one soaks up love like a child, she said.

As you will find out, your children are your heart. Let me give your heart a home, if that's what you're looking for.

I remember reading this on December twenty-eighth at the library, where I'd started to look up information on adoption. In most of the posts I found, women and couples were practically begging, desperate, with long stories about how many years they'd tried to have a baby on their own until they finally gave up and decided to adopt, or God told them to adopt. There were a lot of religious people. There were a lot of people trying to make themselves sound perfect. A lot of people posted pictures of themselves, and every time I saw a picture of one of these men, one of these potential fathers, I worried: what if he turned out to be a Kent kind of a person? I know most men aren't, but some are.

A lot of the sites were run by agencies, and all the communication happened through a between person. Love Grows was different. Just people who posted vague things in public, and then everything specific happened in e-mail. I saw the post on the twenty-eighth and thought about it for a few days, and then on New Year's Eve, while Kent and my mother were out, I got onto Kent's computer to write to Robin. Normally I'd wait until I could get to the library computer, but I didn't want someone else to get her before I did. So I wrote to her and then deleted all my history so Kent couldn't see. The next time I checked at the library, Robin had written back, and we made our promises. I believed in her. Until today, when she and Dr. Yee were talking about me being "allowed" to do things like hold the baby, and when Robin said maybe we should use a social worker.

I can't believe she did that.

She should know that children aren't sponges only for love.

They soak up whatever they've been given.

My whole life has been one big broken promise.

I don't know why I thought this could be any different.

Jill

By Tuesday night at work, I've not only *not* listened to Ravi's messages, I've deleted them. His text only said, "Did you get my messages?" Whatever I told myself about it being no big loss if I messed up with him was clearly a shameless lie; otherwise I wouldn't be so scared to know what he thinks of me.

Annalee is in a pissy mood, closing the register drawer harder than necessary, snapping at Ron the one time he's not at the customer service booth when someone wants help, and striding through the store with her long skirt making angry *I'm too busy to help you* swishy noises that I can hear from six aisles away. When I finally catch her in a standing-still moment, compulsively neatening a stack of remainders, I ask, "Is Ravi... R.J...going to be around tonight?"

"How should I know?" She swishes away from the remainders over to an adjacent shelf, where she continues her needless arranging. "He doesn't work *here*. He works for the *region*. He could be at any of the stores, or none of them."

"Okay."

"I'm not his boss."

"Okay."

"If you need him to come here for some reason, talk to Corporate."

"Okay, but..." I catch Ron's eye from the customer service booth, and he gives his head a tight little shake and clears his throat, which I take as a warning to back off. "All right," I tell Annalee. "Thanks."

She mumbles something else, which I don't ask her to repeat, and stalks off towards the cafe. It doesn't take a genius to gather that something has gone down between her and Ravi.

I'd counted on him coming in tonight; seeing his face when he sees mine will tell me more than any voicemail ever could. I want to apologize. I want to tell him it's not like I *want* to be suspicious of every good thing and push it away before it can hurt. I want to trust the world again. Trust friendship.

Which is a lot to ask of myself, I know, considering how I've exhibited no skill in this area. So if I can't do all that, I can at least give him a Mandy update.

I tried to get her to give the watch over last night so I could take care of it today, but she said she wanted to write a letter to her mother and she needed some time to think. "Well, think fast," I said. "Your mom doesn't seem like the patient type." Then Mandy said, "She doesn't?" I laughed, thinking she was being ironic, but then I remembered that Mandy and irony go together like mustard and chocolate, so I said, "No, she really doesn't."

Over the last couple of days, I've tried to imagine what conversations between my dad and Mandy would be like, the looks he and I would give each other about some of her crazy ideas. I think at first he'd be like, "What the hell?" and then almost as instantly that would turn into affection and acceptance. Maybe I could get there, eventually. Hearing her mom on the phone has already caused some new gear in me to kick in. The one that wants to call that woman back and say, "Hey, bitch, stay away from my family."

I swore to Mandy I'd keep the watch situation a secret from Mom. Mandy doesn't want my mom to think she's a thief, a bad person, trouble. I tried to tell Mandy that Mom would understand, but she begged me to promise, and I did. I understand the desperate need to not disappoint people.

And I'm planning a birthday party for Mandy. I told

Dylan at school today that it's this week and that I want to do something, a surprise.

"Kind of short notice," he said. We've gotten friendlier compared to the polite and careful way we were last week, but still not very boyfriendly/girlfriendly.

"I know," I said. "But it has to be the day of her birthday. Otherwise it's lame. Also, we can make it a baby shower, too, sort of. A birthday-slash-baby-shower. Short notice is good; we won't have time to get nervous and act suspicious."

I didn't tell him about the watch. He'd have an opinion, and his opinion would be that I should tell Mom.

For the party to happen, I need to ask Annalee for Thursday off, something I'd planned to do tonight, but the circumstances aren't ideal for that.

She swishes her way back up to the front with a coffee in one hand, comes behind the counter, and slaps a magazine down. She flips through the pages violently. *Crack. Crack. Crack.* "It's dead," she says, as if she owes me an explanation. "I'll do register two if we get a line."

Just then my phone rings from my apron pocket. It's the theme from *Mission: Impossible*, which I assigned to Ravi's number when I first saved it on my phone. I pretend not to hear it and start dusting the display of gift books behind the counter.

"Go ahead and answer," Annalee says. "I don't care."

Oh, I think you'd care if you knew who it was.

"It's okay."

"Answer it, Jill."

This is no night to test her. I obey. "Hello?"

"Hey. It's me."

"Yes?"

"Me, Ravi."

"Yes." I move away from Annalee, scared she'll hear Ravi's voice. I'm stuck giving him a semi-cold "What's up?"

He pauses. "Are you at work?"

"Yes." I glance at Annalee, who is still looking at her magazine but clearly also listening to me.

"Can we talk later?" Ravi asks.

My heart rises. Then falls again at the idea it could be a bad *Can we talk?* and not a good *Can we talk?*

Still, I say yes, and no matter what, yes feels like an improvement.

When I pull up to my house after work, I call him from my car, heart pounding. Maybe I'm about to get my ass handed to me. But maybe not. Scared as I am, the possibility of never knowing if he and I could really be the kind of friends I think we might be is scarier. For the first time in a long time, possibility conquers fear.

He answers with a hi. Then asks if I got his messages.

I blow breath out. "It depends what you mean by 'got'."

"Got."

"I deleted them without listening."

"Oh. That's..." He sounds relieved. "Why?"

I lean to rest my forehead on the steering wheel, which is freezing cold. *Trust friendship*, I think. *Trust the next moment even though it's unknown.* "I was scared. I thought... I'm sorry for what I said at the coffee shop. I don't know why I said those things."

I can't move while I wait for his reply. I think I'm getting frostbite on my forehead.

"You don't?" He pauses. I don't say anything, waiting to be raked over the coals. When he continues, his voice sounds a little shaky. "I kind of walked out on you before we were really done talking. I'm sorry for that."

Whoa. I sit up. "No, you were right. You should have walked out."

"Okay, yeah, probably."

"Yeah."

And then we have this whole conversation. For nearly an hour. We start off in familiar territory: Mandy. I tell him all about the watch, and he asks me why I think I can handle this information better than my mom can, why I'd keep it from her. Miraculously, I don't get defensive.

"I promised Mandy. She cares so much what my mom thinks and, I don't know, I feel for her. It was smart of her to take the watch, actually, in a way. It makes me see her in a new light. A smarter one."

"You've gone from suspicion to sympathy pretty fast."

It's felt slow to me, in a way, but maybe he's right. Maybe I've got some of my dad's heart in me after all. "I guess I'm tired of expecting the worst all the time. We'll return the watch, and everything will be fine, on track."

Then we drift off into more personal things: memories of my dad, Ravi's trip to India when he was fifteen, my plans or non-plans for college.

"Wow, I assumed you were going," Ravi says.

"I'm going to go, I think. After a year or two off."

"English major?"

"Wrong."

"Creative writing?"

"Really? No."

"I just thought because you work in a bookstore and everything."

"So do you," I say.

"Good point. Um, social work."

"Ha!" Who is this Jill person who would major in social work? What does Ravi see in me that I don't? I ease the seat of my car back and put my feet up. "New topic: in your yearbook, you thanked all these people."

"My family. My mom and dad and brothers and sister."

"What's it like having siblings?"

"Mitali, she's closest to me in age, and she treats me like a friend. My brothers are bossy and really different from me. It's always been like that."

I turn onto my right side so I can see my house, the front-porch light on, the light in Mandy's room off. "But what's it *like*?"

"I guess I've never thought about it too much. They're just always there. Like friends you'll never lose, even if you fight."

"And even if you're different? Like you and your brothers?"

Ravi starts to answer, then stops. "Are you worried about that? With the adoption and everything?"

He's good. "Perhaps a tiny bit of worry crossed my mind."

"Don't. I'll tell you what it's about: shared experience. That's what makes a sibling a sibling. Going through stuff together, good and bad."

We talk more about that and, around midnight, plan to meet for coffee tomorrow afternoon because...I don't know why. No good reason except it feels like our conversation isn't done. He has to be at one of the regional stores at three, so I'll be ducking out of school early to meet up with him.

On Wednesday morning, Dylan's waiting for me at my locker with a huge grin on his face. I'm feeling pretty good myself. "What?" I ask.

"I have the perfect idea for Mandy's birthday-shower thingy," he says.

"Yeah? Hit me."

"Two words," he says. "Casa. Bonita."

I slap my hand on my locker door. "Yes! You're a genius. She'll love it." Casa Bonita is this awesomely tacky Mexican restaurant on the fringes of Denver, with cliff divers and fake caves and enchiladas made with canned cheese. If Mandy likes Pancake Universe, she'll be crazy for Casa Bonita. Just the thought of her there, probably saying something like, "This is the most delicious Mexican food I've had in my life," adds to my cheer. I give Dylan a kiss on the cheek. "Best idea ever."

"Wait – who should we invite? We need to tell people today if this thing is tomorrow."

"Probably just us. Me and you, my mom." I don't know if Cinders and Laurel could get through it without letting on to Mandy the kinds of things I'd been saying about her before I started to come around. "Maybe this guy I know from work that Mandy and I ran into the other night."

"Who?"

"You could invite the band if you want," I say quickly, wondering why the hell I had to mention Ravi. Well, I know why. Because I want to invite Ravi, but I can't invite Ravi, because Dylan knows Ravi is the person I was going to ask for help with spying on Mandy. And also, PS, Mandy thinks his name is Clark. "Oh, Clark." I wave my hand like he is nobody. A speck of dust. "He worked at Margins for like five seconds last year. Mandy seemed to really like him. It might perk her up."

I feel completely transparent, but Dylan is blinded by his happiness about me finally being nice to Mandy. "You're like, a whole different person," he says.

I can hope.

Mandy

Just because you have a watch worth eight thousand dollars doesn't mean you're going to get eight thousand dollars for it, I found out. Robin went to meetings half the day, and while she was gone, I called jewellers and pawnshops and even a couple of antique stores. All of them said they had to see it before they could say how much they'd give me. The only person who gave me a number said twenty-five hundred. Something about street value. "It's not enough," I said, but there are probably people who have started new lives with less.

I have to decide soon. Jill asks me every night if I'm done with the letter to my mother. And I tell her not to worry, that my mother sounds bad but doesn't follow through with things. Except mostly she does, especially things that are for protecting herself.

All through last night I thought about the baby. Having

her. Going through the pain, and the being afraid, and then handing the baby to someone else, someone else who will be her mother. It's like that lady I met at the mall, the one with the nanny, said: once I go through all that to have the baby, I'm not going to want to give her up. When she said that, I was so sure she was wrong, and so sure about what I was doing. Now I don't know what happened.

Robin finally talked to me this morning at breakfast. Again she said maybe we should get a social worker after all, or even hire a private mediator, and write something down, formally. Sign an agreement. "Just so there aren't problems later," she said.

"No. I told you from the beginning."

"But, Mandy," she pleaded, "everything would be the same. The agreement could say anything you want."

I got up and rinsed my breakfast plate and put it in the dishwasher, my head so full of things I wanted to say to Robin, to explain to her. The story about how my father paid my mother so he'd never have to see me. About going to find him, and how he'd moved without telling anyone. The way I used to dream about my father, who he might be and how he would someday come back for me. I don't know why my mother couldn't let me go on thinking that for the whole first five years of my life, why she had to tell me what really happened, drag me everywhere looking for him instead of doing it in private.

I don't want my daughter to ever hear a story or see a piece of paper or know that one exists on which I signed her away. I don't want her to ever think that I didn't want her. No matter what, I don't want to leave any evidence she could find later that she might think proves to her the worst things she thinks about herself on a bad day. Not when she's ten, not when she's fifteen, not when she's forty. Maybe I'll be there to explain it to her, but I can't know that sure enough right now to plan on it. I want it to feel like fate, the way she ended up with Robin. I want to be in her life like a good dream, like someone who might not always be there but who never really left. Her world should feel full of possibilities and open doors, not full of things that are closed and final.

Robin wouldn't understand this, because she's never been abandoned. Mac dying isn't the same thing.

"I don't want to sign anything," I told Robin this morning.

She folded her napkin and unfolded it and folded it again. "Okay." It came out like she was trying hard to be patient. "But we still need to talk. Not just about what's going to happen when you give birth but about everything after. Your plans for your life, how often you'd like to see the baby, what you want me to tell her about you as she grows up... Mandy, there's so much to *talk* about!" For the first time she was getting mad at me, and maybe ready to cry, too. "I only want to *talk*. It's nothing to be afraid of."

"It's confusing to know what the best thing is," I said. Talking sometimes makes me more confused. Like when Kent used to talk to me late at night about how what we were doing wasn't wrong, because I wasn't a child and I wasn't related to him, and I liked it. "Right?" he'd ask. He'd ask it over and over until I answered back, "Right." And I don't want to be talked into something again just to make the other person feel better.

Robin twisted the napkin in her hand. "It is confusing, I know. I thought we could make this up as we went along. But I see that wasn't necessarily helpful for either of us."

I wish we could go back to those e-mails, each of us at computers, knowing exactly what we wanted and how we wanted to do it, and being so sure of each other. "I'm going to lie down," I told Robin.

She stood up. "Mandy, no. Let's keep talking."

"My back hurts."

"I'll come up with you. Or I'll set you up on the couch."

"I want to be alone."

I tried to puzzle it out while I rested. To remind myself why I thought this was the perfect plan in the first place, giving up the baby without really giving it up. Being in charge, making my own rules and all my own choices. It's not that I suddenly think I could do a better job than Robin; I know I couldn't. But the emotions of it. I didn't expect to feel this way, like I want to run. This is too hard, maybe impossible. And then there is the piece about who the father of this baby is. If I knew that for certain, maybe I would understand what to do.

If this isn't Christopher's, I think I might hate it. I don't want to drag around a helpless child, letting her feel all my anger, the way my mother did with me.

If I could wait and make my decisions after I know, get away for a little bit and then come back, depending, Robin would forgive me. I think. She forgives Jill everything. She could give me that one thing, a small amount of time and space.

Except I don't want to leave. The part of me that is just Mandy – no baby, no Christopher, no Kent – wants to stay here for ever.

Jill

Cinders and Laurel think it's hilarious to punch me in the arm every chance they get. It's St. Patrick's Day, and though I'm half Irish, I completely forgot about the holiday and am not wearing a stitch of green. There's something about the energy of their thumps that can't wholly be explained by my failure to adhere to a meaningless tradition. They're punishing me for the last year. Fine. I deserve it, and I'm in a good-enough mood to take it. But by lunchtime there's a bruise growing on my upper left arm, so I sit with Dylan and the guys from the "band" to avoid further abuse.

"Did you call work about getting off tomorrow night?" he asks me.

"Not yet." I haven't called work, I haven't told Mom about Casa Bonita, and I haven't figured out how to get Mandy there and keep it a surprise, or whether I should invite "Clark".

One of the guys – Bo, I think – says to Dylan, "She coming to practice?"

"No, 'she' isn't," I say. "Neither is 'he'. "

"Dude," Bo says, "are you in The Potato Rebellion or aren't you?"

"I thought we dropped the 'Potato', " says another guy, whose name I can never remember. Kyle, Kenny, Chris, Kevin...? "We're just The Rebellion, right?"

Bo shakes his head. "We found out there's already a band called that. Anyway, the 'Potato' part is what makes us indie."

I rap my knuckles on the tabletop. "Sorry to interrupt but the point is Dylan will not be at practice tomorrow. He has a birthday/baby shower to go to."

All male heads turn to Dylan, who laughs and raises his hands. "No. No. Not like that. It's not a baby shower for *us*."

"Good," Bo says. "Because you can't go out on tour with a baby strapped to your back."

Tour? Restraint prevails; I withhold all out-loud sarcastic comments about the future of The Potato Rebellion as a touring band. Instead, I scoop up my stuff and tell Dylan I have to be somewhere after school; I'll call him later.

Ravi's got his suit on, and even though Suit Ravi still makes me slightly nervous, he looks really nice in it. Suit or not, this is the same person I spent an hour with on the phone last night without insulting, demeaning, or dismissing him, and without him shoving my bad behaviour in my face. Again, he's there first, and again he stands, and again I think we should hug hello. Again I don't. And that's starting to mean something. If he were a friend, definitely a *friend* friend, I would. Instead I carry my coffee over to the napkin-stirrer-creamer-everything area and shake cinnamon into the cup. When I come back, he's sitting again.

"If we talk about work, I can say it's a business meeting and stay out longer," he says. Whatever amount of time we were going to spend together, he wants it to be longer. Implying that he enjoys my company.

"Oh. Like...what about work?"

"Do you think you'd ever be interested in working for Corporate?" Ravi spins his coffee cup gently in his graceful hands.

"Maybe. If it would get me out of Denver."

His cup stops. "Why do you want to get out of Denver? Especially now, with Mandy and the baby."

"I know. But I feel like I should. My dad did. He saw the world at my age. If I do like he did, maybe I can..." Be like him? Be *with* him? "I've been planning it."

"You can change your mind, though. If you want."

"I can?" I act shocked, drop my jaw, which makes him laugh his lovely laugh.

"Hey," he says, sitting up straighter, "do you want to go on a stake-out with me?"

"I'm sorry. Did you say 'stake-out'?"

"I did."

"Okay," I say, without any idea what he's talking about. It doesn't matter, because whatever it is, if it's with him it feels like something to look forward to. It hits me how grateful I am, so unbelievably grateful, that circumstances led to my elbow strike to his face. I almost think...no. I don't believe that stuff.

On the way out to his car, he explains that he suspects an assistant manager at one of the stores in our region of aiding and abetting theft. "His wife comes in to say hi, and suddenly a bunch of cookbooks are missing, stuff like that."

"Sneaky."

It's a pretty nice day – chilly, but you can definitely tell it's more spring than winter. When we get into his car, an oldish sedan, Ravi says, "I brought you something," while reaching behind my seat, and when he does, his shoulder is right by my face. And: chemistry. That thing that I couldn't place almost a month ago when he came into the store and we walked through talking about shoplifters and he stepped close, that thing I felt as nostalgia, homesickness.

And the first night he came in, when he apologized for surprising me at closing, that thing that made me think Dylan was looking at me. Chemistry. I must have had it with Dylan when we met – you know, how before it's love, it's something more basic. But I don't remember it being like this. This intense. And one thing I've never understood about chemistry is if the other person feels it, too. They must, right? If it's truly chemistry, it can't be one-sided. If Ravi's feeling it, he's doing a good job of pretending not to.

He sits up and he's got his senior yearbook in his lap. "I thought maybe you'd want to see what you wrote to me."

He flips through the book, and I hope that I wrote something at least nice and at most something like he wrote in mine, something that showed maybe I thought we could be friends, too, even if I don't actually remember him from back then.

"Here." He hands it over.

I signed on the first page of the sophomore section. *Raji – Have a nice summer.* And I signed my name. My heart sinks. I couldn't even get his name right?

"Oh. *Raji?* Sorry." I stare at my handwriting, loopier than it is now, neater but also kind of childish-looking. Written by the hand of the Jill I used to be. I wonder: the day I wrote on this very piece of paper, was it a good day for

Dad and me? Did I tell him I loved him? Chances are more than good he told me he loved me.

Ravi laughs. "I'm over it." Then he leans over and flips through some more pages, and his shoulder is still magnetic, and my breath is shallow, and I don't know if it's chemistry or if I might be about to cry over my dad again, but it's a buzz up the back of my neck, in my fingertips. "This is my favourite picture of you."

"You have a favourite picture of me?" He's pointing to one of the candids pages. I don't remember myself being on a candids page. But there I am, leaning against Cinders and smiling so big, like I'm in the middle of a laugh. My hair is lighter. Much lighter. I'd forgotten how light it was. When I went dark, I went *dark*.

"I don't remember that," I say, running my finger over the Jill who would smile so big. "So, you have a favourite picture of me, and you've been staring at it for two years?"

He closes the yearbook and takes it back. "No, no. It's not like that. I only remembered that I knew you when I said your name aloud that night at the store. And I went home and looked up your picture, and it all came back."

"What all came back?" I want to understand. I want to know.

"You." He starts the car and we pull out. "I was shy. You had a lot of personality in that class. Trust me, I'm not the

319

only shy guy who sat there thinking he wished he were your friend."

We drive along. I have no idea where we're going, which store, how far. "What kind of personality?"

"Smart. Funny. Like I wrote in your yearbook."

"Was I *nice*?" I ask, dreading the answer.

"Yeah," Ravi says. "I mean, you seemed nice. And you seem nice now, so I'm sure you were."

"I do? How can you say that after—" Then we round a corner, and there's the city cemetery, coming up on our left. It's too weird. How are we driving by it right now, when I've managed to avoid it for almost a year? "Can we go in there?" I point to the gates.

"Oh. Sure." We wait to turn left, and drive on the main path, rolling hills dotted with gravestones on either side of us. "Where am I going?"

It's hard to remember. You'd think your body would have some sort of compass that would make you remember things like where your father is buried. If pigeons with brains the size of peas can find their way home, humans should be able to accomplish this simple task. "I think all the way to the other end, maybe."

Ravi drives. I try to picture where it was. There was snow on the ground then. There is now, too, but it's patchy, and there might be new trees or bushes or something, and honestly my focus was not on landmarks at the time.

"Pull over," I say. "Maybe we should look on foot."

"Right. And...what are we looking for now?"

I turn to him and say, steady as I can, "My dad is buried here. Somewhere. I haven't been back since the burial. I haven't seen the headstone."

Ravi holds my gaze, and if he's stunned or horrified to hear what a terrible person I am to have gone nearly a year without paying my respects to my dead father, he doesn't show it. "Ah. What...was his name?"

"Gavin MacSweeney."

Some of the gravestones have potted clover beside them, green foil, even leprechaun cut-outs. HAPPY ST. PAT'S, some of them say.

It's chillier than I realized, and as we walk around the cemetery for what feels like for ever, I shove my hands deep into my jeans pockets and begin a kind of teeth-chattering shiver I can't make stop. Pressure builds in my chest; we're never going to find it. Why don't I *know* where it is? What kind of a daughter am I? Mom comes every couple of weeks, I know she does, even though she stopped inviting me months ago when I yelled at her that I didn't need to see his grave to remember that he's gone. A tear gets out. I brush it away. Ravi is walking on the other side of the trail so we can cover more ground, and he can't see me. Another drop rolls out, down my cheek, soon followed by one on the other side. I remember exactly how my voice sounded, saying that to my mom – a completely yelling voice, utterly lacking in anything even close to tenderness while talking about the forever gone-ness of my dear, dear, dear father, my mirror, the only person who would understand my yelling in even that moment. I'm brushing tears away every second now, wiping the back of my hand on my jeans, returning it to my pocket, taking it out again, brushing, repeat, repeat.

"I think I found it," Ravi calls to me from the top of a small swell of grass. Yes, it was on a hill. A view of the houses in the neighbourhood below.

By the time I get to Ravi, my teeth are rattling in my head like a machine gun; I can't stop shaking from the cold. My eyes are leaky taps; the tears just come and come and come.

GAVIN J. MACSWEENEY
1957–2010
LOVING FATHER AND HUSBAND

"Not real original, is it?" I say, my voice tight with cold.

"I think it's good. 'Loving father and husband' is underrated. I mean, that's a lot. It's really a lot."

I nod. It's everything.

Ravi removes his suit jacket. Puts it around my shoulders, presses its warmth around me with a tight side hug. I let myself lean against him, and he circles me with his other arm, still staying to my side, rocking a little bit. And I look at the headstone, thinking, *Did Dad send Ravi to me?* Is that something I even remotely believe is possible? Because however he got here, Ravi has been exactly what I need, and is sticking with it like he's on assignment from God.

"Dylan wanted me to come here with him," I say. "I could never do it. I don't know why. It just seemed like he wanted this big, dramatic...I don't know what. It felt like everyone wanted to tell me what to do and how to feel and ways to cope."

Ravi is quiet. He drops one arm, leaves the other around my shoulders.

"It probably sounds weird," I continue, "but it's like my grief is all I have left of my dad. It's private. I save up my crying for the middle of the night, when no one can hear. So it can belong to me only."

"That doesn't sound weird."

We stay there awhile, until I worry about Ravi getting too cold without his jacket.

It isn't until we're back in the car and driving out of the cemetery that Ravi says, "So, maybe you've mentioned him before, but I'm not sure... Dylan is..."

I swallow, look out the window, finger the edges of the yearbook now on my lap. "My boyfriend."

"Oh."

Oh.

Mandy

Jill's getting anxious about the watch. There's only so much longer I can tell her I'm still writing the letter to my mother. Two nights ago she came into my room, late, midnight, and sat on my bed in the dark, talking low. She said we have to mail it by Friday. Tomorrow. That we're just lucky my mother hasn't called again, and we can't wait any more. "Unless you decide you want to go ahead and tell my mom about it," she said.

"No," I whispered.

"I get it. You don't want her to think you messed up. You didn't, okay, Mands?"

Mands. No one ever gave me that nickname before. I didn't know what to say to that.

Jill nudged my arm. "It's really not a big deal. We can go tell her right now if you want. She's down in her office. No secrets, no worries."

If this were only about me wanting Robin to think of me a certain way, Jill would be right. But the part I can't tell her is that I might need the money. I can't tell Robin I want to keep the baby and then expect her to write me a cheque. Even I'm not that stupid about how the world works. The watch is all I have. That, and the baby. But without the watch I don't have the baby, because without money I can't do anything, and I won't go back to Council Bluffs, no matter what. No matter what.

"No," I told Jill. And I felt bad lying to her, but I said, "We'll mail it by Friday. I promise."

Last night we had dinner early; Robin had to go to a meeting, again, afterwards. "A few more days of this," Robin said, "then it's all over. As soon as I present the feasibility study, my part is done and we can focus on... everything else." Meaning me, the baby, the decisions we haven't made, the conversations we haven't had. Since dinner was early, Jill ate with us instead of running right off to work. She looked a little bit like she'd been crying – by now I've seen her cry enough to know her different faces – but she sounded and acted happy.

"Still soup?" she asked. We've been eating this soup since Sunday.

"Unless you'd like to whip up a rack of lamb," Robin said, putting out bowls.

"It's good," Jill said. "Just eternal." She looked at me, then, and made a face. Like we're friends, or sisters. *No secrets, no worries* might be true, but also having a secret together has made us closer.

She took the newspaper from the top of the recycling bin in the corner of the kitchen. "I think that's yesterday's," Robin said, putting out spoons, napkins.

"That's what I want. I'm testing the wisdom of the universe."

"What do you mean?" I asked.

"Oh, this argument I got into with someone from work who totally believes in astrology. I want to see if yesterday's horoscope came true." She flipped through the pages and read aloud: " 'You're not as clever as you think you are, Aries'. That one's for the baby." She leaned over and said to my stomach, "Not as clever as you think! We're onto you! Okay, now me. Capricorn. 'Don't let what you think you know...' " Jill kept reading silently.

"Go on," Robin said, laughing. "That sounds like you, all right."

"This is obviously b.s."

"Oh!" Robin turned to me, suddenly, from the stove. "Do you realize your due date is right around Mac's birthday? April second. Wouldn't it be something if she was born on his birthday?" She sounded far away. "Wouldn't it, Jill?"

"It would." Then Jill got up and decided she needed to go straight to work after all, leaving the newspaper in a pile at her place at the table. On her way out, she said, "Mom, try to stay up, I want to talk to you about something when I get home," and I don't mean to be paranoid, but it sounded like the thing she wanted to talk about was me. Otherwise why would she say it like that? "Something" instead of "work" or "school" or normal things. Maybe she'd figured out from her laptop what I'd been looking at about the value of the watch and where I could get money for it. I'd cleared all my history, but she could know something I don't know about computers.

The truth is that earlier yesterday I was a little calmer. More sure about staying here and following through with all my plans. Confident that Robin and I would work it out, and everything would be all right somehow. But when Jill said that, I knew she was going to tell on me for taking something that wasn't mine, trying to get away with something. That I might be a thief. That I might wind up stealing from them.

Then this morning they both acted normal and I thought, *No, Jill didn't tell. Maybe I'll stay.* It's so hard to know what to do, and I go back and forth like that, all day, every day, since Monday after Dr. Yee. I look at Jill and Robin and think, *Yes, I can trust them; this is a good situation.* Then I see Robin at her computer and think maybe she's not doing work for her meeting, maybe she's e-mailing lawyers.

I picture it all:

Me at the hospital. Giving birth. It hurting and taking a long time. Robin will be there helping, but it's only because she wants this so bad, this life in me, someone to give her love to who is new and isn't ruined like I am. And the baby will come out, and Robin will hold her, and she and Dr. Yee will whisper and take my daughter away.

And disappear.

Then it's me. Alone.

The nurse will say, "Mrs. MacSweeney packed your bag for you, and here it is. So you don't have to go back to the house for it."

It will be like at the train station in Omaha when the taxi driver left me and I walked through the snow and the dark, only this time I won't even have my baby, or anywhere to go.

That is how it's going to happen, I just know. That's how my life has been. That's how it will be, unless I do something different.

So all of that means this is my last day here.

At breakfast this morning I took in every detail to remember in a week, in a year, in twenty years: how Jill looks before she puts on her eyeliner, the way she stands in the middle of the kitchen eating her peanut butter toast instead of sitting at the table, because she's always in a hurry. The sound of Robin's feet on the stairs and how they're different from Jill's – lighter and more cheerful.

Robin had to rush out, too.

"This is the last day," she said to me, touching my head, like she does sometimes. I closed my eyes and felt each fingertip. "After tonight I'm done. If they need anything else from me, they'll have to get it by phone. Okay? I promise."

"It's fine," I said. "We'll talk about everything tomorrow." I gave her my most convincing smile and reached up from where I was in the kitchen chair and put my arms around her neck. Powder, coffee.

Remember this, I think.

Jill

All day Thursday I can't shake a peculiar feeling. Mrs. Espinoza has the window cracked, and there's a spring breeze that's almost warm, smelling at once carbon-y and grassy, old snow and new plants, growth, life. Everything's off somehow, unsettled. It feels almost like: the future has already happened. Graduation is over, Dylan has gone off to college, Mandy's had the baby, and I can see my mom holding her, gazing at her. The only thing I can't clearly see about the future is what *I'm* doing in it. I sort of picture myself in Denver. Which is all wrong.

Spring fever. Senioritis, maybe. Confusion about Ravi, certainly.

Meanwhile I have to plan a surprise party, call Annalee about work, and get that damn watch back to Iowa no later than tomorrow. And PS, I also have to be at school and perform my trained-monkey-high-schooler duties: showing up on time, paying attention or pretending to, and somehow not checking out before it's all over. Just because I'm not going straight to college doesn't mean I want crappy grades for my last semester of high school.

But, something's got to go, and I'm afraid it will be government and chem, aka the latter half of my day of learning.

In English while we're supposed to be writing, I make a checklist, try to break it down to one thing at a time. Dylan, who sits two seats ahead and one row over from me, casts a look back every now and then, and I can tell that *he* can tell that whatever I'm writing in my notebook, it ain't an essay about William Faulkner.

Call Annalee.
Call Mom.
Buy presents.
Figure out how to get Mandy to C.B. without telling
her what's going on.
Invite Ravi to C.B.

I tap my pen on the Ravi sentence. *Tappity-tap.* I cross it out. I write it again. I tap. Dylan looks back at me, and Mrs. Espinoza also gives me the eye.

I want Ravi to be there. For Mandy. She likes him, and

it will even out the boy-girl thing and make her feel good. Don't tell me that even at eight months pregnant, you don't want to enjoy a little social interaction with a boy. Also, I don't want him to be there. The situation is full of all kinds of potential awkwardness. But...man. I just want to *see* him. Like, I can't go a whole day without seeing him. It's bad.

When the bell rings, I tell Dylan to meet me in the school parking lot at lunchtime – we have to go shopping. "That's okay for me," he says. "I don't have any unexcused absences yet this semester. But you're kind of on your last leg with that, right?"

"Oh no, now I won't get into Yale."

He starts to say something, then shuts it down. I take off to the bathroom to make my phone calls. Annalee answers her cell phone. The sound of her voice in real time instead of her voicemail makes me wince. After a bunch of excuses and a lot of hard-core negotiation that results in me being scheduled for the next five Friday nights, I get the night off work.

Mom doesn't answer her phone at first but calls me back while I'm leaving her a message. "What, honey? Everything okay?"

She's in a big rush, that's clear, maybe even in a meeting. Her in a rush and me sitting in a bathroom stall do not add up to the right time to tell her about Mandy's surprise party, which, with everything else that went on yesterday, slipped my mind. But I tell her, and she says, "Tonight?"

"Yeah, tonight. It's her birthday."

"It is? How did I not know that? A party, Jill, that's... thoughtful. But I have a neighbourhood meeting tonight to present the feasibility study. The one I've been working on for the last six months? I may have mentioned it *once or twice*."

Crap. "Oh yeah."

"And by the way, explain to me why you want to go to *Casa Bonita* anyway?"

Mom doesn't appreciate the awesome badness of Casa Bonita. "I think Mandy will love it. So I'm sorry I forgot to tell you, okay? And don't tell her – it's a surprise."

"Fine, fine. Have fun. Take pictures. I want to see this."

The break between lessons is well over, and I'm alone in the bathroom. If I'm going to invite Ravi, it's now or never. I scroll through my phone in order to simply reread one of his text messages and accidentally brush the touch screen where it says CALL RAVI DESAI. The universe has made my decision for me.

"Hey, Jill." He sounds subdued.

"Are you okay?"

"Yeah. What's up?"

"I wanted to see if...I mean, I wanted to tell you thanks for yesterday."

He's quiet.

"That was good for me," I say. "To go there."

"Good."

I wait for him to say more. I stare at the bathroom door, freshly scrubbed of graffiti. "Also, we – I'm throwing this little surprise birthday/baby shower thing for Mandy tonight. I thought maybe you could come. As Clark."

"A baby shower? Isn't that a girl thing?"

"More her birthday, but the presents will be baby stuff. At Casa Bonita."

He pauses. "Who all is going to be there?"

Someone comes into the bathroom. Through the space around the stall door, I can see whoever it is looking at herself in the mirror. "Me. Mandy. Dylan. Maybe some other people."

"I don't know."

"You can bring a date," I say in a rush, with too much enthusiasm. "You can bring Annalee!" Digging my fist into my thigh keeps me from punching myself at how absurd it is to say that. As if I don't know Annalee can't take off work tonight because I'm going to. As if I don't know she's mad at him or they're broken up or whatever.

"Not likely."

The person in the bathroom is waiting for me to leave, I can tell. "Really, I just thought Mandy would enjoy it."

"I guess I don't see the point, Jill."

No, no, I think. We were doing good. We were talking openly. We were figuring it out.

On the other hand, he's right. It's a bad idea, and there is no point except my selfish desire to see him again, which isn't fair to him and not fair to Dylan and not fair to me, really, since I'm so mixed up anyway. Which makes me angry at myself. Usually when I'm angry at myself, I take it out on people who mean something to me. This time I try to be different.

"Ravi, it would mean a lot to me if you were there, but I totally understand if you can't or don't want to. Casa Bonita. Six thirty."

After a few seconds, he says, "Let me think about it."

"Okay."

My angry-at-self-plus-confusion mood is still evident when Dylan finds me in the school lot, waiting in my car, with what I'd guess – based on how it feels on my face – is a pissed-off expression. "I'd ask what's wrong," he says, getting into my car, "but I'm scared, in case it has something to do with me."

"Not everything is about you."

He laughs. "I *know*. Lately not anything is about me."

I resist the urge to drive over the speed bumps as fast as possible. "Meaning?"

"Nothing, Jill."

Not just *nothing*. *Nothing, Jill*. And in this context, in this tone, you can pretty much substitute *bitch* for *Jill*.

In an attempt at redemption, I ask with all sincerity if The Potato Rebellion is coming to the party.

"Nope."

"You could go to Casa B early and get us a good table. Up near the divers. Then I could bring Mandy, and I'll just tell her we're going on an errand or to a drive-through or something like that. Then—"

"Jill," Dylan says, "I forgot I promised my dad I'd help him change the brake pads on his car when he gets home from work. It shouldn't take long, but I don't think I can get there early for the table."

We're at a red light. I throw my head back and let out a huge sigh-slash-growl. "Seriously?"

He speaks slowly, as if to a toddler throwing a tantrum. "*You* go early and get the table. *I'll* pick up Mandy. It will *all* work out. Okay?"

It's an effective approach. "Actually, that's a good idea. You guys kind of bonded; she'll go anywhere with you.

You can make something up."

We work out the details of the plan on our way to Cherry Creek, where as soon as we see the tiny, adorable baby clothes, we're overcome with the cuteness of it all and it's like we were never fighting. We pick up some practical things, like blankets and bottles, but my mom can worry about most of that stuff. We're clothes-crazy.

"I want a baby," Dylan says, holding up a miniature knit cap with a turtle on it.

"Don't look at me."

We wind up dropping nearly two hundred dollars between us, requiring more than one trip to the ATM. Afterwards we stop for lemonades and look at all of our purchases again.

"Do you think you'll ever be a mom?" he asks, holding a lamb beanbag toy and touching its little ears.

"I can't picture it."

"Really? I can totally see myself being a dad. And I want to be a young dad, you know? So that when the kids are in high school, I could still potentially be a little bit awesome."

"Kids?" I ask. "How many are you thinking?"

"Three?"

Our eyes meet. I love Dylan. He loves me. We're each other's first. But we're not going to be together for ever. We've both known it, I'm sure. He's going to college right after graduation; I'm not. He wants a bunch of kids, apparently; I don't. It's not like we've ever talked about for ever. But we've also not made a habit sitting around talking about our future adult selves in a way that makes it this obvious we'll be on different paths. And letting go of Dylan means letting go of another piece of my life as it was when I still had my dad.

I'm the first to break our gaze, stabbing at my crushed ice with my straw. "It makes me sad," I say to my cup. "To think about it."

"Me being a dad?"

"Ha-ha. No. You'll be great. That's not what I meant."

He places the lamb on the table between us, its beanbaggy legs splayed.

"Yeah, I know. You know what else is sad?"

"What?"

"It just kind of occurred to me that we're giving this stuff to Mandy for her birthday, but she's not really going to be around to see the baby wear it or use it or whatever."

I pick up the lamb, hold it to my face, feel like I could cry. Because, holy hell. That *is* sad.

Mandy

In the afternoon, while Robin is gone – to the copy shop for her presentation things, to clients' offices, getting her hair trimmed – I spend some time in every room in the house: lying for a while on Robin's bed, then on Jill's. Sitting at the big kitchen table, where I've had my breakfast with Robin almost every morning for the last month. Touching the metal napkin rings that are cut-outs of moose or elk or some animal like that. Standing in her office with my hand on the back of her desk chair. Looking at the pictures from the ultrasound that first day at Dr. Yee's. Studying the baby's face. Who will she be? Whose will she be?

In each room I wait for a feeling of certainty that will tell me what I should do. Maybe this is panic. Maybe every woman who is planning to give up her baby feels exactly this way, but I don't know about every woman, I only know about me, and what I feel is that I need to think. For the longest time I sit in Jill's father's chair. Sometimes when I think about Mac and the stories I've heard about him, I'm jealous of Jill. Why do some people get a father like that and some get what I got? It might be better to have a dead father like Mac than an alive one who doesn't want to know you. As for my baby's father, I don't know. The ghost, the shadow of Mac that's left here would be a better father than Kent. But if it's Christopher...

The phone rings. I let the machine get it, scared I might hear my mother's voice.

"Mandy? Hey, Mandy, pick up if you can hear this. It's Dylan."

Dylan. There's another person Jill has and doesn't appreciate like she should. "Maybe you're taking a nap or something. Crap. I hope you get this in time! Why don't you have a phone? Everyone has a phone. Homeless people have phones. Okay, the deal is I'm going to pick you up at six tonight, and I can't tell you anything else. I do promise it'll be the most fun you've had since you got here. Maybe the most fun you've—" The machine beeps, cutting him off.

A few seconds later the phone rings again, and again I don't answer. I don't think I'm strong enough to talk to someone as nice as Dylan right now. "As I was saying, six o'clock. Just wear whatever's comfortable."

The machine robot voice says the time. Four fifty-eight

p.m.; later than I realized. I don't know if I can do what I need to do before six. Not that I have that much stuff, but I'm slow now, and I haven't figured out how I'm getting to the pawnshop and then the train station, or even if I'm taking the train or maybe the bus, or where I'm going. East. West.

I get up to make and wrap some peanut butter sandwiches and take them to my room to pack. I put my vitamins in a bag, too, and fill a plastic bottle with water. Everything needs to fit in my duffel, and it can't be too heavy. I remember my trip here, dragging my bag in the snow, no one offering to help. And here I go again, alone. I rearrange everything to be more compact and have to leave behind a few of the heavier sweaters that Robin bought me. Of all the things that could make me cry, that's what gets to me.

I sit on the edge of the bed. My whole body is pain: my feet, my back, my rear, even my fingers, which are puffy and tight-feeling. All I want to do is rest a little bit. It will be a good chance to go through the plan in my head, anyway, so I lie back and stretch out. This will be the last time I sleep on a bed this comfortable. The final time these hopeful orange walls are the last thing I see before closing my eyes.

* * *

"Mandy?" There's a hand on my shoulder. I open my eyes. Dylan.

"Hi," I say, groggy.

"Hey."

I sit up and Dylan stares down at me and I finally wake up, realizing what he's seeing: me, and all of my things laid out on the bed beside me – the duffel with my clothes in it, the sandwiches and the water, my coat and the scarf Robin bought me that day at the mall. My Bible.

"Um," Dylan says, and he sounds worried. "Are you going somewhere?"

He's my friend. He hugged me. He understands about my mother. "I have to leave," I tell him.

"No no no!" He puts out his hands, his voice getting higher with every "no". "You don't have to leave. No leaving. I know Jill can be a bitch, but if she's been acting weird the last day or two, it's only because—"

"It's not Jill." To help Dylan understand, I make it about the father. Dylan's the one who said that if it were his baby, he couldn't let it go so easy. "I need to talk to the baby's father."

"Can't you just call him?" He starts to take clothes out of my duffel and put them into the dresser drawers.

I sit up and go to the drawers. "Imagine it's your baby. I have to try to find him, one more time." I move the clothes back to the bag. He watches me, and I can tell from how conflicted he looks that he believes me.

"You can. Tell Robin. She'll understand; you know she will. She'd even go with you." He looks at the clock on the dresser. It's ten after six. "You can't leave, Mandy. You can't."

"You're my friend, Dylan. You can help me."

He clutches the sides of his head. The more excited he gets, the calmer I feel. "No, I can't. I mean, I can help you *stay*. Talk to Robin. I'm telling you. You want me to do it for you?"

How can I explain to Dylan what I don't understand? It's motherhood, it's fathers, it's fear, it's the known and the unknown. It's biology, an instinct that tells me to go, go. "I'm coming back," is all I can say just so that he won't worry so much.

"If you're coming back, then why are you taking everything?"

"I'm not." I open the drawer and show him the sweaters that are too bulky to take with me.

He glances around the room, worried, as if someone might come out of the closet and catch us. "Mandy, I totally agree that you should find the baby's father and talk to him. As a dude, I am for that. It's only right. But don't run away."

We stare at each other. Dylan's a good person; he's

trying to decide what's more right out of two things that don't feel right. I turn and zip my bag.

"I'll make you a deal," he says, pulling the bag towards him. "Come with me now. Bring your stuff. This was supposed to be a surprise...Jill is throwing you a little birthday party at this crazy restaurant she thinks – we think – you'll love. Don't tell her I told you. Come with me, please." He takes a deep breath and holds it. "Afterwards, I'll take you wherever you want to go."

A birthday party? "It was Jill's idea?"

"Yeah. You gotta eat anyway, right?"

The train east leaves around eight. The train west doesn't leave until the morning. The buses, I don't know. Dylan is holding up my coat now. I put my arms into the sleeves. "Is Robin going to be there?" I wouldn't be able to face her.

"No. She has her meeting." He pulls the coat around me as far as it will go and keeps hold of the lapels. We're standing so close, I can smell the cinnamon gum on his breath. "I'll help you, Mandy. I promise."

It's hard to think clearly so soon after a nap. Dylan's hands on my coat make me feel safe.

"Well, I am hungry."

Jill

Any trip to Casa Bonita is in itself weird, but it's extra awkward to be sitting at a dimly lit Casa Bonita table with Ravi. We've been waiting for Dylan and Mandy long enough for that awkwardness to build in scope and intensity. Our food, which we picked up on our way in, because that's how it works in a fine establishment such as this, is getting cold. But we do have a prime table, thanks to me getting here crazy early and begging the host. I never went home this afternoon for fear that I'd start acting weird around Mandy and spill the beans. When Ravi showed up, looking so nice in his glasses and sweater, I had to resist literally jumping up and down.

He sips his virgin margarita and looks everywhere but at me. "Wow, this place is..."

"I can't believe you've lived in Denver your whole life and never been here."

"Gross parental neglect. Clearly."

I check my phone again for a reply to one of the three texts I've sent Dylan to ask what's taking so long. Half-naked cliff divers run past us to climb the fake rocks that are built into a fake cliff in the cavernous restaurant. Mariachi music plays loudly. It's all very festive – or it *would* be, under different circumstances.

"We should eat," I say. "The food is bad enough when it's hot." As I cut into my enchilada, bright orange cheese oozes out. "Thanks again for coming."

He nods grimly but says nothing and takes a cautious bite of his rice.

"Remember that you're Clark."

"I know."

Cemetery Ravi is long gone; I try to reel him back from the deep sea where I've allowed him to drift by being stupid. When we first met, there was no reason to tell him about Dylan. Dylan wasn't even talking to me then. It all snuck up on me.

Nerves make me all chatty, in hopes I can make Ravi more comfortable.

"So you know that conversation we had about college and stuff?" I ask. "I was wondering if you were planning to stay in Denver longer, keep working for Margins, or what?"

"I don't know. It's a pretty good job. Part of me still wishes I could make my parents happy, achieve the American dream, make all their hard work and sacrifice worthwhile."

"See, that's the problem with doing stuff to make other people happy. If they really love you, and you wind up miserable, how can they be happy? Me going to college would make my mom happy, but my life can't be about that." I run our little Mexican flag up its pole to try to get some chips. "The American dream is kind of stupid, anyway. Slave ninety per cent of your life so that you can spend the last ten per cent of it doing nothing?"

"I wouldn't say it's stupid, but—"

"And there's no guarantee you even make it far enough to enjoy the fruits of your labour."

"True. I just think there *is* some value in—"

"Look at the state of the world. At this rate it's all going to implode any second, anyway, and you could...*die* unexpectedly. So you should do what makes you happy."

He takes a big bite of food.

"Right?" I ask. Then I spot Mandy's blonde hair, fluffy once more, coming our way. "Finally." And here is where my enchilada threatens to come back up, and not just because it's kind of cold and gross but because Ravi and Dylan are about to meet. Why did I ever think this was a remotely good idea? I wave at Mandy. If I stay focused on her and the baby, we'll get through it.

Dylan, trailing behind her, doesn't look very happy, considering how excited he was about this idea initially. I opt not to make a scene about them being late. I don't give Dylan a hug or a kiss. I introduce him to "Clark". I explain to Mandy how the flag works. I point to the little stack of presents at the side of the table and say, "Surprise! Happy... birthday!"

She smiles, just barely, not looking all that surprised. "Thank you," she says. "You didn't have to." It's maybe the most forlorn and sincere I've ever seen her. She seems sad and far away, and she keeps her hand on her belly like it's a security blanket. I have this impulse to hug her and tell her everything is going to be okay, that by this time tomorrow the watch will be out of our lives, and between me and her and Mom we'll figure everything out.

It's not the time.

Dinner is nice enough, for what it is. We get a good view of the cliff divers and of the floor show, which involves a guy in a gorilla suit. What it has to do with Mexico, I cannot say. Dylan eats his weight in sopaipillas but doesn't seem quite all here. He's distracted and anxious-looking, and I worry that Ravi will think he's rude, or that Dylan thinks Ravi is rude. Ravi is acting weird, too, and I don't blame him. Considering how into him Mandy was when they first met, she's barely talking to him or to any of us. He tries to start a few little conversations with Mandy; the music is loud, and Mandy is out of it, so he gives up.

And then when Mandy opens her presents...well, I don't know what I expected. Some excitement? Or emotion? When she holds up the little onesie with ducks on it, her face is a sheet of ice. Dylan shifts in his seat. "I picked that one out," he says, sounding incredibly uncomfortable.

"Oh."

I'm an idiot. I should have made the time to get a couple of things just for her – non-maternity T-shirts, her very own straighteners – and wrapped them up quickly to mix in with the other stuff. Or in place of the other stuff. I should have thrown a baby shower for my *mom*, not for Mandy. It's so obvious now, way too late.

Ravi excuses himself and asks me to point him towards the restrooms.

"I'll show you," I say. "I have to go, too." Which is a lie.

We weave our way through the tables, dodging a pair of cliff divers, moving to let an escaped toddler by, and narrowly avoiding collision with a sopaipilla-bearing waitress. When we get out of the main dining area, I admit to Ravi that I'm lost and I think the bathrooms are on the other side of the indoor lake.

He turns and says abruptly, "I think I'm going to head home."

I knew this wasn't going well, but I don't want him to leave. "I wish—"

"I just—" Ravi turns away from me, gazing off at the waterfall. "Jill, you really..."

I know what this is. I do know. I've been pretending I don't, but I do. I know why I said those things to him at the coffee shop when he brought up Annalee. I know why I haven't felt right lately being back together with Dylan. I know.

Ravi stares at me now, with his kind brown eyes behind glasses, and shakes his head slightly, then starts walking away. I follow.

"That's not the exit." He's totally not listening. "You're going to wind up in the caves." I follow him into the caves, little kids running by us, salsa music pounding. It's dark. He's walking fast, towards an area that's partially blocked by a sign: PLEASE ACCEPT OUR APOLOGIES. THIS AREA IS CLOSED. "Ravi...wait." I feel silly, ridiculous, chasing him through this dim, fake world, when he clearly wants to get away from me. "Holy shit, Ravi, why can't you—"

He turns and in one movement pulls me towards him by my arm. Not hard. But certain. We squish against the wall to hide from the Casa Bonita authorities.

"Ravi, what—"

"Maybe you could stop talking for a second."

I do. He's looking at me in this way that makes my breath rapid and shallow. His hand is still around my forearm, firm enough that it would be hard to get away. In a different kind of a situation, I would pull another self-defence move. I would twist my wrist and jerk it towards myself at the weak part of his grip, where his thumb and fingers meet. Then I'd put my hand on his face and push his neck around, using leverage to throw him off balance and put him on the ground, leaving him to be trampled by small children hopped up on soda and fried ice cream.

I don't do any of that.

"I'm not with Annalee. I never really was," he says, and waits.

Oh, I think.

"It's hard for me to see you with your boyfriend," he says, and waits some more.

My vision blurs; my heart races.

"Aren't you going to say anything?" he asks.

"You asked me not to talk."

He pulls my forearm against his chest. He puts his other arm around my waist. Bends his knees to get closer to my height. I stand on my toes to get closer to his. It happens.

Lips, tongues, hands.

352

Joy. Revival.

Oh.

I reach to take off his glasses without stopping what we're doing.

There are giggles. A couple of junior high girls have stumbled upon our little scene here. "What are you looking at?" I ask over my shoulder.

Ravi pulls away. The girls leave. "I think I'm going to head home."

No. No. "Yeah, you said that before."

"Now you know why."

"Why'd you even come tonight?"

"Morbid curiosity? To see what I'm up against? Because you asked? Definitely *not* because I thought this would be the perfect place to make a smooth move."

Even though what I would like to do is scream "Fire!" so that everyone gets out of the restaurant and Ravi and I can stay in this cave for hours, reason prevails. "Come say goodbye to Mandy. Otherwise it will seem weird. Please?"

"Jill," he says in disbelief. "The things I do for you."

"Thank you."

"Act normal."

We travel back through the cave – the memory of Ravi's hand still on my arm – past the lake, among the patrons, and find our table...empty. A waiter is clearing the plates.

The presents are gone.

"A guy and a girl were here," I tell the waiter. "A guy with eyeliner and a really pregnant girl. Did you see them?"

He doesn't look up. "They left."

Mandy

Dylan is keeping his promise. I wasn't sure he would. When we drove to the restaurant, we passed several pawnshops and I wanted to stop then, not wait. This is a time for seizing moments, because you don't know if you're going to get another one. But he was so worried about how Jill was expecting us and didn't want to be later than we already were. I thought maybe it was a trick. That when we got there, he'd tell on me to Jill and she'd call Robin and they'd keep me locked up until it was time for the baby to come. Then they'd abandon me at the hospital.

But he didn't do that. When Jill and Clark went to the bathroom, he looked at me and said, "We'd better go now."

He put all the presents into a bag, and we got our coats and left. Dylan said he'll keep the presents for me until I come back and get them. I took the duck outfit and the turtle hat and made them fit into my bag, in case I don't end up coming back.

Now we're driving in the part of town where most of the pawnshops are; Dylan keeps not stopping. He'll slow down at one, or even stop for a few seconds, and then something makes him change his mind and he keeps driving.

"We need to pick one and stop," I say. "I still need time to buy my ticket and get the train." Or the bus, or whatever I'm going to do. Dylan shouldn't know too many details. Even though he's keeping his promise now, it's better to leave him partly in the dark.

At the next shop there's a police car out front with its lights flashing. "Nope," Dylan says.

"Here," I say, pointing to another coming up on our right.

He pulls into one of the four spaces in the small lot out front, and we look into the store.

"Do you even know how this works?" he asks, the engine still idling. His cell phone rings; he ignores it.

"No."

"Me neither." He glances at me and laughs a small laugh. "I'm sorry. I guess I'm scared."

"We have to just do it. They'll tell us what to do." I start to take off my seat belt, and a man comes out of the store and lights a cigarette, the whole time staring a hard stare into the car. He takes a step towards us, gesturing to Dylan to roll down his window.

"Nope," Dylan says again, and backs out into the street faster than is really safe, and the tyres squeal a little. "Sorry," he repeats.

I should have done this on my own. People like Dylan and Jill and Robin – they might have had some bad things happen to them, and they might have pierced eyebrows and lips, and Jill might act tough, but when it gets down to situations like this, they don't know how to be truly strong. You have to dig down and find some part of you that doesn't care what people think, doesn't care if it's hard, doesn't care if it hurts, doesn't care if you have to momentarily experience humiliation, uncertainty, fear. I know.

"Tell you what," Dylan says. "I'll stop at an ATM and give you what you need for the ticket and as much extra as I can take out." His cell phone rings again. We know it's Jill.

"It won't be enough." All of my chances to sell the watch whip by in a blur of lights.

"It'll be something."

We stop at a bank drive-through. He gets money and gives it to me with an expression on his face that tells me he wishes he'd done better.

"Thanks."

By the time we get to the station, it's past eight. The train going east, the one that would take me back to Omaha, will have already left if it was on time. Still, I don't rush Dylan or say anything when he takes too much time finding a place to park. Staying calm is an important part of survival and getting from one moment to the next. He helps me in with my bags, watches them while I go to the bathroom. After I pee and wash my hands, I look in the mirror and take deep breaths. I could walk out into the station and tell Dylan to take me back to Robin's. Nothing has changed yet. Nothing has been ruined. There's still a window of hope for me here if I'm willing: go back. Figure out with Robin what we'll do after I give birth. Trust.

Trust. That's the part that makes my willingness stumble. Everything in me says I can trust Robin. But sometimes trust isn't something you can just choose to do even if it makes sense. All my life the only reliable person, the one I could count on, the one who hasn't abandoned me, is me. What I can't figure out is what staying means and what leaving means.

If I stay, it means I'm willing to abandon my daughter. If I leave, I think maybe I'm abandoning myself. And that's one thing that, through all of this, I've never done.

When I come out of the bathroom, I go to the ticket window and talk to a woman there. The train going east is delayed.

"By how long?"

In a friendly voice she explains that the passenger train shares the track with freight trains, and if freight trains have troubles, everything else gets off schedule.

"I didn't ask why. I asked how long."

She frowns. "It's about an hour out right now. But all I can do is guess. Sometimes they make up time."

"What about the train to California?"

"Westbound is on schedule as of now. But after eastbound makes it out of here, we close the station until morning. You'll have to go home and then come back. A coach fare..."

I walk away while she's still talking. "It's a little behind schedule," I tell Dylan so that he'll keep believing that where I'm going is east, to look for the father.

"You want me to wait with you?"

"No, thank you." I'll have to think of somewhere to spend the night.

He puts his hands in his pockets. I sit on the wooden bench. I already feel like I have to pee again, but I just want Dylan to leave before anything happens to me. Emotionally, I mean.

"Good luck with everything," he says. "You have my number?"

I nod.

"Mandy..."

"What?"

"Sorry about how I didn't come through exactly."

"It's okay."

He sits on the bench next to me. His arm touches mine. "You're gonna come back, right?"

I look at him.

"I mean, once you talk to the father and all, you'll come back and have the baby like you planned."

And give her to Robin, he means. The answer is that I don't know.

"Yes," I tell him.

He exhales and gives me a sitting hug. "Okay. Call me if you need anything, any more money or anything."

I nod against his shoulder. He's a friend, even if he partly failed at his promise tonight. He's the only friend I have after right now, I think. I squeeze him tighter, as tight as I can with my belly between us, so that he knows I'm not really mad about him being scared of the pawnshops. Not everyone can be brave.

Jill

Mom is beside herself, a babbling wreck. She keeps asking me to explain how this happened, as if there could be an explanation, as if I personally have control over the actions of everyone in the world.

"How could you lose track of Mandy?" She's frozen to the couch, exactly where she first sat when she came home from her meeting and I told her Mandy and Dylan were sort of missing. She's still got her laptop bag half over her shoulder.

"I didn't lose her. She left." I'm not doing so great myself – furious with Dylan and at myself because what if it was the stupid baby stuff we bought her that put her over the edge? What was I thinking? And at Mandy. I thought we had a deal; I thought we were a team, and she lied to me after all. Maybe I was right about her in the first place. The only thing I feel calm about is Ravi. Well, relatively calm.

"Why won't Dylan answer his phone?" Mom asks.

"I don't know, Mom. I'm not Dylan."

We've tried calling his house, against my advice. I told her it was too soon, that we should wait a little longer, that maybe Mandy didn't feel well and they stopped at a drugstore for something to keep the enchiladas down.

I didn't really think that; they wouldn't have left without saying goodbye.

"He would have called, or answered," Mom said, and she was right. Now we've got his parents all upset, on top of everything else.

Mom wants us to go out looking. I tell her to remember what Dad always said: in case of an emergency, stay right where people would expect you to be. *Dad, Dad. Be here now.* I've never seen Mom like this. Eleven months ago this scene was reversed: it was the day of the accident, me a statue on the couch, her taking care of things and making calls and telling me it would be okay, it would be okay, and now I remember she brought me a glass of bourbon from Dad's stash. So now I get her some wine and make her watch the public television station instead of the news, just in case there are any horrifying car crashes around town or anything. Public TV is showing a special on the history of domestic cats. In between texting and calling Dylan, I refill her wine, make her talk about the cats. I take off her shoes and slip her bag off her shoulder and tuck a blanket around her.

"How could Mandy do this?" she asks me, forlorn.

"We don't know if she's done anything. As long as she's with Dylan, I think she's okay."

"Then why won't Dylan answer?"

It's a circular conversation that keeps winding up back here. I suggest that his phone could be dead or lost; it happens. Then she repeats, "How could Mandy do this?"

Finally, frustrated with not having an answer, I say, "She doesn't belong to us."

"She does, though." Mom runs her hand up and down the blanket. "Don't you think she does? That we all belong together?"

"I don't know."

"You were right. I should have gotten a lawyer."

Yes, I was right. But in this moment I don't want to be right. "Signing something wouldn't necessarily guarantee anything," I say. "People are free. Things happen, and you can't stop them, remember? And Mandy is..." Mandy is what? Crazy? Stupid? Those are words I would have used to describe her a month ago. But what would I do, in her shoes? How would it feel to carry a baby for this long only to give it away? "You know what Dylan said about her once?"

"What?"

"That she's the one who needs a mother." As I say that, an idea, a memory, shimmers for a fraction of a moment in the back of my mind, but it's gone before I can figure out what it is.

"That was astute of Dylan." Mom has a little trouble getting the word "astute" out, and I know the wine is working. "Even though she's eighteen...nineteen now... she's such a child. I'm scared for her to be out in the world on her own."

Mom's eyelids droop. "If I didn't think it would be too confusing for the baby, and for Mandy, I'd have let her stay with us. She has no idea the lengths I would go to for her. If she did, she wouldn't run away. I should have done a better job of this. I should have gotten a lawyer. You were right."

She goes on like that, repeating herself, repeating me. I top up her wine and put a pillow behind her head as she lies back. "I bet when you wake up, she'll be right there in her room, like always."

"Mmm."

Soon she's out.

Up in Mandy's room I check one more time for any clues as to what might be going on. The Bible is gone. Her new clothes are gone, her bag. My straighteners. I dig through her trash and find an envelope addressed to her and get all excited, thinking there will be answers. But the single sheet of paper inside simply says:

Please stop writing to me.
— Alex from the train

I go back down and sit in Dad's chair, watching Mom, watching the door. My phone, which I've got on vibrate, buzzes with a text and I scramble for it. It's Ravi.

Ravi. When we were leaving Casa Bonita, he asked if I wanted him to stay with me, if there was anything he could do, but I sent him home so I could focus on this situation. Now he wants to know if there's any new information. *No*, I text back. *Thx for checking.*

I go over and over the whole night in my head. Dylan and Mandy being so late, acting so strange. Could something be going on between them? No, that doesn't make any sense. Mandy is nuts and pregnant, and one thing I've never doubted is Dylan's faithfulness to me, even when I've been less than faithful to him.

My phone buzzes again. This time it's Dylan.

He's outside my house in his car, and can I come out? I bolt for the door, grabbing my keys and my coat. It's freezing outside; I run out to his idling car and jump into the passenger seat. "Where is she?"

Dylan looks terrified. "I took her to the train station."

I don't even blink before saying, "Take me. Right now."

"Jill...you don't get it. Imagine if—"

I hold up my hand, concentrating on containing my fury. There isn't time to say everything I want to say. "I trusted you. I told my mom if Mandy was with you, we had nothing to worry about."

"Imagine you were a guy who got a girl pregnant. Wouldn't you have the right to know?" He's impassioned. "Wouldn't you want to have some *say* in what happened to your baby?"

I open the car door. I'm not here to debate parental rights. I just have to get Mandy back so that my mom isn't shattered all over again. "If you won't take me, I'll go myself."

"She's coming back," he says with less confidence. "She said she would. She—"

The rest of his words are muffled and then lost as I slam the door and walk to my own car to start scraping ice off the windshield. I hear him get out and follow. "Are you listening to me? No, of course not, because you never listen to anyone."

"Why would I listen to bullshit, Dylan?" My fingers sting with the cold.

"Not everything is bullshit!" He's loud enough now that

if my mom weren't stone-cold out, I'd worry he'd wake her. I move to the rear windshield, Dylan staying close. In an only slightly quieter voice, he says, "Ever since your dad died, you—"

"Don't, Dylan. Don't 'ever since your dad died' me." The ice scraper falls from my numb hands. I pick it up. "I haven't changed. I've always been this way."

"No, you haven't."

"Okay, well, I don't remember that Jill." I hold my hands to my face to warm them up, to press back tears. "I don't remember. I'm sorry. And I can't *be* her now, and I'm never going to be her again," I say, my voice rising. I realize it, finally. This elusive old Jill I've been chasing isn't someone who can be found. Short of my father coming back from the dead, it's not happening. Which doesn't mean I can't change, just that I can't change *back*.

I recognize hysteria coming when I see it; I can't afford it right now. My hands drop, and I take deep breaths of the lung-burning air. "If I could, I would...and I wish...I'm sorry."

Dylan is miserable, staring at the ground. "This sucks."

I open the driver's-side door, throw the scraper into the car. "Was she trying to sell a watch?" I ask.

He pulls his head back, a little surprised. "Yeah."

"Did she?"

"No. I...I chickened out. I thought we were going to get

stabbed outside a pawnshop or something. I gave her some of my own money instead."

At least there's that. "Go home," I say. "Your parents are having a shit fit."

Mandy's sitting on one of the high-backed wooden benches, looking ten times as lost and helpless as she did the day she got here, even though her clothes are better now, and at least this time she's got on a decently warm coat. At the sight of her, tears spring to my eyes. Tears of relief, I guess. Such incredible relief. Also, I feel something for her. Something like pity but more like affection, more like compassion. Because imagine. Having a mother like that, being pregnant, having the balls to leave home and go through with it all. And I wonder where she's planning to go now, trying for another fresh start. As mad as I am at how close she's come to getting away, there's something admirable about how she can take care of herself, be this strong.

I sort of want to let her go. I still think my mom is bonkers for wanting to take on a baby at this point in life. And if the baby has half Mandy's kooky genes, it's going to be interesting. I also know my mom would give that baby a great life and love her even when she's an ungrateful, bitchy teenager like me, love her more than she deserves. Not that Mandy couldn't love her, too, and I'm not saying money necessarily makes a life better, but they had a deal. Does it matter that it might not hold up in a court of law?

"Mandy," I call, breathless, from where I am, maybe three metres away.

She turns her head and stands up. "Hi, Jill." And she waves, as if we're just running into each other at school or something. I'll never get this girl.

I take a few steps towards her. "Where are you going?"

"I was just deciding."

Someone at the ticket counter shouts into the station that it's closing in five minutes.

"Did you miss the train?"

"One of them."

My breathing slows.

Her bags are at her feet. She's got something in her fist. "Is that the watch?" I ask, coming closer.

Mandy lifts her hand, opens it. "Dylan was going to help me pawn it."

"He's not that tough. He won't even go into a 7-Eleven if there's a homeless person out front."

I get close enough to touch the watch in her open hand. "We're mailing this back to your mom."

"No," she says with more emotion than I've ever heard

her use about anything. She closes her fist back around the watch, puts it in her pocket.

"Mandy, I don't know what kind of crazy family you come from, but after five seconds of listening to your mom, I know it's scary, and I know why you wanted to get away. The last thing we want is this dude Kent coming around here causing all kinds of trouble." At "Kent" she flinches. "We send the watch back, and it's over. And then whatever you decide, at least you decide it with a clean slate."

"He owes it to me."

I don't know what to say to that, what it means, exactly.

"It's all I have." There are tears in her eyes, and fear.

God. I can't imagine feeling that way. That all I have in life is a stupid object belonging to some guy who is obviously someone to be terrified of. And I think about all I have, and all I've rejected. The support, the friendship, the comfort that I've refused from people who actually love me.

"That's not true," I say.

She stares, expecting more.

"I know how I was to you when you first came here," I continue. "I was in a bad place. I wasn't on board with this whole thing, I admit it. I thought it was a terrible idea; I wanted to protect my mom. But I sort of get it now."

"You do?" She smiles a little bit, her eerie eyes boring into mine. "Because I don't. I don't know what I'm doing."

I swallow. "Well, I don't know what you're doing. Or what I'm doing. But I think I know what we want."

The station agent comes over to us. "Ladies, we're closing up. If you need information about a shelter..."

"We're fine. Thanks." I pick up Mandy's big bag.

She stares and stares. Waiting. "What do we want?"

What do we want?

"Something different from what we have now." I want what I felt when Ravi kissed me, not because of the romance of it but because of how I feel about me when I'm with him. I get a feeling of possibility and, more than that, a glimpse of myself as someone who would be *open* to possibility.

I want to start again. Not necessarily in a relationship but for myself. I want to start again with me, as the me I've become without Dad here. Good and bad and all of it.

Mandy picks up her other bag. "I don't know what to do."

"There's this coffee shop. Mom and I went there the morning we came to pick you up. We could—"

Before I even finish talking, she says, "Okay."

Mandy

I wake up surrounded by the hopeful orange walls. Despite wanting to believe this is real, again I think it could be the last time, because I still haven't faced Robin and she could hate me now. I could be repacking everything within a few hours.

When Jill and I got back home last night, Robin was asleep on the sofa, and Jill put her finger on her lips and we crept up the stairs. Jill helped me unpack. We put the new maternity clothes back in the drawers, put my Bible back on the nightstand. I gave Jill the watch because I didn't trust myself not to get scared again, and I also gave her the address for where to send it.

"I'll take care of it," she said.

We were too tired to talk for very long at the coffee shop. Instead of discussing what to do with my future, Jill talked about the past. She told me how it was the morning

I arrived. How she'd fought with Robin about me. How she was mad about Pancake Universe. How she was sure I was only here for money or something. It made me feel bad at first, but then I could see that her point was she'd changed her mind.

"I get why you ran," she said.

She thinks she gets it. She doesn't know all the reasons.

"But I'm still mad at Dylan," she added. "I can't believe he gave you money. I can't believe he didn't bring you right home."

I admit I didn't listen to or remember every single thing she said about it. I was tired. What I remember is that I asked, "Can I still be friends with him?"

She didn't expect me to ask that, I could tell. First she said, "But you're not really friends..." Then she stopped. Then she started again. "I mean, you've only really talked to him once or twice."

I stared at her.

"And it's not like..." Then she looked at me, and down at her tea, and back up at me. "Yeah," she said. "You can. Not that you need my permission." She nodded, her eyes on the cafe wall behind me. "He's a good friend to have."

She said she was sorry she wouldn't be here this morning to help me talk to Robin but that she couldn't miss school again, and that I should let Robin lead the conversation because maybe she had enough wine that she wouldn't remember I was missing for a few hours. I told Jill that I'd had lots of experience with people drinking too much and that you'd be surprised what they remember.

Jill comes into my bedroom now, all dressed for school in her usual dark, drab colours and too much eyeliner. "Hey," she says, sitting on the bed. "Mom is still on the sofa. When she gets up, remind her to drink lots of water and eat a good breakfast."

"Tomato juice with hot sauce."

She smiles. "Right. You know about these things, I forgot."

"Not because of me," I tell her. "I've never even tasted alcohol. But I know from my mom and Kent."

"If you have any other secret cures, let her know. She's going to be feeling profoundly shitty. She hardly ever drinks." Jill shifts her backpack to her other shoulder. "Well, good luck today."

"Wait..." I wiggle and scoot across the bed so I can reach the nightstand. I take a folded-up piece of paper out of my Bible. "Put this in with the watch. Don't read it."

She comes closer, takes it. "I won't."

Of course, Robin remembers everything. A little bit too much wine isn't the same as a bottle of whiskey.

"We're going to have a long talk," she calls to me in a croaky voice from the couch when she hears me in the kitchen. "As soon as I can think."

Jill was right about one thing: Robin is very sick. She throws up three times in the first couple of hours after waking up. I offer her all different things to eat, but everything in the house is so healthy. "What you need is a doughnut," I tell her, standing in the downstairs bathroom doorway. She's on her knees in front of the toilet, elbows on the seat, resting her head in her hands as it hangs over the bowl. "Alcohol makes your blood sugar go low, and you need to get it back up."

"I can do that with fruit," she mumbles.

"It's not the same."

She spools a few squares of toilet paper onto her hand and wipes her eyes and mouth. "Mandy, I'm sorry, but I don't feel like taking nutritional advice from you right now."

"Okay." I sit on the padded top of the clothes hamper. "I have a glass of water here if you need it."

"I'd really rather you leave me alone completely until I'm done throwing up and have had a shower and coffee." She retches again; nothing comes up. She moans a little and then crawls to the tub, sitting on the floor with her back against it. When she sees that I'm not going anywhere, she asks me, "Were you very sick during your first trimester?"

"Not really." I felt good. I acted normal. My mother had no idea. The only reason she knew is because I told her.

"When you got here that day on the train, I felt bad that I'd already missed so much of your pregnancy. I wish I could have been there for every moment, to support you and help you through it. I felt like a mother would feel with a pregnant daughter. I felt connected to *you*. I always have. It's—" She stops herself and stares at me the way a person does after just realizing something important. Maybe it's striking her that she does hate me now, how deeply I betrayed her, that she only wants me to leave. Her fingers go to that spot on her face she always touches when she's thinking.

"Here." I hold out the water. She takes it. "Small sips at first," I remind her. "How did your council meeting go last night?"

"The council meeting?" She laughs and leans her head against the shower door. "Fine. Brilliant. Everything went great until I got home and found out you'd run away."

I know I should say that I'm sorry. My hand automatically goes to my belly and starts circling. "I didn't run away. I'm here."

"What if Jill hadn't gone after you?"

What if questions are always hard for me to answer.

"Mandy?" Robin's voice is shaky now. "Were you really going to leave?"

"I don't know."

Robin closes her eyes and starts out soft, asking "Why?" and gets louder, "Why? Why?" until on the last "Why?" she sets the water glass down too hard, and it breaks against the tile. Her hands curl into fists and pound against her thighs. Her eyes are still closed. "Why?" I don't know whether she's even asking about me any more.

I get onto the floor, which isn't easy, and crawl over to pick up the glass before she accidentally cuts herself.

"I've done *everything* your way, even though I clearly know better than you do." Her voice seems extra loud here in the bathroom. She opens her eyes. "I've ignored – leave it, Mandy! – I've ignored everyone who has been telling me to be careful, to not trust you. Especially Jill, who warned me and warned me."

The big pieces of broken glass are in my hands; I was already mostly done cleaning up when she said to stop. I shuffle on my knees to the trash can and let them fall in with a *clink*. Still on my knees, I reach to take a hand towel off the rack, reach again to dampen it in the sink, then shuffle back to wipe up any small pieces of glass that might be there. We're next to each other now, and I lean my back on the tub, too.

"All of our e-mails, Mandy, everything we talked about... I thought we'd developed trust. A relationship. What could

I have done differently to keep you from running?"

It was at the doctor's office, I want to say, *when you were talking about not letting me hold the baby.* But I don't want to blame her right now, and maybe that's an excuse, and really it was only Dr. Yee saying those things. "Nothing."

She exhales a sigh. Her breath is sour; I turn my head away a little, but not so much she'd notice and feel bad. "The father," she says, "if that's what this is about – we'll find him. I'll do everything in my power. We'll hire someone if it helps, only promise we'll talk about it, do it together."

The father.

"Mandy? If we find him and get his explicit consent, would that make you feel better? I'm *trying* here," she pleads. "I'm racking my brain, I—"

"I don't know who the father is."

I said it. It's out.

Robin pauses. And then, "I'm confused. I thought you said there was only one person it could be?"

"There are two people it could be."

Robin draws her cardigan around her body, takes several deep breaths. "Mandy. You told me you couldn't find the father. That you tried. If it's someone else, someone you *could* find, don't you see that changes everything?"

"I know." I'm not trying to make her madder, but that's what I'm doing, and I understand it. I don't blame her.

I haven't told the whole truth about something important. Something I should have told her right at the beginning. But I didn't want her to see me that way, see that part of who I am, the part that feels ugly and ruined.

"I mean, do you think this other man would *want* the baby?"

"I don't think so."

"Okay," she says slowly. "Well, we could have a paternity test done. Of course, we'd have to get a sample, and it might take...anyway, we can get it all cleared up somehow. It might take some time, and meanwhile you can stay here. The point is there's a solution."

"No."

"Mandy, you say no to everything!" She scoots away from me, still against the tub but just out of arm's reach, like she wants to get away. "You have to start saying yes to something. Anything. Say yes. Tell me what you *want*."

It's easier to say what I don't want than what I want, since I'm not sure what I want. "One of the people...the one I sort of tried to find, if we could find him, I wouldn't want him to think it could be anyone's but his. The other person. I wouldn't want him anywhere near her."

"Yes, Mandy," she says, still frustrated, not really listening. "I'm sure it's complicated. It won't be easy. But it's the right thing to do."

I look at her beautiful profile. Profile because she won't look at me right now. *Trust, Mandy. If there's anyone in the world you can trust, any place in the world you're safe, it's here in this bathroom, with Robin.*

"One of them," I say, "is my mother's boyfriend. Was."

This stops her frustrated momentum. She's waiting for me to say more.

"We..." This hurts my throat. "He..."

I know what the word is. I say it in my head all the time. And I argue with it, and feel wrong, and feel right, and wonder what it means and doesn't mean, about him, about me.

"He..." I need to say it. "He abused me. Sex."

I could never say that to my mother because she wouldn't believe me. She'd find a way to make it my fault.

"All the time, he abused me," I continue.

My mother would say, *All the time? Amanda, maybe once you can call it that, but if you let it happen again, it's something else.*

"So you can see if it's his, I don't want him to know."

Robin finally looks at me. Looks and looks and looks, eyes searching mine. Am I telling the truth, she's wondering. I meet her eyes. Yes. She scoots back over towards me, sour-smelling and sweaty, and puts her hand on my leg. "Mandy."

"I'm sorry if you don't want a baby that was made like that."

"I don't care how it was made," she says softly.

"I do." And this is where I start crying. Even though all those baby books tell you how emotional you get and you'll probably cry all the time for nothing, this is the first time since leaving Council Bluffs that it happens for real. Maybe it's wrong that I said it, but I *do* care. I don't want this to be a baby from fear and sadness. I want this to be a baby from cornfields and Ferris wheels and stars.

Robin puts her other arm around me, and it's awkward here on the bathroom floor, me so big but her trying to envelop me anyway. "Of course you do. Of course you do." She presses my head to her shoulder and lets me cry.

"I'm sorry," I tell her after a long time.

She doesn't let go. "Either way, this little girl is innocent, and I'm going to love her with all of my heart." Her whisper is fierce. "I have no doubts."

When I'm not crying so hard any more, I say, "How can you know?"

She takes my head gently in her hands and pulls me back a little so she can look me in the eye. "Because I already know, Mandy." She taps one finger very softly against my cheek. "This little girl is innocent, too."

Jill

Because I've vowed to myself not to cut again for the rest of my high school life, and also because I'm avoiding Dylan with a zeal that puts my past avoidance behaviours to shame, I use lunchtime to ship the watch. I send it insured, for Saturday delivery. Of course I put Mandy's note in, too, and even though I said I wouldn't read it, I do. Let's face it: Mandy's judgment is the tiniest bit questionable. I just want to make sure she didn't say anything that's going to cause more problems. So, sitting in my car outside the shipping store, this is what I read:

Here is the watch.

I turned nineteen yesterday. Maybe you remembered my birthday. Sometimes you do.

What nineteen means is I've reached the age of majority. I bet you didn't even know that I know *what that is. It means I can do whatever I want, be whoever I want.*

So even if you cared enough to ever find me, you have no say over my life.

I belong to myself.

Amanda

PS: Everything you think about me is wrong.

I have to say, the letter sends a tingle up the back of my neck and to my scalp. I read it a few times. That Mandy. She might not be the smartest person ever to walk the earth, but she has a kind of power about her you have to admire. I hope her mother really is a horrible-enough person to care about the stupid watch more than her own daughter and will leave her alone for good.

And that's it. The watch is out of our lives.

On the drive back to school, I remember what flashed in my mind last night when I told my Mom what Dylan said about Mandy needing a mother. At least, I remember part of it; I need to ask my mom the rest, and I want to do it right now, but her cell phone goes straight to voicemail and the house phone goes to the machine.

Between school and work, I go home and find both Mom and Mandy fast asleep in their rooms. There's a pizza box in the fridge with two slices left – I can't believe my mom let Mandy have pepperoni, and it's not even the soy kind. I guess everything is okay. Maybe Mom really did forget the details of last night. Maybe they talked it out. I'm dying to wake up Mandy and ask a million questions, and I even creep close to the bed in case she's resting and not really sleeping, but she's out like a light. She's got the prettiest face, truly. I almost reach out and touch it. Instead I leave the tracking slip for the watch tucked in her Bible and look in on Mom. Same deal: dead to the world. Too bad.

I shake her awake. "Mom."

"Mmmph."

"Open your eyes."

"Jill. Not now."

I prise open the lid of her right eye with my fingers. "I'll make it quick. I have to go to work."

She bats my hand away and sits up, clutching her pillow to her chest. "Speak, child."

"Remember when you and Dad volunteered as educational surrogates? For those teen foster kids?"

What I remember: Dad coming home from the first training, brushing snow off his coat and saying, "Hey Jilly, I found out tonight that adults can adopt other adults. So when you're eighteen and sick of us, you can farm yourself out and get a fresh set of parents." I said, "Awesome. Best news I've had all year." Then we went to the kitchen and ate brownies.

Now I have Mom's full attention. "Go on..."

On the way to work, I have time to ponder the Ravi situation. I've been sending him very brief text updates throughout the day, but nothing serious.

It wasn't a surprise, what happened in the cave. What it means, though, I have no clue.

Dylan tried to talk to me this morning right before first period.

"I'm still too mad at you," I told him.

"I know. I'd be pissed at me, too. So...after school."

"I don't think I'll be ready today, Dylan. Probably not this week. Angry Jill isn't good at communication." The look on his face broke my heart. We both knew. I touched his arm. "Please. Don't give me more opportunities to say stuff I'll regret."

"Call me when you're done being mad," he said, and fortunately the bell rang to drown out his last couple of words, which were tear-choked and full of a final kind of sadness.

Now I text Ravi to see if he's coming into the store tonight, and he says he's not sure, how is Annalee's mood?

Not good, is my reply, and I stick my phone in my apron pocket before Annalee catches me. She's been terse with me since I got here, all snippy about me taking a night off. "We got slammed," she says. Tonight we get an hour-long rush of customers during the post-dinner hours, everyone wandering around after their mall meals or movies, looking to rack up a few more credit card charges.

It's all I can do to keep my eyes open and stay upright at the register. During a lull Annalee says, "You're not asking people about the frequent-buyers club."

"Sorry."

"And you're not smiling."

"I'm really tired. Sorry." I smile hugely at her, gritting my teeth. "I still got the magic, see?"

That's the kind of thing that would have made her laugh a week ago. She turns away. "You know, Jill, there was a secret shopper here a couple of weeks ago. You did not get a good report."

"For real?" I always get great marks from the secret shoppers. I'm helpful, friendly, and always try for an add-on sale.

"You told her that Jake Lamonte doesn't write his own books."

Damn. So one of our regulars went to the dark side. Usually I can smell a secret shopper from a mile away.

"Well, he doesn't. It's not really a secret."

"That's not the point. You made a negative comment about one of our products."

"It wasn't negative," I argue. "It was neutral."

She lunges over the counter and grabs a paperback from one of the front dumps and waves it in my face. "Jill, if you go to a restaurant, do you want the waiter to tell you that your chicken parmigiana comes from a chicken parmigiana factory instead of the tender loving care of the restaurant kitchen?"

I laugh. "It's not like we're writing the books in the back room..."

"Let people form their own opinions about the products. If they want to find out about Jake Lamonte's 'writing process', they can go online. If you want to be all conversational about how books are made, and pretend you read the *New York Times*, maybe you should go work for one of those dirty little bookstores with a mangy cat in the window and no cafe or Internet."

She's totally picking on me. We've both been making snotty comments about Jake Lamonte all year. She slaps the paperback down on the counter and tears the plastic wrapping off a roll of dimes.

A few more customers line up, and we play nice. I get one person to sign up for the frequent-buyers club, and sell one mini *Bhagavad Gita* from the spinning rack at my register. When those customers are gone, Annalee turns to me. Her face is red. Her eyes are shiny. "I know we only went out twice, but I really liked him, Jill."

Oh no. "Who?"

"As if you have to ask." She slams her register drawer shut and swooshes past me, walking back out into the store.

I slip my phone out of my pocket to see Ravi's reply to my last text: *She knows.*

I write back, *Um, yeah.*

Despite my exhaustion, despite my headache, despite the fact I just want to close my eyes, I follow Annalee. "Am I really in trouble about the secret shopper?"

"No," she says curtly. "It's your first negative report." She picks up a cookbook that a customer has left with the fiction and walks away.

My phone rings. It's my mom's ringtone – Barry Manilow's "Mandy", which Dylan set as a joke about a week ago – super loud and super embarrassing.

Annalee turns around, her eyes fierce. "Do not answer that. You're not on break."

"It's my mom. She never calls me at work unless it's an emergency."

"If you answer that, Jill..."

You came and you gave without takin', my apron pocket sings. I don't want to lose my job but considering what happened last night, I reach for the phone. "We've got this pregnant girl staying with us."

"Don't, Jill!"

I turn away from Annalee, answer.

"Mom?"

"Meet me at St. Vincent's," she says. "Mandy went into labour."

Mandy

It hurts.

A lot.

I know that Robin is in the room with me, that she's next to me, with me, but I can't hear her or see her or feel her any more. It's like I pictured it, only now I'm sure that she'll still be here after my daughter finally comes out. Soon, I hope.

At first the pain only came in waves, and we even laughed a little bit on the way to the hospital. "I knew I shouldn't have let you have that pizza," Robin said.

Mostly I was scared. "Is it bad to be this early? We didn't take our birthing class yet."

"It's not ideal, but you're within the safe zone. It will be fine."

"Is Dr. Yee going to be there?" As much as I don't like Dr. Yee, I wanted to know what was going to happen and what I could expect, and I wouldn't mind a familiar face.

"I had her paged, so I hope so. But since it's early, there's no guarantee."

My seat was tilted back at a slight angle. I could see the street lights and phone wires and tops of buildings. "How does it feel?" I asked Robin. "How did it feel when you had Jill?"

"It feels...well, it hurts, Mandy. I won't lie. It's going to hurt," she said, flying through a yellow light. "But it's something completely indescribable, too. And it's yours, it's totally yours. It's strange that way – an experience women have all over the world every minute, but at the same time something so *yours*. Not anything that anyone else can ever understand or take away from you. And it's so worth it."

If this had happened two days ago and Robin had said that, I would have thought, *That's what women always say, but the women who say that are mothers, and they're talking to women who are also going to be mothers. What about for people like me? Is it still worthwhile?* But now everything is different. We decided what to do. The idea of it being worthwhile for me is more real than ever. Still, after I waited for another wave of pain to pass, I asked her, "Are you sure?"

"Yes. I'm very sure."

We got there fast; getting admitted took longer. Robin

yelled at the nurses a lot. I had to tune her out, go away in my mind, because she was causing me stress. Finally we got into a room and as Robin helped me get out of my clothes she said, "You're going to be a good mother, Mandy. I promise you."

Jill

The hospital feels so empty at this time of night. And it's sad. Mandy's family should be here. I mean, not her biological family, because they suck, but there should be people to join in the waiting and excitement. The person I want to invite is Ravi. I want to see him, have his company. But he's not really anyone that important to Mandy, and I think about how she asked if she could still be Dylan's friend. It meant a lot to her – that was clear.

I call him, even though it's past eleven now. It's Friday; he'll be up.

"You're already done being mad at me?" he asks.

"Mandy's in labour. Can you come?"

"Oh shit. Yeah, wow."

I tell him how to find us, and then ask, "Can you stop on the way and get her some trashy magazines?"

"Done."

Absolutely crushed with fatigue and a headache, I wind up dozing off in the waiting room. When I wake up, Mom is there with me, her feet up on the coffee table. Her eyes are closed, but I know she's not asleep.

"Anything happen yet?" I ask her.

"Not really," she says without opening her eyes. "She's been having a hard time. She's trying to take a little rest, but it's rough going."

I move to the chair next to her and rest my head on her shoulder. "Is it anything to be worried about?"

She puts her arm around me. "No. Birth is never easy. That's all there is to it. The body is sending you all these signals that it's time for new life to happen, but it also resists. It wants to quit. Fighting it hurts. Not fighting it hurts. Helping it hurts. There's no way around it."

I slip my hand into hers. I've always loved her hands. Strong, capable. "I can imagine."

Mandy

I don't know how long I've been here, but I've had time to think about everything. Every moment at the fair with Christopher, all the meals Robin has cooked me in the last month, and the ones I liked best. The crêpes were good. The little clothes that Dylan bought for the baby. The music at the restaurant last night and how happy I was to see Jill walk into the train station.

I try to think of being on a long, slow-rocking train ride. The land flicking past. That I'm moving, moving, moving forwards into my new life and new family, away from the old one. My hand goes to my neck, and I feel the blue-beaded necklace Christopher gave me. I put it on after Robin and I finally left the bathroom this morning, before we went downstairs to work on—

"Push!"

I don't know who's yelling it. Maybe Dr. Yee, maybe

Robin, maybe someone else, I don't know. All I know is that whenever something is yelled at me, I do it, even though I think I might die.

Don't die, Mandy. You finally have life.

But it's hard. It hurts, like Robin said it would, and it goes on a long time and hardly any rest in between now.

Someone puts ice in my mouth. Someone squeezes my hand. Someone gives me a shot of something. And I can't help it: along with everything else, I think about my mother.

Nineteen years ago this was her, in a hospital in Fort Dodge, Iowa. She was young. Not as young as I am, but still young, and my father, the married man – well, I guess he wasn't there. And I know her mother wasn't there, because she told me. So it's the same for us, and for a few seconds I'm able to understand how hard it was for her, and for those few seconds I wish good things for her. For her to find what she's looking for. For her to know love like I have. And I don't mean with Christopher.

Also I know that what Robin said is true: this is an experience all yours, and whatever kind of relationship you have later with your baby, it ties you to them for ever. My mother is tied to me, and me to her, even if we never see each other again. And I can feel sad and let some of these tears be for her.

About the hundredth time someone yells at me to push,

I think, *No.* I would say it out loud if I thought I had the strength. I'd look at Robin and say it, but I know what she'd say back. That I have to start saying yes.

I have to start saying yes.

I give my whole body to yes.

Yes to trust, yes to a new family. Yes to hope. Yes to staying.

Yes to my daughter.

Yes to me.

Yes.

Jill

When Dylan gets here, we sit with one seat between us and keep our eyes on the nurse's station. I tell him everything I know. We look at the magazines he got for Mandy. He did a good job; they're super trashy, full of gossip and pictures of celebrity cellulite. We say nothing about anything until Dylan says, "I should have answered my phone that night."

"Why didn't you?"

He laughs. "Hello, because (A) I'm scared of you. You're brutally frightening sometimes, Jill. And (B) – and this is the big one – I really thought I was doing the right thing. Something about Mandy, like, moves me. That day she told me about her mom. I mean, me and you…" He shifts in his chair, touches my arm, and I worry he's going to say something about us and our couplehood and how we'll work through this and go on. "Me and you have no freaking way to *begin to begin* to imagine growing up with a parent who treats us like that. My parents are cool, and yours—"

He freezes. He's scared to mention my dad, because of the way I react when he does, the way I've reacted every time. Tears are already working their way up when I tell him, "Go ahead."

"Your dad. Loved you. Like crazy. *Crazy*."

I dissolve. I melt. And let Dylan scoot one chair closer and hold me and comfort me exactly the way he's wanted to for eleven months, without me resisting or getting mad or pretending I'm okay. "I know."

"You guys were like twins," he says into my hair.

"It hurts so much." And it hurts to say it hurts. The words themselves plus saying them brings on another wave of pain. "I've just felt...lost."

"I know. I'm really sorry, Jill."

After a few minutes, when I'm sure I can say it coherently, I reply. "I'm sorry, too."

"I know."

I sit back in my chair and make use of the box of tissues on one of the side tables. "Why have you put up with me?" I ask.

Dylan leans on his elbows. "Because I love you. I mean, I know this is kind of it for us. It's time."

I nod.

"But I'm still going to love you, always. And in the rock-paper-scissors of life, love is rock. Fear, anger, everything else...no contest."

Love is rock.

"That's deep," I say. "You should write a song about that for The Potato Rebellion."

"Maybe I will."

After a little while I get up and buy a bag of pretzels from the machine in the waiting area. When I turn around, Dylan's head is in his hands. I go to him and rest my hand on his back. "I'll always love you, too."

"I know."

Mandy

They do like Robin promised. They lay her on my chest right away, and they say, "Here she is, Mandy. Here's your daughter."

She's covered with goo, and I can't see her face very well, or what her skin is like other than red and slimy, but now I understand why Robin says it doesn't matter how this baby was made.

She is miraculous and innocent.

All possibility.

Love.

Later, when she's washed and dried, Dr. Yee holds her up in front of me, and even Dr. Yee is smiling and maybe even a little bit emotional.

"A good head of hair on this one," she says, beaming, stroking my daughter's black, black hair.

I nod and touch the beads around my neck. "Just like her father."

Jill

There's a flurry of activity down the hall – we look up. Mom rushes into the waiting room, looking like crap but gigantically happy. She presses her hands to her mouth and nods. The doctor follows behind her and extends her hand to me. "Congratulations on the birth of your niece."

I stand and shake the doctor's hand. "Thank you. Thank you."

Dylan stands, too. "Niece?"

I hug my mom, and hug her and hug her and hug her.

"We'll explain it later," Mom says to Dylan over my shoulder.

The doctor puts her hand on my back. "Wouldn't you like to see her?"

Mandy Madison MacSweeney

In sixty to ninety days, that will be my legal name. Then we'll get an amended birth certificate for Lola, and she'll be a MacSweeney, too. Jill will be my sister. And Robin will be my mother.

And I'll sit at this table each morning at breakfast and each evening for dinner and wake up to the cheerful orange walls, without secrets or worrying that I might mess up or thinking about when I have to leave.

Really it was Jill's idea.

She remembered something from three years ago. Robin and Mac volunteered to help do something with foster kids. I don't remember what. But when they did it, they learned about how some foster parents really wanted to adopt their foster children but couldn't, because the biological parents wouldn't give up rights or other complications. But then when the children turned eighteen and could make their own choices, the foster parents adopted them.

If it was possible to adopt adults, could Robin adopt *me*? Instead of the baby? Jill asked. *Jill* asked. That day after I thought I wanted to leave.

When Robin finally wasn't throwing up any more, we went down to her computer and looked online. She called her friends in the government.

"We could do this, Mandy," she said, getting more excited with every phone call and piece of information.

And I said, "But you wanted a baby. Not a nineteen-year-old."

I didn't believe it could be that easy. Nothing in my life is that easy. Nothing ever has a solution that makes everyone happy. You don't get anything without giving up something. And I knew Robin would be giving up something, and I wanted to make sure she was thinking of that and not just being scared to lose the baby completely.

She rolled herself in her office chair around to where I was sitting in another chair, across the desk. "Here's what Mac's death taught me about life, Mandy: be prepared for detours. We had a whole plan. For our marriage, for Jill, for retirement and old age and burial."

"Death changes things," I said. "It happens and you can't stop it. You don't have a choice. This is different."

"Life changes things, too."

And then, like Lola had heard us and couldn't wait three more weeks to change our lives with hers, my water broke. Robin started the paperwork for adopting me as soon as I was home from the hospital.

And that's how I belong to her and she belongs to me and we all belong to each other and I'm home.

Jill

He's there already, at our table, wearing old, ratty jeans and a sloppy sweater and glasses, looking devastatingly gorgeous. I can admit it to myself now without all the anxiety: Ravi Desai is one of the best-looking guys I have ever known.

Even though he's dressed so casually, I wish I'd tried harder to look nice. But I didn't want to seem like I was trying. Yes, we are still in that complicated phase.

"Hi," I say, and sit down.

"I got you an au lait." He slides the mug towards me. "That's what you like, correct?"

"Correct."

Mandy's dossier is on the table between us. "Why did you want me to bring you this?" he asks, tapping it. "I assumed case closed."

I slide it towards me and flip through it, running my finger over Ravi's handwritten notes, his printouts about adoption scams. "Hey, look." I hold out my phone to show him the latest picture of Lola, who I'm falling for fast.

Ravi takes it. "Wow."

"You should see her in person. She's totally serious. Furrowed brow, stern looks. Like we're all in trouble with her. Considering she has none of my dad's genes, she's an awful lot like him."

I close Mandy's file and push it back towards him. "I was thinking you could help us find the baby's father. Mandy doesn't know his last name. He lives on a reservation in South Dakota. She thinks. She knows the general vicinity."

He puts his palms on the table. "At this point...I should probably confess: I don't actually know how to find people. I mean, I have your basic Internet search skills, but that's about it."

"But when I asked about Mandy, you made it sound like—"

"Yeah. Because I wanted to impress you."

"It worked."

"I know."

I laugh, and we spend a good number of seconds grinning like the fools we are.

"Did you ever think," I say, "the night I elbowed you in the face, that we'd wind up here?"

"I hoped."

"You did not! Did you?"

"If you're asking when terror turned to lust, it's difficult to pinpoint the exact moment."

"Lust? Is that all this is?" I'm playing, helping to keep things as light as he's trying to. We both know that there's a lot going on right now for me, too much to get as serious as we sometimes feel.

"Isn't that always what it is, at first?"

"No. At first it's friendship." I sip my au lait and say, as if I'm indifferent, "I'm moving away, you know. Or travelling. After graduation."

"So you've repeatedly claimed."

"You don't believe me?"

"You're an aunt now. And a sister. Family ties."

While I still sometimes struggle to feel connected to Lola, who is alien in her baby-ness, it's easier and easier to think of Mandy as my sister. We bicker like siblings. I'm bossy, like Ravi's brothers. We're different. But we experience the same life now, together.

"Do you think, maybe, you'd like to come over for dinner next week?" I ask.

"As Clark?"

"No. As you." I hold up my au lait in a toast. "And I'll be me."

Mandy

The view from the train back to Omaha is different from the trip to Denver. The time of day is different, the light is different, and since then spring has come and summer is coming. Wild flowers are up, trees are leafing.

Jill, in the seat next to me, yanks out one earphone. "How long did you say? Nine hours?"

I nod. Jill groans. "I know taking the train is all meaningful for you, but I still think we should have driven. I'm going to get some coffee. Want anything?"

"Something sweet."

"Of course." Then she leans over Lola in my arms and talks in the voice she always uses with Lola, low and silly and with her lips pursed, trying to make Lola smile. "How 'bout you? Tea, coffee? Raspberry scone? No? All you ever want is milk. So predictable."

Then she looks at me again and frowns, reaching to fix

my hair. "You should keep it off your face. The whole point of this haircut is to show off your eyes."

"Okay."

After Lola was born and I could walk around again, I told Jill I wanted shorter hair, and she took me to the place where she goes. The man who cut my hair had a shaved head and three nose rings. I got scared and told him, "Don't make me look like Jill."

Jill put her hands out, pretend strangling me, and they laughed. I don't know why that was so funny. The haircut turned out good, though. I'm still me, only more free-feeling.

"Mom?" Jill asks Robin, across the aisle from us. "Want anything?"

"I'd love some tea, honey, thank you."

They've been getting along better. We usually all eat breakfast together now. Since Jill's done with school, she's not always rushing, and she'll come down and eat at the table and not stand in the middle of the kitchen like she has somewhere else she wants to be. Sometimes if she's up late, she'll even sit with me in my room when I'm nursing in the middle of the night. One night I told her she didn't have to do that, she could go to bed.

"Remember when you told me liking some people takes time?" she whispered.

I nodded.

"I'm starting early with Lola."

Jill

Mandy thinks that once she sees the fairgrounds, which she knows how to get to, she'll figure out how to find the reservation. It all sounds a little overly optimistic to me, but my ideas about optimism might be changing. Mandy's been wearing the necklace Christopher gave her, and sometimes Lola reaches up and grasps it in her fingers, and Mandy is convinced this is a sign of something.

It was a summer one-night stand. Mandy says it was love. She says love is love whether it happens in five minutes or five years. Usually I just try not to laugh. But once in a while, I decide that I don't always have to be right.

As we drive in the rental car out of Omaha and into the country, where it's just acres and acres of green, I put my hand out the window. Life is always moving forward, forward, forward. Relentless. If someone offered me a time machine right now and I could go back to before my dad died, I would, of course, if only to see if I could save him. But then I'd want to come right back here, to face the next unknown moment and the next and the next.

Lola becomes her most quiet, serious self. Mandy says she can sense Christopher getting closer, closer. "I can feel his energy," she says.

My dad would laugh. He'd call it all mystical bullshit. He'd say, "Take your dreamcatcher and sell it somewhere else, sister."

But he was a romantic. Tender-hearted and sentimental.

Secretly he'd believe.

And so secretly, secretly, as the cornfields fly by, I believe, too.

A message from the author

Years ago I heard a piece on the radio about something called "adult adoption". Usually, it's an arrangement made between foster kids who have turned eighteen, and the foster parents who always wanted to adopt them, but couldn't – often because one or both biological parents would not give up parental rights. But sometimes, people over eighteen with no fostering connections use the adult adoption laws to legally become a new family. It's a way for biologically unrelated people to make a claim for each other: "You're mine, and I'm going to take care of you always."

The notion of choosing your own family has long fascinated me; it's a theme I've explored indirectly in all of my books. The process of growing up is partly about loosening your biological ties and beginning to create a community of people for yourself. This community may be made up of friends, non-parent adults, a church community or social group, selected family members, or all of the above. It's a community where you're safe, and accepted, and cared for – a circle of people that make you feel at home.

Mandy has never felt "at home". Fearful and confused, she's been betrayed by the adults in her life, with no community, and no one she can turn to. When she sets out on her journey, she thinks she's only looking for a home for her baby. But consciously or not, she's also searching for a home for herself.

In the e-mail message that begins *How to Save a Life*, Mandy writes to Robin: "No lawyers. No agencies. That's why I am on this site." "This site" is a fictional online message board called Love Grows, where people who want to adopt babies and people who have babies they are giving up for adoption find each other, without the burden of home visits, waiting periods, or other requirements of bureaucracy in the USA. This scenario is sometimes referred to as "grey market adoption". Birth mothers and prospective adoptive parents may connect through acquaintances, "baby brokers" or, as Mandy and Robin do, the Internet. Whatever way they find each other, birth mothers and adoptive parents may, for their own reasons, come to a private agreement outside of the legal system. Money may or may not be exchanged. Either way, it's not technically legal.

However, it's a crime not easily prosecuted, because if something goes wrong or either party changes her mind, neither usually wish to invite the scrutiny of law enforcement. One of the major problems with this kind of arrangement is that it leaves both parties vulnerable, with no one's rights truly protected. Robin could change her mind and put Mandy, pregnant, out on the street. Mandy could change her mind and disappear with the baby. Or, as Jill points out, Mandy or the baby's father could come back in five or ten years – at any point, really – and take the child back, leaving Robin no legal recourse. But Robin is an impulsive and impatient woman, desperately seeking a new start. She doesn't have time for bureaucracy. As for Mandy, she's been at the mercy of others her whole life, and has no interest in letting anyone else control her situation from here on out.

Robin and Mandy like to talk about their plan as if it's an "open adoption", a form of legal adoption. Information about the adoptive and biological parents is freely exchanged, and there may even be a visitation agreement whereby the birth mother can stay in touch with her child, though the adoptive parents have legal custody. In truth, this isn't the case with Robin and Mandy's arrangement, as Jill well knows.

Since the death of her father, Jill has also lost her sense

of "home" and "community", pushing away her mother, her friends and her boyfriend, and clinging ever tighter to her grief. Though she doesn't know it in the beginning, Jill, too, needs the changes Mandy brings with her.

Robin, Mandy and Jill are all vulnerable, although in very different ways, and the questionable adoption arrangement forces them into a level of trust that would be difficult for anyone. Ultimately, though, it is this leap of faith that finally helps all three of them find their way back home.

I knew from the beginning of this story *that's* what Mandy needed – not just some well-off person to raise her baby. She needed home and family in ways her mother never could provide. When Robin makes an undisputed claim on Mandy by adopting her officially and legally, in essence she says those words Mandy has needed to hear her whole life: "You are mine, and I'm going to take care of you always."

Through the process of adult adoption, Robin, Jill, Mandy and Lola make a new family. Not just in spirit and through good intentions, but in name and by law. And all by choice. Which I think is a beautiful thing.

About the author

SARA ZARR was raised in San Francisco, California. She now lives in Salt Lake City, Utah, with her husband. Her debut novel, *Story of a Girl* was an American National Book Award Finalist. *How to Save a Life* is Sara's first book to be published in the UK. To tune into Sara's podcasts and keep up-to-date with her blog, log on at **www.sarazarr.com**.

Discussion Questions

- *How to Save a Life* opens with the Flannery O'Connor quote "*The life you save may be your own.*" What relevance do you think this has to the book?

- What were your initial impressions of Jill and Mandy? How long did it take you to connect with the characters? Did your feelings towards them change as the book progressed? If so, why?

- How did the use of two narrative voices affect your reading of the novel? Did you prefer to read from Jill's or Mandy's point of view? Why do you think the author chose to tell the story in this way?

- What do you think about the methods used by Robyn and Mandy to initiate the adoption process?

What do you imagine might have been the outcome if Mandy and Robin had gone ahead with their original adoption plan?

- There are many real and hypothetical mother/daughter relationships in *How to Save a Life*. Discuss the various mother/daughter relationships in the book, and the impact they have on those involved.

- Fathers and father figures are also central to the book, despite being absent or lost in some way. Compare the characters of Mac (Gavin MacSweeney), Kent and Christopher and discuss what it means to be a father.

- *"Try a little tenderness"* is the one piece of advice from her dad that Jill regularly invokes. What do you understand by this, and why do you think Jill finds it so difficult to do?

- Early in the novel, Mandy explains that she sometimes tells strangers that her baby's father is in Afghanistan. What other lies does Mandy tell in the book? Why do you think she does this, and how did it make you feel about her?

- Discuss the significance of the various e-mails, letters and notes which are sent and received throughout the novel. What impact did reading a character's personal correspondence have on your attitude towards them?

- *"When someone lives a certain kind of life all the time, it's hard to describe to them what it looks and feels like to someone who lives a certain other kind of life"* – Mandy. Compare Mandy's and Jill's lives before Mandy arrives at the MacSweeney's. How do their different experiences affect their ability to relate to one another?

- *"Dad was my mirror, and without him I can't see myself"* – Jill. Both Jill's and Mandy's view of themselves changes profoundly over the course of the novel. Why and how do you think this happens?

- *"Adding someone to a family...is major. Life-changing. Permanent. When someone's been subtracted from a family, you can't just balance it out with a new acquisition"* – Jill. Consider your own definition of "family". Has reading *How to Save a Life* changed or challenged this?

- At the cemetery, Jill tells Ravi; *"Dylan wanted me to come here with him... I could never do it."* Why do you think Jill was able to visit the cemetery with Ravi, but not with Dylan?

- Mandy says that Robyn has a way of doing things that *"just makes you feel good. She knows how to make a home even out of a table. Not everyone can do that."* Discuss the concept of "home" as explored in the novel, and in the author note.

- The book ends with Robyn, Mandy and Jill travelling back to Omaha in search of Lola's father. Do you think Mandy will find Christopher? Does it matter to you if she does?

Acknowledgements

With grateful thanks to the following folks for research help: in Denver – Susan Bettger and Scott Kingry for hospitality, happy hour, rowdy stories, chauffeuring, and three memorable trips to Casa Bonita. Steve Inman for additional insights, tales, and bar service. In and about Omaha – Mark Peach, Jaafar Talha of Happy Cab, the Bookworm, the staff at the Magnolia Hotel Omaha, Sarah Sproul, Lois, Kaylie and the guy who drove me to the train station so that I wouldn't have to haul my bags through the snow like Mandy, and the man next to me on the plane who answered all my questions about corn. Also – Mitali Perkins, Sherman Alexie, Melissa Marr, Dr. Bernadette Kiraly, and that person on Twitter who named the bookstore that employs Jill.

A debt to Bret Anthony Johnston's *Naming the World*, which contains the prompt that inspired me to write this story.

Tara Altebrando is a generous and smart reader and friend. Top secret thanks to Bob.

Love and gratitude to Mike Martin, my second self, whose friendship saves my life a little every day.

Thanks to Pam Garfinkel, Victoria Stapleton, Zoe Luderitz, Barbara Bakowski, Ames O'Neill, Andrew Smith, Megan Tingley, genius Alison Impey, and the whole incredible LBYR crew for everything that helps keep the wheels of this career turning. Special thanks to Stephanie King at Usborne for her careful attention to the UK edition.

I would not be the writer I am without the guidance of my editor, Jennifer Bailey Hunt, who also gave me the time and space and encouragement needed to make the process good again. Thank you, Jen, for your particular wisdom when it came to this story.

Love and gratitude to my agent, Michael Bourret, who, along with God, makes all things possible.

And, always, my heart to Gordon, for being my home.

If you loved

how to save a life

you may also love...

Kathryn
Erskine

Mockingbird

American National Book Award Winner

Mockingbird

by Kathryn Erskine
AMERICAN NATIONAL BOOK AWARD WINNER

*"Erskine's moving and insightful masterpiece delivers a
compelling message for all."*
Publishers Weekly

Caitlin misses her brother Devon. Since his death, she
has no one to explain the world to her. And for Caitlin,
the world is a confusing place, full of emotions and
colours that she can't understand. Dad tries to help, but
he also spends a lot of time crying in the shower.

So when Caitlin reads the definition of "closure" in
the dictionary, she decides that's what they need. And
as she struggles to find it, she learns how to let a world
of colour into her black-and-white life...

**A bittersweet story told in the unforgettable voice of
a young girl with Asperger's syndrome.**

ISBN: 9781409538585
EPUB: 9781409541677   KINDLE: 9781409541684

Yankee Girl

MARY ANN RODMAN

Yankee Girl

by Mary Ann Rodman

"*Moving and powerful.* – The Bookseller

Valerie's voice is as sweet as honey. She's the obvious choice to star in the Nativity. But this is Mississippi, 1964. Things are far from simple. There is uproar when Valerie is picked to play the angel...because she's black. As one of the first black children to attend Parnell School, she has to face violent protestors outside and vicious bullies inside the classroom.

Alice is torn between standing up for Valerie, and being popular with the in-crowd, especially as she's found it hard to make friends since moving to the Deep South. Struggling between guilt and fear, it takes a tragedy for Alice to find the courage to act.

A truly resonant story about racism and doing the right thing, based on the author's own experiences.

ISBN: 9780746067499

For more exceptional YA reads
log on to www.fiction.usborne.com